COATTAILS AND COCKTAILS

MURDER STRAIGHT UP WITH A TWIST

RUMER HAVEN

fallen·monkey

Also by Rumer Haven

Seven for a Secret
What the Clocks Know
Four Somethings & a Sixpence

Fallen Monkey Press

First edition, September 2017

The characters and events in this book are fictitious.
Any similarity to real persons, living or dead,
is coincidental and not intended by the author.

ISBN: 978-1-9998197-0-5

10 9 8 7 6 5 4 3 2 1

Cover Design by RoseWolf Design
Interior Book Design by Coreen Montagna

Printed in the United States of America

To Gracie and Ollie

PROLOGUE

the mixology of murder

*D*rip, *drip, drip…*
Crystal-cold beads drop from the countertop, a sleek head breaking their fall to the floor. Easing down smooth flesh, past an unflinching eye, the droplets curve and crawl lower until they bleed into fine fibers. No sign of entry, no trace of a weapon. Only the shapeless ice that keeps melting over the one who had it coming.

A body clearly shaken, but not stirring.

Apéritif

to whet the appetite

A scream that could curdle cream rang out across the tennis court. The singles match had turned into a game of keep-away—but the one "keeping away" only kept getting caught. On purpose, it seemed.

Another shriek pierced the humid air, followed by a peal of giggles.

"And critics say she can't act," Edith Warne commented from the terrace of her Belleau estate, with more smile in her voice than she was inclined to share on her face. "I like when she can't *speak* either."

She raked her fingernails along one of the portico's stone columns, making her companion shiver. With that, Colonel Ransom Warne tapped the iron railing twice with his knuckles before leaving Edith's side, trotting down the steps and into the sunshine with a flourish of indifference. Or so it would seem to the untrained eye.

Edith followed her husband with her gaze until the courtside cacophony ensued.

"Put me DOWN!" shrieked the otherwise silent actress. She draped from her leading man's shoulder, baring more of her assets than would grace the silver screen. With her pleated dress wilting around her hips like a dying daisy, Lottie Landry bounced in rhythm with Noble Howard's steps across the lawn. She beat against his back in another fit of laughter.

A few yards farther, though, the blonde-bobbed head went quiet. Looking up from Noble's rear, Lottie wasn't smiling any-more—at least not until she met Edith's eye. At once, Lottie flashed her pearly whites again and playfully snatched Noble's flat cap from his head.

"Lottie, dear, your cocktail's lost its cool." *Seems the cocktease has, too*, Edith thought, not letting that stage smile fool her for one second. Well, the girl only brought it on herself, flirting her way out of what could've been a proper tennis match, had Lottie possessed any more talent on the court than she did on the screen. What was her *real* game, anyway?

Lottie lowered her head and gave Noble one last smack with his hat. He obliged by dropping her on her feet. Taking his cap back, he escorted her petite frame toward the portico while Lottie patted her hair back in place behind a silk bandeau. Edith slapped on her own fake smile to greet them.

But Lottie suddenly broke off in the opposite direction with a wave to Ransom, who'd been standing in quiet contempla-tion—or contempt—between the porch and reflecting pool. Arms swinging, she clopped through the grass to where the middle-aged gentleman cast an imposing shadow on the lawn. "Handsome Ransom," Lottie trilled within Edith's earshot. She stood on tiptoe to remove his Panama hat and muss his black hair. In turn, he pinched her pointed little chin between his forefinger and thumb.

Watching them from the terrace, Edith tapped her finger-nails on the sweating highball glass still sitting unclaimed on a silver tray.

"Why don't you take this one, Noble dear," she said when the matinée idol climbed the stone steps. "I'll mix her a fresh Mary Pickford instead."

Noble's brunet waves lost their sun-kissed luster once he joined her under the portico's shade. Shaking his head as he received the highball, he *tutt*ed with his tongue and brought the glass to his temple.

"We'll tell her it's a pink lady," Edith compromised.

"She'll know the difference."

"As any lady ought." She glanced at the couple on the lawn once more.

"You're not talking about the drink, I think." He chuckled, augmenting his fine pencil moustache with a conspiratorial leer before taking a smooth sip from his glass.

Edith raised her brows and gave an innocent pout, saying nothing more. Before long, Lottie tapped her way up the porch steps.

"Now, darling, did you sneak my giggle water?" The young actress slinked toward Noble, the backs of both hands propped on her swaying hips.

"I was just leaving to fix you a fresh pink lady, sweet." Edith tapped the underbelly of Lottie's chin with her fingertips as she strode past.

She entered the grand home, the door slamming closed behind her.

Lottie held her saccharine smile for exactly two seconds after the door had banged shut behind Edith. Then she dropped her lips just as fast as she reclaimed her highball from Noble.

"Must she always be so patronizing?" With her free hand, Lottie fanned the lapel of her loose vest away from the sleeveless tennis dress beneath.

"Must you always be so attentive?" Noble cocked his head toward the lawn, his ice-blue irises particularly piercing. "Look, you've overheated yourself."

Lottie turned on her heel to stare him down from head to toe. "That color doesn't suit you. No, it doesn't at all."

Rolling the cuffs of his striped yellow shirt, he assessed his white vest and trousers. "I think it suits me fine."

"I mean green. But then, *jealous lover* never was your strongest role."

He stepped closer and fondled the bow hanging from her sailor collar. "Remember your place here," he whispered firmly, then poked the skin above her neckline but once.

"I am. Everything at Belleau is mine to enjoy, too."

"You flatter yourself, my little four-flusher."

"As if you're not counting on that being the case."

Noble matched her steely stare until a throat cleared behind them.

"Lovers' quarrel?" Ransom bellowed from the top step.

Lottie and Noble spun apart, her bow untying while still in his grip. He dropped the ribbon to give Ransom a robust pat on the shoulder. "Your little ward is only unhappy with her drink." He seized the glass back from Lottie, leaving her to fist a now-empty hand onto her hip.

"That so?" Ransom frowned. Standing tall and broad in a cream linen suit, he stuffed his hands into his trouser pockets. "It's not like Edith to mix a bad batch."

"Everything's jake, don't worry," Lottie said. "Just a little bitter on the tongue, that's all." She squinted at her costar with a wan smile as he downed her drink. "Luckily, Noble is dreadfully parched."

"I only want to drink *you* in, my love." He gave a little snort before swigging another deep sip.

Lottie clenched her fist for two beats, but willed herself to snake it around Noble's back and slide against him. "Aw. You always deliver the right lines, baby."

He tossed his cap away to wrap his arm around her waist, too, swinging her around to stand face to face.

"You never miss your cues either, doll." Pressing her close, he brought his lips to where her earlobe peeked out from her bandeau. "Now stick to the script," he murmured into the silk.

Lottie grinned with a breathy exhale and drew her face to his. But she became overwhelmingly aware of Ransom in the corner of her eye, an audience she didn't want to play to anymore. Kissing Noble on the nose, she took a step back.

"Lottie, sweet," Edith announced just then. The porch door slammed behind her once more. "I'm sorry for the wait."

Lottie accepted the proffered cocktail with a theatrical curtsy. "Ain't *she* sweet." She raised her crystal coupe in a silent toast to the others before puckering her lips at its rim for a dainty sip. An unexpected tartness shot through her jaw.

Edith's long fingers played with the ruffles on her sleeveless shift dress — a pretty floral one, Lottie thought, if a trifle matronly for a childless woman in her early thirties. As with her chestnut hair, which Lottie had encouraged her to bob, but Mrs. Ransom Warne preferred to pin her long waves up.

"Something wrong?" Edith's eyes sparkled. "Should I have let you choose your poison?"

Lottie's pursed lips stretched into a grin. "It's only that I've never had a pink lady with rum. Or pineapple." Smiling around clenched teeth, she held the glass at a distance. "In fact, if I didn't know better, Edith, I'd think this was a Mary Pickford."

Edith brought those claw-like fingers to her chest. "Oh! There's no mistaking a Mary Pickford when you've seen one — I mean *tasted* one, of course. This heat has muddled my mind. Here, let me make you another if she's too strong for you."

"Don't be silly, Edith. I can handle it fine."

"If you're sure you can take her down…"

Lottie leveled her with a stare. "Quite sure." In one long, elegantly dramatic sip, she swallowed nearly half the cocktail.

Noble's charming laughter sliced the thick air. "As long I get the cherry!" He plucked it from her glass and dangled it by the stem while, behind him, Ransom grew as red as the fruit. "There now, that's my coquette."

Ransom stepped forward just as Noble turned and waved a hand at him, tottering a little as he did so.

"Talking about the drink, good man. Its namesake, the actress. Mary Pickford, *Coquette*, you know? I wager she'll get an Oscar for that one. You seen it?"

Stopping where he was, the Colonel shook his dark head.

"Oh, where's your mind, Ransom," Edith said. "We viewed it on our own screen."

He rubbed his fingertips against his thumbs, furrowing his brow in that brooding manner he had. But then his ebony eyes softened and he bounced on the balls of his feet. "Yes, yes. Fine actress, Pickford. But she approaches twilight while our star here's on the rise." As a smile peeked from beneath his thick yet impeccably trimmed moustache, Ransom pinched Lottie's chin again and raised it. "Chin up. Eyes forward," he said to her. "Let no one stand in your way."

Holding his gaze, Lottie nodded and feared her lip would tremble above his thumb if given enough time.

"Anyway," Noble said, "I don't know what all this Pickford comparison's about when my gal's a dead-ringer for Davies."

"Yes," Edith chimed in. "Now that's a more apt comparison. I don't think *she'll* see any Oscars...however." She appended the last word like an afterthought. "As one difference between you two, I mean." Narrowing her eyes, she smirked at Lottie.

"Davies doesn't need a trophy," Noble said. "She *is* one. Lottie's got a newspaper man behind her, too, ay, R.W.? More competition for W.R.?"

A weight bore down on Lottie's breast like a wet sack; she thought even Edith went a little white at that. He'd just *had* to bring up William Randolph Hearst, Marion Davies' lover and patron, not to mention Ransom's chief rival. And he'd spoken it on Warne soil.

When his host only stared at him, Noble added, "Oh, I'm yanking your chain," as he literally did so with Ransom's pocket watch where it looped through his vest. "So…Davies' first talkie's out any day now. *Marianne,* reshot with a new cast, sound, everything. Lottie would've made the better French girl, though, huh? I'm sure they could 'elocute' that accent right back."

His gum-beating faded to incoherent jibber the more Lottie struggled to breathe under the porch's Neocolonial edifice. Seeking escape, she swiveled on her heel.

"Hey, where you off to?" Noble asked.

"Just ankling off my *Coquette*-tail. Turns out, she *is* too strong for me."

"Shall I join you?"

She shook her head as she skipped down the steps, calling back, "But I'll return in time for the others." Splashing her drink into the hedges—then discarding the glass into them altogether—she stomped away across the lawn.

Ransom followed.

"What's eating them?" Noble asked Edith. He tipped back more of the highball he'd pinched from Lottie as he walked to the railing.

"Oh…" Edith flicked her hand as if the Hearst comment hadn't gotten under her skin, too. "That's just Ransom. Lottie as well. Almost twenty-one yet still storming off like she's eleven. I'm sure you'll find her in the stable."

Noble leaned against the nearest column with customary swagger. He fixed his eyes on Edith, and she didn't quite know how to interpret his grin. Then he looked off into an imaginary distance. Closing one eye, he held up two L-shaped hands to frame the image he was about to paint: "Lottie as a littlun, throwing a tantrum. I can absolutely picture it. Those same baby-doll eyes throwing knives. Did she curse in French, too?"

Edith looked out into the real distance, the one her husband was gradually disappearing into with the young starlet. She compressed her lips.

"Only ten or so when she first arrived…but already such a beauty. All the time of the world on her side." Losing her focus on the horizon, she softly smiled at the thought of such youth. Lottie's, hers.

"My dear, you say that as if you're not also a choice bit of calico." Noble adjusted his position against the pillar as she approached the railing, but he didn't move his gaze or that disarming smile the slightest bit. "You may've raised that tomato, but you're not old enough to be her mother."

"Yet he's old enough to be her father." She delicately placed her hands on the railing.

A light wind ruffled the leaves, thinning the air a bit. Noble quietly sipped his drink.

"He doesn't finance her films, you know," Edith added after a while.

"Course I do. It's my business to know where the money comes from." He winked. "But oh, look, I only brought ol' W.R. into it because of his papers and, you know, Hollywood connections. Business affairs, not, ah, affairs of the heart."

Edith could almost feel the heat of Noble's eyes withdraw from her to search the lawn, too. Gripping the iron rail, she warned herself to tread no farther down this path. There was no decorum—or sense—in entertaining any such ideas, raising any hackles. This weekend was about reuniting, celebrating. Entertaining and hunting. All the same, she suddenly wished she'd worn a more attractive day dress, something more current and baring a little more skin. But to impress whom? She expelled a light laugh.

The warmth of Noble's gaze penetrated her again. She knew it without looking. Swallowing, she willed herself to face him. And there it was, that funny little grin again.

"I like your face when you smile." He lifted his weight from the column to stand beside her. "What amuses you?"

She dropped her chin to her chest before swinging it around to peer at him. "Me, I think."

Her shoulders shook with a more genuine laugh this time. A more girlish one, the kind she used to tempt Ransom with when she'd been Lottie's age.

And what did Edith think she was doing now, flirting? Noble was practically Lottie's fiancé, and *he* was only exuding Hollywood charm.

All the same, it was nice to see a young, as-yet single man waste any sort of charm on her. Still trying to win over the future in-laws, of course, or at least the closest thing that Noble would get with an orphan like Lottie — much as Edith loathed becoming the standby mother-in-law of a man her own age. It didn't hurt for Noble to get in the good graces of an influential newspaper tycoon either; when Ransom's papers spoke, the nation listened. And now his local military influence was growing, too, through the Illinois National Guard.

Colonel and Mrs. Warne had already become acquainted with Lottie's suitor over a few occasions, Noble and Edith getting on famously from the start. But this was the first time at Belleau, the Warnes' own home. And for an entire weekend, with nowhere to hide.

On that score, Noble would do well to slow down on his liquor — and cease *altogether* the remarks about Hearst and Lottie's "cherry" or whatnot. Edith shouldn't have encouraged such teasing. At *all*, let alone in Ransom's presence. Whatever offense the Colonel might take on Lottie's behalf, he certainly had the right as her former guardian. He had taken the girl in after the passing of an old war friend, promising to raise her as his own. Just how "fatherly" he felt toward his former ward now, though, Edith couldn't be certain.

She turned around and rested her lower back against the railing, her hands propped on either side. "I'm only having fun with her," she said. "You know that."

Noble rotated halfway to face her, leaning his hip on the railing, too. "Of course, dear. It only goes to show how close you two are."

Edith inched nearer. "She's always been a spirited girl, and…" She picked at her fingernails. "I do believe in her and her…talent, and…like Ransom, I simply don't want her to sell herself short. Pickford's had her heyday as Queen of the Movies, and, well… now it's Lottie's time."

Noble nudged a little closer, too. "Thank goodness she's a better actress than you in that case." He raised his glass—now filled only with melted ice—to toast her.

Edith raised empty hands.

"I can fix that," he said. "I'll serve you somethin' stiff." Winking again, Noble made his way inside.

His wake smelled of lavender and musk, enlivening the air. Unsettled yet excited, Edith spun around and rested her elbows on the porch rail. Folding her hands, she rubbed her thumbs together, no longer able to see Lottie or Ransom.

Have fun, she told herself. *But be careful.*

2

Hearing the soft crunch of footsteps behind her, Lottie waited until she'd passed the reflecting pool to slow her gait. She wasn't at all surprised to see the Colonel fall into step at her side. Together, they entered an avenue of elms.

She elbowed him lightly. "I'm sorry about that back there. I haven't grown up much, have I?"

He grinned. "On the contrary, you've grown so fast. Whenever I look at you, I can't believe the woman you are."

"With a child's temperament."

"With a soldier's determination. You don't lie down, you march forth."

"By running away?"

"By finding your room to breathe. Even in that big house, you never got much of that, did you?"

"Not by your fault."

"Not by hers either. Not deliberately, anyway." He paused. "She never expected to be a mother, Lottie."

"She never wanted to be, you mean."

He lowered his head, watching his feet or the grass beneath them. "She also never wanted to get in your way."

"No, she stayed quite clear of that. And still, what a smothering effect it had. Funny."

Ransom wrapped his long arm around her narrow shoulders. "Karlotta, you're an adult. Maybe Edith wasn't the mother or even sister you needed, but you can be your own woman now, pave your own way. You don't need her approval or anyone's."

The farther they strolled from view of the porch, the more Lottie did feel she could breathe. She rested her head on Ransom's shoulder and cuddled into his side. "I need yours." With her chin on his lapel, she looked up at him. "You know how I do."

Kissing her forehead before laying his cheek on it, he gave her arm a squeeze. "I need yours, too, dear girl. More than you know."

They walked on silently like this beneath the canopy of trees. The summer air within the allée was thick, but with the branches keeping the late-afternoon sun at bay, there was a cushioned coolness to the atmosphere, sweetened with floral fragrance. Lottie felt she could be floating through the enchanted forest of her childhood fancies if it weren't for the solid anchor of Ransom's embrace. He'd always kept her grounded, holding her down in a way that somehow held her up, too.

A little farther on, he straightened and, with arms akimbo, took her hand in both of his. As he intermittently squeezed and patted it, a swell of emotion buoyed her. For half her life she hadn't known him, but now she couldn't imagine a world without him.

She parted her lips to say, "There's something I've been meaning to ask you," at the same time he said, "There's something I ought to tell you."

Laughing, Lottie insisted that he go first. He reluctantly conceded.

"Well, you see," he began, "there's never been a right time, and…I don't want to lose the chance, while there still *could* be a chance, so I…"

His palms grew hot around hers, and she didn't believe she'd ever seen this quiet, collected man break a sweat at his brow like he did now. He tugged her toward one of the great elms lining their path, where she leaned her back against its coarse trunk. Still holding her hand as he faced her, Ransom had some difficulty finding his words, let alone looking her in the eye. Instead, he focused on retying the bow at her breast.

She studied him, his uncharacteristic countenance, how time and trial had streaked his black hair with gray. Both eager and wary of what he might say, she ventured, "Is it to do with Noble and me? You don't approve?"

That got him to look up. He searched her face. "Do you need me to? It's serious, then?"

She knew the Colonel to be a man of few words and fewer expressions, but there was no mistaking how whatever light had sparked behind his eyes just moments before now dimmed. The weight of his disappointment dragged her own gaze to her feet. But, on an inhale, she raised her face and gave a slight nod.

He patted her hand. "Lottie, I…"

She closed her other hand on his knuckles to still him.

As he clenched his square jaw, his inscrutable lips wavered somewhere between a smile and a frown. Swallowing, he nodded, too. And then he pulled her into a hug like he would never let go.

Running her fingers through the black mane beside her, Lottie couldn't stop replaying what Ransom had said to her. How he'd looked at her. There was more burning in his mind than just Noble, an intimacy he'd looked desperate to share if her interjection hadn't dried the words in his throat.

The dark hair softened with her every caress. "There, now," she cooed. "That's it. That's my precious boy." She pressed her lips to her companion's bristly jaw.

"He's been missing your special touch, Miss Lottie." Hands on hips, a man stood in silhouette at the stable's entrance.

"Feeling's mutual. Oh, how I've missed my Dusky. *Mon amour*," Lottie baby-talked. Inhaling the stallion's warm, earthy scent, she gave his mane one more stroke before trotting toward her visitor, who grinned and offered a bow. "Now, Ernie, that's no way to greet a lady!"

She threw her arms around him and laughed delightedly. When she took a step back, she saw him flush and dig the toe of his work boot into the earth, always so shy when they first reunited. He stood not much taller than her but quite broader.

"Just doin' my job, miss." He tipped his cap.

Coming of age under a war-hero-turned-media-mogul's roof, only to rapidly ascend the throne of Hollywood royalty, Lottie had grown accustomed to people humbling themselves in her presence. But she hadn't started out that way. With her own modest beginnings in rural France, she hadn't had any more nor less than most members of her agrarian community. Ransom's own modesty, despite all outward appearances, had helped preserve if not encourage that humility of heart, as had the natural wonderland of his Belleau country estate, named for the French woodland that the U.S. had recaptured from Germany a little over a decade ago. Instead of a battlefield, though, Lottie found peace and perspective here. It was Hollywood that dug at her roots, pulling her up from them to pot her in its own dirt like a hothouse flower.

But she wasn't in California now. And Noble hadn't plucked her just yet. She wouldn't let him while she was here. Here, she *would* be her own woman, as Ransom encouraged.

And here, she wouldn't let childhood friends feel inferior. "Ernie, what have I told you?" She fisted a hand at her hip. "Don't you dare 'Miss' me."

"But I do. It's not the same without you here."

She giggled. "I mean don't *call* me 'Miss.' I'm Lottie to you—*sir*."

Ernie blushed deeper, his boot scraping along the ground again. He bit his upper lip in that same funny way he had when he was just a boy. He removed his cap from his mop of dusty blond hair and wrung it in his hands a moment before replacing it on his head.

She took his hands in hers. "But I've missed you, too. I can't tell you how pleased I am you're still here. How's your father?"

His tawny eyes lit up at that. "Strong and stubborn as ever. But I'm no different, I s'pose." He raised his shoulders toward his ears. "You know, together we're readyin' a new garden for next spring. Filled with iris and lily, just for you to enjoy when you visit, and maybe remind you of home? Your homeland, I mean?"

She brought her hand to her chest. "Ernest Hart, you are a soul truly living up to his name. If I miss your daddy today, I hope to see him tomorrow." Giving another giggle, she returned to Dusky, who'd grown restless as soon as she'd left his side.

"Now, now, you," she said to the bobbing head, "there's enough of me to go around."

She smiled and turned back to Ernie, who was now nowhere to be seen. Soon emerging from the shadows of another stall, though, he walked over and handed her a brush.

"May as well make yourself useful," he said with a playful, growing confidence that reminded her more of the boy she once knew.

"Remember how we'd dream of running away, you and me?" she asked, cheerily setting to work on the thoroughbred's mane. "We were going to ride Dusky and Betty into the sunset. Me, to get away from Edith, and you, those rotten bullies. How lucky you've escaped *your* problem. I'll always have that ol' nag." She whinnied gently at Dusky.

Ernie curled a corner of his lips and reached into the adjacent stall to slap the ashy hide inside it. "Sure couldn't take Betty now. The old gray mare ain't what she used to be, as they say." He softly patted the horse's face. "Cataracts in both eyes now, and the arthritis only gets worse."

Lottie stopped brushing to give the aging beast a thoughtful look. "Promise me you'll be there if she has to be put down."

He nodded. "I'll do it myself."

Offering Betty a silent moment, Lottie resumed her task.

"Take Dusky, then," she said to brighten the atmosphere. "You know, if you still want to get away. Ransom wouldn't mind."

She glanced over at Ernie and grinned. "You'd probably have hell to pay with Edith, though."

"Who would *you* ride?"

"Oh—" she swung around and twirled the brush in the air "—any of the others would do in a pinch."

He continued to smooth his hand along Betty's face. "The others aren't worthy of you."

Her smile faded, and Lottie returned her attention to Dusky. But she couldn't block thoughts of Noble, of the other stallions that ran wild out west, threatening to trample her. Good, loyal Ernest couldn't know how true his statement was. Could he? Maybe it was just an old friend's sixth sense kicking in. Maybe it was enough to read the papers; maybe no matter how good of an actress she was, her face would always be an open book with plenty to read between the lines. Or maybe he was simply talking about horses.

She closed her eyes and shook her head, embarrassed of how easily she could make everything about her. Perhaps she'd just done the same with Ransom, and that's why he'd so abruptly ended their talk to return to the house. Maybe what he'd almost confessed beneath the elm tree had nothing to do with her. Maybe it really concerned Edith, or just himself. It could've been anything—an issue at the paper, a complication in his health.

The heaviness returned to her breast, and Lottie lost her smile completely. She just concentrated on Dusky's heavy mane as she brushed, brushed, brushed…

Ernie left her to her silence until she began dreaming aloud.

"Do you ever still imagine it, though?" she asked, the haze of hay and dust an incense to her nose. "Just that feeling of riding away, with all you need in one sack on your back?"

"Why would you want that now, mi—Lottie? Why run with nothing when you have everything?"

She dimly smiled again as the mane's strands blurred to blackness. "But I *don't* have everything. I know it looks that way, and I don't mean to sound ungrateful. I've lived a fine life. But…"

Rocking her entire torso with each brushstroke, she lulled herself into deeper reverie. "It's not the one I expected, out there. Fame isn't—it isn't real, you know? You can't touch it, can't hold it... but people want you to believe you can, just so they can place you in the palm of their own hand, carry you in their pocket, then shine you up, swap you, toss you away. People are only good to me because they think I'm somebody, and knowing me means getting to know somebody else who's somebody so they can become a somebody, too. And they just keep meeting and creating and crushing somebodies. Yeah, I'm somebody, all right. Until I'm nobody anymore."

An icy chill shivered her out of her spell, and, blinking, Lottie caught her breath. She'd said too much. Brush still in one hand, she wiped a tear with the other and dried it against Dusky's jaw. Then, she kissed the horse's sleek face and turned to kiss Ernie's cheek as well.

Placing the brush in Ernie's palm, she held her curved pinky finger out to his other hand. He looked down at her finger with a raised eyebrow, but eventually he nodded with a warm, if hesitant, smile. He hooked his pinky around hers, just like when they were kids, and that was enough for Lottie to trust her old pal wouldn't tell a soul.

3

"Heavens, Noble, you weren't kidding about a stiff one. I don't know where the rest of the rickey is, but I sure taste the gin. Just try this, Ransom."

Hampering a hiccup behind her fingers, Edith passed her glass to the Colonel. He declined with a shake of his head.

"Killjoy," she chided and turned back to the actor. "Now, Noble dear, when is your next picture? I can't tell you how much I enjoyed the last one. The, uh…oh, you know, the one with that actress?"

"Lottie, you mean?" he teased with gin-glittering eyes. "She's in *all* my latest pictures, doll."

Edith swallowed back another hiccup and shook both her head and hand at him. "No, no. I mean that marvelous brunette who absolutely stole the show."

He gave a long, low whistle. "There've been quite a few of those."

Closing her eyes, she pressed the back of her hand to her forehead and snapped her fingers until it came to her. "*Devil's Daughter...Devil's Spawn?* No, I'm fairly sure it was *Devil's Daughter.*"

"The man had top billing in the film, dear." Ransom looked to Noble. "He knows which one you mean."

Hand in pocket, Noble smirked and rocked on his feet. "*The Devil's Damsel*, madam. The damsel being our devilish Lottie, of course, who I'd say stole the show ahead of that ghastly Ethel. That one's nothing but a chorus girl who had a stroke of good luck."

That he would discredit her opinion so bluntly made Edith bridle a bit, but "Oh, of course," she said to keep their allegiance alive. "No, I was thinking of a different picture with a different brunette entirely. Yes, that Ethel you mention, she was ghastly."

"He means off-screen, don't you, darling?" Lottie said from the porch steps. She carried a white oxford shoe in each hand, and goodness knows where her hosiery had disappeared to. "Ethel certainly did get lucky. But her performance must not've been strong enough to land a longer-term contract. Isn't that right, Noble?"

"No chemistry, you see. With the cast in general," he seemed quick to add, laying it on thick with his most charming of smiles for Ransom and Edith.

"Yes," Lottie said. "Auditions for a competing love interest have remained open for *such* a long time now."

"Still waiting for *your* screen test, Sheba," Noble muttered into his glass.

Lottie clapped the soles of her canvas shoes together. Ransom scratched the back of his neck and made his way inside the house.

Edith shook her head. "Oh, are they reshooting *Queen of Sheba*, too?" Of course, she wasn't so spifflicated from Noble's concoction that she couldn't surmise what his remark meant. Nor had she forgotten her intention to go easier on the actress. But she'd also promised herself some fun today, so she was having it.

Lottie looked to the stone floor, her jaw set. Noble just kept rocking on his feet, running his tongue between his bottom lip and teeth before sipping his drink through the sustained silence.

"So, she was a chorus girl, you say?" Edith tried again. "I've never seen one of those shows, you know. Ziegfeld Follies and the sort. How lucky that our Lottie could skip the demeaning process of working one's way up." She mock-shivered. "I suppose this Ethel didn't have the ear of the studios. You know, through as influential a connection."

She looked down to take another brave gulp of her gin rickey and, doing so, saw Lottie's grip on her shoes tighten. The girl might take aim if Edith wasn't careful.

"Perhaps you should put those back on, dear," Edith said. "And where are your stockings?" No sooner had she asked than hellos rang into the air behind her.

Entering the porch arm-in-arm were Helen Conroy and Frederick "Rex" Rainger, freshly arrived from Chicago. Ransom and his butler followed, the latter rolling out a bar cart.

"I don't *believe* it!" Lottie squealed as she dropped her shoes and ran to the newly arrived pair, spreading her arms to hug them both at once, though she could hardly circumnavigate Rex's barrel-chested form. "I knew you'd come, of course, but to see you actually stand here, it's a dream! A lovely little dream!"

Taking both by the hand, she drew them farther out onto the portico where they could greet the others.

Once Lottie detached from Rex, Helen wrapped her old university friend in a tight embrace that rocked them both side to side. "You marvelous gal, you," she cried, "how *are* you? Rested from your journey?"

"Mm-hm," Lottie replied, "and pleasantly wasting the day away. Though I must say I'd hoped you and Rex would come earlier for a doubles match. Keep Noble on his toes."

"That's my fault," Helen said. "Lost track of time on a dead-line and realized I hadn't even packed for the weekend."

Only a year older than Lottie, Helen already enjoyed a de-gree of success as a society and fashion columnist for the *Chicago Chronicle*, Ransom's flagship newspaper. Standing tall and lithe, her brown bob peeked out from a smart summer cloche hat that complimented her cream drop-waist dress with black geometric trim.

"Then we hit a patch of traffic on the way out," Rex said.

"Too bad, too," said Helen. "I wanted to breeze in that breezer of his."

"I'd have hated for you to lose your pretty hat." He tipped his own straw boater to her.

"Oh, I've lost my pretty head anyway."

Rex turned his smile on Lottie. "*You* look spiffy."

She poked a finger into her dimple and held out the hem of her pleated dress as she curtsied.

"Always perfect for the occasion, pet," Helen said, patting Lottie's head scarf. "*This* is cute. I do wonder about the footwear." She looked pointedly at the actress's bare feet.

"Oh, just wanted to feel the grass between my toes, you know?"

"Now *that's* the berries. Let's go."

Without any hesitation, Helen removed her own T-straps and chucked them aside before taking Lottie's hand and leading her down to the reflecting pool. Whooping, the ladies skipped right into the shallow water, dancing, kicking, and singing.

Edith *tsk*ed at how they risked dampening and dirtying their frocks, not to mention disturbed the pond's plant life. But then she remembered her own manners and quickly mixed up a cocktail for their new guest.

Beside her, Ransom directed Rex's attention to Noble. "I believe you gentlemen have met?"

"Rex Rainger, good to see you again." Noble gave him a hearty handshake. "Congratulations again on your film debut. Quite a different world for you."

"Rex is plenty used to public attention," Ransom said with renewed vigor. "He's been famous in these parts since he could practically walk."

Frederick Rainger was now known nationwide for his half-back position on the Chicago Cardinals, but he'd been a local football hero long before that. His unmatched record on the

Wheaton High School team had carried on to downstate victories for the Fighting Illini, too, at the University of Illinois. He'd been nicknamed "The Red Fox" in those early days for his auburn hair, pointy nose, and quick thinking on the field, and over the years the moniker had shortened into just "Rex." So, Rex he became, and Rex he'd remained.

"First recipient of the *Chronicle's* Pewter Pigskin award, in fact," Ransom continued.

Noble leaned in to elbow Rex. "Pays to know the publisher, right?" When Ransom's expression turned to stone, Noble stood straight again. "But, really, Rainger, with your individual record, don't you think you're wasting yourself on a losing team? Isn't it time to move across town?"

"Halas has been trying to sign him ever since he graduated," Ransom said on Rex's behalf as the athlete accepted his drink from Edith. "I assure you he can do what he wants when he wants."

"Gosh, I don't know about that," Rex said, "but it *is* a privilege to hold the Bears' interest. I'm confident the Cardinals will turn it around this year, though, and I've been their fan from the beginning, so…"

Ransom side-eyed Noble. "He'll be loyal to the end."

The actor coughed into his hand. "So, ah, will I be seeing you again in Los Angeles? Made quite a splash out there, too." He slapped the athlete's back and clinked glasses. "To *The Renaissance Man!*"

"A talkie at that," Edith remarked. "Not even Lottie's done one of those."

Only too late did she realize the implication of what she'd said. No, Lottie hadn't done a talking picture yet, which was fair enough given both she and the medium were still new to the industry. But Noble Howard had been in the business for quite some time. Lottie would've already ridden his coattails to the soundstage if he'd been offered a speaking role himself.

"Though the great Howard and Landry must be slated for the next one, of course." Edith downed the rest of her gin as if that could further cover her gaffe.

"Yes, of course," Noble echoed, all smiles if not all truth. "Biggest budget yet, too. But, really, Rainger, even for a smaller production, hats off." He pantomimed the gesture with his hand since he wasn't wearing a hat any more than he likely meant an ounce of this humility. "And Lottie was sure on cloud nine to see your mug. Practically threw herself at you like the other dames. You score on all fields, don't you, pal?"

He punched Rex on the arm—pretty hard, Edith thought.

"I don't know about that," Rex replied with a sheepish grin, hardly flinching at Noble's contact, "but I did have a lot of fun and am flattered with the offers. For more pictures, I mean." He blushed and ran his hand up and down the side of his neck. "But I haven't decided if I'll do another film. We'll see how this next season goes."

Noble finished off his drink and bit down on a chunk of ice. "Why, sure. I imagine you felt rather out of your element, without training and all."

Rex straightened and dropped his hand from his neck, sliding it into his beige trouser pocket instead. "Wasn't so bad. I had a good director. And, well—" he chuckled "—portraying a football player wasn't too hard, I guess."

"Even so, athletes usually do make awkward actors. Babe Ruth couldn't even play himself convincingly." Sniggering, Noble chewed on more ice.

"The man just hit his five hundredth home run and continues to count them," Rex said. "All *he* needs to play is baseball."

"Oh, but you did just fine, kid," Noble went on, seeming not to hear him. "I couldn't do what you guys do, handling your balls and all that."

Rex's smile hardened. "You look like you could use a refill there, sport." He went to take Noble's glass, but Edith snatched it first and set it aside.

"No, I think perhaps he's had enough. We want to see you at dinner, Noble." She raised her brow at him despite tottering a little on her own feet.

"Yes," Noble said, "making whoopee all afternoon, I could do with a lie-down, in fact. Make my excuses to the girls, will ya? And tell Lottie to see me?"

Rex saluted the actor—and laughed with Edith when Noble made a conspicuous grab for a whiskey decanter on his way inside.

"He might be drinking his dinner." With a softer smile, Rex leaned in to kiss Edith's cheek before shaking Ransom's hand. "Thanks for having me, Colonel. Always good to be home."

"Good to have you here, my boy," Ransom said. "Belleau's always open to your family, and it was kind of you to drive Helen out. Pity your father won't be here tonight, but we hope he's still joining us for the hunt tomorrow?"

"Far as I know." Rex nodded. "He sure appreciated the invitation, sir. Hunting's just more his scene than dinner parties. I hope you don't take offense by that."

"Course not, of course not. If anyone deserves evenings off after the time he's served, it's him. I respect the peace your father kept in this community, and, safer as I'd feel on his watch again, I don't begrudge a man a quiet and private life well-earned."

"How he managed those hours while raising you boys, *all* on his *own*," Edith said warmly—and rather over-dramatically, she realized, as the words came out. She wouldn't have thought her mouth had room for *both* feet, but now she'd done it, broaching a personal subject her tongue wouldn't have dared touch when sober.

Yet the Warnes and Raingers had been fond friends for years now, getting to know each other fast and familiarly in this small and relatively peaceful community. The rail and motorways invited riff-raff into its streets, however, which Chief Rainger had chased for years—most often as Wheaton's twenty-four-hour, one-man police force due to budget constraints. While someone of Ransom's status would naturally want to ingratiate himself with anyone of authority in the region—indeed, nation and world at large—Lewis Rainger, now retired, was a gentle giant, and it took no effort or agenda to befriend such a kind soul. And from the looks of it, his sons were following suit. Losing their mother at such a young age would've broken lesser individuals, but their family's strong physical stature was mirrored in their will, making them quintessential Americans in Ransom's favorable eyes.

"It was all he could do to manage both. Toughest man I know." Rex smiled and looked down into his drink, clinking his ice in the brief silence that followed. He cleared his throat. "Lottie looks well. As if she ever hasn't." He chuckled again and shook his head, and Edith saw another faint blush bloom in his cheeks. "Like Noble said, I got to see her in Los Angeles not too long ago. Only briefly at a party. It'll be nice to catch up properly this weekend without so many people around."

"Yes," Ransom said, squinting at Rex before looking out at the girls in the pool. "It's good to have her home."

Edith bit her lip and tapped her nails on her glass. Swaying slightly on her feet, she brought the drink to her lips to polish it off, only to realize she already had. But its fumes lingered between the ice, and when they reached her nose, she began to swoon. The brickwork of the house's rear wall rippled like water, and oh, how she dearly wished Lottie would stop splashing in it already with her precious porcelain feet.

It was slipping from her grasp…all of it…

Dully, she could almost physically feel it. The life leaving her hand…and her heart coming crashing after.

"Mrs. Warne?"

"Edith?"

The two men each grabbed her under her shoulders before she could sink into the shards of her shattered glass.

"The heat, you think?" Rex asked after helping Ransom lay Edith on the porch's sofa.

Chauncey, the butler, had made every effort at sweeping up the glass slivers before retrieving a maid. Ransom thanked them both, then sat in a patio chair next to Edith, holding her hand and patting it as he looked at Rex and shook his head. "She enchants guests with her mixtures yet can't take her own medicine. Usually just wine at dinner. I don't know what's gotten into her today."

"I hear you, Ransom," Edith said weakly with her eyes still closed. "Don't worry your handsome head about it."

Their words held the weight of something more, but Rex knew it wasn't his place to speculate, already uncomfortable in the heavy air beneath that porch's heavy roof. When he and Helen first arrived, Lottie hadn't changed her expression quickly enough to hide how sallow she'd looked, emptied of air with Edith at her side speaking in low, scolding tones.

An old memory came calling—of Edith's voice, yelling from Belleau's front patio for Lottie to get off the ice truck that instant. *"Let them do their job, girl. You're only getting in the way."*

It had been a hot and sticky summer day like this, Rex recalled, and he'd been on one of his shifts for R.C. Johnson's Ice Company at the old and responsible age of sixteen. His twelve-year-old brother Henry had come back from the playground with another local boy and an overheated and cranky Lottie. The second Rex had seen the little French girl's wrinkled brow, contrasting so sharply with her lively yellow ringlets, he'd laughed and invited the kids onto the ice truck during his deliveries if it would cool them off and cheer them up. Thus began a new summer tradition that Old Man Johnson was happy to oblige so long as no one got hurt—and no one had until Edith spied her ward's skinny legs hanging off the back of the truck. Reprimanding her in front of the boys hadn't hurt anything more than Lottie's feelings, granted, and Rex stepped in to rightfully take the blame. But seeing that pretty little brow still pinched in that same way just now...

Well, if his presence could've had anything to do with restoring color to those dimpled cheeks today—and that night in LA—Rex was glad of it.

Silently, he walked to the bar cart and wrapped a cloth napkin around some ice. He brought it to Ransom to lay on Edith's forehead.

"Thanks, son."

"Yes, thank you, Frederick," Edith said kindly. But Ransom had no sooner received the cold compress from Rex when Edith grabbed it and applied it herself. "That racket doesn't help," she muttered.

Meeting Ransom's eye, Rex grinned amiably but felt increasingly awkward as the Warnes' third wheel. Their tension only thickened the humid air. At some point, the breeze must've stopped.

In Edith's defense, the ladies on the lawn were still singing and laughing and somehow growing louder. Rex stepped over to the railing to see Lottie and Helen walking back toward the house — yet not the porch. They veered east instead, and, as they were already quite wet, he guessed where they'd head next. Two screams followed by two splashes and more screams confirmed that suspicion.

"Not the swimming pool," Edith whispered.

Rex laughed to himself with an itch to join them.

"Where have all the ladies gone?" She sighed and shook her head beneath the ice. "Ransom, really, you cannot fill that in soon enough."

"Oh?" Rex asked. "Not getting your use of it?"

"*We* certainly aren't," said Edith. "And now he doesn't like a pool so close to the new library, which he just *had* to build another porch off, too."

Rex ignored the ill humor and nodded.

"We couldn't have a Montpellier without a Monticello, now could we?" Ransom boasted. "Son, this southern edifice on which we stand is modeled after the great President Madison's porch. The new one is Jefferson's."

"A noble homage," Rex said. "So, is this the pool's last season?"

"'Fraid so, my boy." Looking to Edith's resting face, Ransom appeared to take advantage of her closed eyes by flashing a mischievous grin. "You should enjoy it." He cocked his head eastward, adding with a wink, "Dive in while you can."

Rex had never seen this side of the Colonel's disposition, wondering now if his request that Rex drive Helen here had been with ulterior motive. But Rex didn't regard Miss Conroy in that way, didn't doubt that feeling was mutual, and he worried what Mrs. Warne would think of him joining the present spectacle either way. He also hadn't thought to bring a bathing suit.

Then again, the young ladies hadn't bothered, and with the sun lowering in the sky, the wet heat trapped beneath his shirt, and the sweet siren song of Lottie's laughter rippling on the waters, he couldn't resist. He removed his hat and set it on the cushion of an empty patio chair. Peeling off his jacket next, he folded and laid it neatly over the chair's back.

"And how, sir," he said before hopping down the Madison porch steps.

Paddling in and out of view as he neared the Jefferson porch, the girls simulated a water ballet. They squealed when Rex charged at the pool as if going for the touchdown — and positively shrieked as he belly-flopped onto them.

Rex was first out of the water so he could retrieve towels for the saturated ladies in white. Dripping, he was made to wait at the back door on the Madison porch while Chauncey fetched the linens. The Colonel and Mrs. Warne had since retired indoors. They would rest in their respective bedrooms until dinner.

"My hero!" Lottie cried with expertly executed melodrama as Rex returned with the towels and knelt to help her out of the pool. He averted his eyes until the bath towel could preserve her modesty—or he at least tried to, as he had to ensure she made it safely out and onto the grass. In the brief seconds of that safety check, he could see the lacy texture of her brassiere beneath her transparent white blouse, which clung to every contour of her—

He caught Helen watching him from the water's edge, smirking.

His cheeks blazed, and Lottie's cool body pressed to his until he could wrap her in the towel. He rubbed her arms to help warm her but then quickly sent her on her way so he could lift Helen out next. Lottie snatched her discarded vest and hairband from the grass and swayed from side to side while she waited for them.

Helen's white dress suffered the same lack of opacity, but she emerged confidently and helped herself to her own towel. She picked up her hat and, still grinning, elbowed Rex as she passed by him to follow Lottie. "Keep your eye on the prize, all-star."

Patting himself dry at the pool's side, Rex squinted at the east-wing Jefferson porch and the library windows beyond it. He raised a hand to shade his sight against the sun's journey west and exhaled when he saw no prying eyes.

Walking arm in arm with Helen up the rear porch steps, Lottie shook off a residual shiver as the pool water evaporated into the early evening air. A mild breeze had picked up again.

"You sure know how to show a gal a good time," she told her friend.

"By drowning her?"

"By throwing a life vest when she was already drowning." Lottie dropped her volume on the last few words as they entered the Warne mansion via Ransom's study. No one was there, and before they crossed into the foyer, she held Helen back a step.

"Maybe it's none of my beeswax," Helen ventured, "but, you need to talk about it?" She gestured for Lottie to take the desk chair.

Lottie could hear the occasional clank of dinnerware as the staff set the table in the next room. She remained standing but took Helen's hand in hers.

"Very much. But—" she glanced at each doorway again "—not now. Not here."

"All right," Helen said. "But tonight? You seem urgent."

"Tonight." Lottie nodded. "If I can. There's something I might need to take care of first."

"First? You sure you don't want tell me beforehand?"

Tried and true, Lottie's lower lip trembled as she opened and closed her mouth on the words she couldn't say. But there was no hiding anything from Helen's investigative gaze.

"Oh, Lottie, I think we need to have that conversation sooner rather than later."

Doing her best to keep composure, Lottie nodded and sniffed. "All right. I'll try." Just then, she saw movement out the window. "Well, well," she said, recovering her shaking voice as Rex entered. "What happened to you, fella?"

"I just saw Ernie Hart on the east lawn on his way up the terraces, about to head home. Says he works here?"

"Practically grew up here, silly goose. You knew that."

"I knew his father maintained the grounds, but good for Ernie! Seems the labor's done him very good indeed. He's built like a baby grand. I nearly didn't recognize him."

Lottie's chest lightened with laughter. "Not the pipsqueak with the nosebleeds anymore. You know he helps old Mr. Johnson, too?"

"For the ice company? Well, I'll be! He sure didn't stand a chance lifting those blocks back then."

"Not everyone was the hulking brute you already were by the tenth grade. And he was a few years younger, besides."

Rex folded his arms and widened his stance. "I remember the little runt you were, too."

She smiled up at his amused eyes. Along with his fine nose and gentle lips, they nicely offset his strong brow and jaw. "Good thing you were there to protect us both, then."

One corner of his lips twitched upward. "I did, didn't I?"

"Mm-hm." Holding the ends of her towel at her chest, she twisted side to side. "The poor little French girl and even poorer pipsqueak. *Mon héro.*"

Rex reached to wipe wet strands from her forehead and out of her eyes. "*Toujours, ma chère.*"

Always, my dear.

"When'd you learn that?" she asked softly.

"You taught me, remember?" He seemed to blink more rapidly. "Strange not to hear a trace of your accent now."

Tipping her head to the side, she rewound the flickering newsreel in her mind to her first years in America, before schooling and theatrical aspirations had assimilated her tongue. She pressed her lips together and shook her head.

"You know," Rex said. "The ice truck. I let you and Ernie tag along."

"Ah, yes. Of course. But only because Henry asked."

He laughed. "That's right, my brother the philanthropist."

"Hey!" She released a hand from her towel to slap him on the arm. "We were his friends, not a charity case. At least until he grew big like you."

Still laughing, Rex bit his lip. His gaze dipped below her shoulders, reminding her of her revealing, as-yet wet garments. She pursed her lips into the smile-pout she'd become famous for and held her eyes on him as she swung the loose end of the towel back around her.

"How is Henry, anyway?"

"Good. Has his degree now and sights set on a new crime detection lab in Chicago. It's only just opened, and he's not nearly experienced enough but hoping to get under someone's wing there. Meeting with some affiliates this weekend, in fact, which is why he can't be here."

"Won't he follow your father in DuPage county?"

"Naw, not as a long-term career, anyway, and Pop's glad of it. The way it was when we were growing up, it wasn't a life. Not for him, at least, not outside law enforcement. And Henry wants to explore the *science* of crime. Guess there's more to forensics than fingerprints." As if punctuating his sentence, he raised his index finger.

Lottie did the same, pressing the pad of her finger to his. "Oh, I don't know," she said with a side-grin. "I think fingerprints are still effective. In the right places."

A snort burst from across the room. Helen, who'd settled herself at Ransom's roll-top desk during this exchange, had apparently reached her limit on silence.

"Oh, don't let me interrupt, darlings. Must be all this nature getting to me." She swiped a hand over her nose. "City girl, country allergies. Unless I'm catching cold from our swim?"

Grasping the chair's wooden arms, Helen shivered from her head to torso. "Time to dip in a warm bath." She gathered her towel as she rose and draped it like a mink stole around her shoulders. "Carry on." Waving her hand, she exited to the foyer.

Rex grew redder than his hair and shoved his hands into his pockets. Though not nearly as risqué as her and Helen's pool-soaked frocks, his wet, pale shirt clung to him in rather interesting ways, which Lottie took the opportunity to notice while he shyly looked to the carpet. She stepped closer and released one end of her towel again to lay her fingers on his wrist.

He shifted on his feet.

"I," she began, then stopped when he met her gaze. So used to fans' stares and critics' jeers, women's glares and men's leers, she rarely met a sincere eye. To chance on one like his, she wanted to preserve it forever.

But like fame, so much was fleeting. The only ones who'd stood the test of time so far were Ransom, Helen, and, sure, Ernie could count, too. And not that she'd ever *dis*counted Rex, but until he'd appeared in Hollywood this past spring, she hadn't seen him since her high school years. He had already moved on to greener football fields by then, and after only one year at college, she herself had set off for golden shores.

"I," she tried again, shivering still from the cool water, "should probably…freshen up. And dress for dinner. You, too."

Drawing his lips into a soft smile, Rex only nodded.

"Poor fellow, dragged into the deep as soon as you got here. Has Chauncey even shown you to your room?"

He chuckled lightly. "He tried to, but the Colonel grabbed us by the elbows and practically shoved us through the house and out the back door. I don't think Chauncey had any choice but to grab the cocktail cart to at least offer us drinks."

"Oh, dear." Lottie laughed into her chest. "That's Ransom for you. Either the stoic man of the world or the silly boy on his playground."

"Quite a playground it is." Rex looked around the mahogany-furnished office. Paintings of the 1893 World's Columbian Exhibition in Chicago adorned the walls, while Edith's porcelain bric-a-bracs from various trips to China collected dust on shelves. On the desk stood a framed letter from Abraham Lincoln requesting a back-issue of the *Chronicle* from Ransom's grandfather. "There's real history here. I've never had that."

"You're making it," Lottie said with a gentle poke to his firm stomach. "Rex Rainger, I'm real proud of you."

"Not doing bad yourself, Lottie Landry."

Her cheeks burned at how his tongue had curled itself around the *l*s of her name. He took her hand and, after rubbing her pruned fingers a bit to heat them, raised them to his lips to press an even warmer kiss on her knuckles. And just like that, her thawing was complete.

Lottie and Rex exchanged shy smiles as she escorted him up the main staircase to his lodging for the night. His and Helen's suitcases were absent from the entrance hall, so they assumed Chauncey had already delivered the luggage to their respective rooms. Being alone with Lottie in such tight proximity—and getting to watch her from behind—was nice. But Rex instead pretended to admire the framed Chinese needlepoints and sketches hanging on the walls.

Rounding up from the last landing, they crept wordlessly onto the third floor to avoid disturbing Noble or Helen in the adjacent rooms. At the end of the hall, Lottie spun around and gestured through an open door.

Rex took one step across the threshold before turning back to her. "Thank you," he said quietly. Her towel hung loosely around her shoulders now, so he reached to wrap it around her more snugly. "I look forward to continuing our conversation at dinner."

"Me, too," she whispered, "and thank you."

"For what?"

She gently burrowed her lips into the terrycloth swaddled at her neck. Then she looked up at him again with those big brown eyes.

"For being a gentleman. Here and…"

She propped up on her toes to kiss his cheek. Her lips lingered there longer than they probably should have, though not nearly as long as Rex would've liked. Nodding with a last, departing smile, she spun on the ball of her dainty foot and padded away.

Rex leaned against his doorway and watched every step of her light tread down the hall. She slowed as she approached one closed door, pausing outside it for a few seconds. He saw her tentatively reach for it, but before her fine fingers could grace its surface, she snatched her hand back. Clutching her towel to her neck, she tiptoed swiftly to the stairs and down them.

The sound of running water trickled into his awareness from the room next door, but Rex held his stare on the closed door that had drawn Lottie to it like a papery moth to a devouring flame. No one had told her that Noble had asked to see her, he just remembered. If Rex followed her now, he could catch her in time to relay that message. Yes, if he just followed her now…

Backing into his guest room, Rex shut the door and looked for his suitcase to unpack.

5

On the second floor, Lottie slowed her stride with safe sanctuary in view. Her bedroom, the same she'd had since Ransom had taken her in. Her refuge after losing her mother and then her motherland—and from Edith, who'd been poor compensation for either. But Lottie had Ransom, and she had this room. A space of her own to breathe.

She inhaled deeply as she opened the door and ambled to her en-suite bathroom. Dropping the damp towel to the floor, she discarded her wet frock and undergarments as well and replaced them with a silvery-white silk robe. Wrapping it over her bare form, she examined her reflection in the mirror above the sink. The glistening fabric molded over her curves much as her soaked blouse had. Emerging from the pool that way and into Rex's waiting arms, she'd felt like Aphrodite, born of sea foam to love and tantalize. And hadn't she tantalized right then, the way Rex's eyes had fallen on her body until decency guided his chin away.

But I've already played that role, she thought as she ran her hands over her contours, the screen goddess of love. Born of industry gods castrating each other on that Hollywood Olympus, where the almighty Studio had arranged her marriage, too. Except Noble didn't resemble the humble, disfigured smith Aphrodite was betrothed to. He was more Ares, the volatile god of war that the goddess took as her lover. And Noble's battlefield was behind closed doors, where he took as *his* lover any leggy brunette he fancied. What the camera didn't catch never happened, and all was fair in Love and War as long as they both played their parts.

If only Lottie hadn't been so foolish as to actually love him… once. Noble Howard had become a household name during her formative years, risen from the obscurity of Howard Noble, the Ohio traveling salesman. Up until four years ago, she'd only seen his photos in the paper. Ransom's private theatre in Belleau's basement was only a recent innovation that he now entertained with on weekends, and special trips to the city's cinemas before that had been few and far between. So, it was 1925 when the local Wheaton Grand Theatre first set Noble's image in motion for a seventeen-year-old country girl. And Lottie had liked what she'd seen. Very much.

So much so that after only a year at the University of Chicago and brief experience in local theatre and modeling, she'd felt it her Manifest Destiny to push farther west on American soil. She'd accepted money from Ransom to make the move possible—but only as a loan, she insisted. She wasn't the opportunistic "four-flusher" Noble and Edith made her out to be and had already paid that loan back with interest. She'd likewise agreed that Ransom could arrange one dinner meeting with a Los Angeles contact but nothing more—and she'd done it only to please her guardian, whom she so liked pleasing and knew would arrange the meeting regardless of her consent.

As it happened, one introduction to a studio executive was all it had taken. She'd had to audition on her own merit, but fit the bill now that Noble's previous leading woman had aged away from her roles. And though elocution lessons had significantly Americanized Lottie's diction, what French influence remained gave her voice richness in tone and silkiness in texture—rendering her ripe for the talkie transition.

Above all, the Howard-Landry chemistry was undeniable. And Lottie would be lying if she said she hadn't fallen in love with Noble on film. His glossy hair and crystal eyes, that debonair moustache, the sophistication of his gait—they leaped off the screen but knocked you to the floor in person. And to have the full intensity of that charm trained on you...

She hadn't stood a chance.

Even now, standing in her bathrobe, alone on the cold tile, actively avoiding the man himself, who was only just upstairs... she could still feel the thrill, the expectant elation of receiving that first kiss. Not a character's kiss, but Noble's, the real man whose real breath brushed her face. Whose real hands stroked her waist, her back, her cheek, and promised so much more when she was ready. She had only to be ready. And meanwhile, wasn't the studio happy for its publicity stunt to actually hold water? Planting stories in the press that these two were the real deal, so thoroughly and convincingly that even Lottie herself had, for a time, believed it.

Sighing, she tied the sash at her waist and bent over the tub to stopper the drain and draw some warm water. While she waited, she stepped into her bedroom, raised the window behind her cherry wood vanity table for some air, and then sat to brush tangles from her frizzed hair. She'd no sooner lifted her silver-filigreed brush from its tray when a dark movement in the mirror made her start.

Noble, reclining on her bed in a terrycloth robe. Nothing more, as far as she could tell. She stared at his reflection over her shoulder.

"You've kept me waiting," he said.

"Why aren't you in your room?"

He shrugged. "Yours was closer."

As he sat up and set his feet on the floor to stand, Lottie turned around to see the crystal whiskey decanter had accompanied him in there, its volume visibly diminished. She gripped her brush handle.

He staggered just a little as he sauntered to her. "Oh, baby, why the icy mitt, huh? We don't get much chance to be alone."

Turning back to the mirror, she sulkily brushed her hair. "Bank's closed."

"Aw, c'mon. I've missed you. I've wanted you." The carnal musk of his fragrance wafted from behind, undiluted by the soft breeze breathing through the window. He laid his hands on her silken shoulders and began massaging them. "Haven't you made me wait long enough?"

For all his alcohol consumption, he enunciated clearly. Practice made perfect. Only his glassy, reddened eyes gave away his chemical state. Now was not the time to have a serious talk with him.

Meanwhile, his fingers made their own impressions. Lottie moaned before she could help herself when he moved over a pressure point; he did know how to hit the sweet spots. Since there was no point in talking now anyway—and she was still rather stiff from their long train journey—she dropped her head as permission to continue. He did, and his lips found her neck.

"What are you doing?" she whispered.

"Spoiling my appetite before dinner," he murmured as he nipped at her earlobe.

His hands stroked down her back, and after kneading above her tailbone to elicit more sighs, he eased his palms around her waist. Lottie tipped her head to the side to bare her throat to him, and he carried his kisses there accordingly.

Opening her eyes, she watched her and Noble's reflection, a perfect cameo of lovers encased in the beveled oval mirror. In that moment, she realized he was right: they were alone, really alone, for the first time in a very long while. So, when he beckoned her to stand, she did, entranced. She didn't stop to understand why.

Stepping around her upholstered stool, she accepted his hand and let it draw her to him. She pressed against him while his fingers roved through her hair and down her back. She received his lips as if she could lick the whiskey off them and further this intoxication, which made him groan and grip her hips against his.

"Baby," he whispered into her skin before drawing his head away to penetrate her with his eyes, their ice blue brought to melting point.

Lottie breathed shallowly through slightly parted lips, her gaze not leaving his. Noble caressed up her waist, rolling his thumbs over the side swells of her breasts. Her breath released on a measured yet shaky exhale. Then his lips melded to hers again, and, slowly, his hands slid down to untie her sash.

Lottie broke away. "Not yet," she panted. *Not ever*, she should've said. But when it was just the two of them like this, when he was so attentive, it warmed her heart to the tender moments she believed they *had* shared and gave her hope.

Returning one hand to her waist, he brushed his fingers through her hair and over her ear. "But I want to love you, Lottie," he crooned, kissing her lips, face, and neck. "Let me love you, won't you?" He slid his hand down her cheek and toward her chest.

She closed her eyes, vaguely aware of the water still running in the next room. "But we agreed," she whispered as she took his hand away and interlaced their fingers.

"We're good as engaged, baby," he said into her neck. "After this weekend, the world will know."

His mouth moved lower, but she took his face into her hands and raised it to hers. "Then it won't be much longer to wait." And maybe that could still be true. She pecked his lips. "We'll make our plans swiftly." Another kiss. "We can have the celebration here at Belleau, and—"

"I'll celebrate *this* here, too," he said as he grabbed her bottom.

"Don't be silly." Giggling, she spun her back to him, but he trapped her in his arms before she could escape. Holding her close, his hands roved over her from behind.

Her knees could've given out when he started suckling her earlobe once more. Yet when his fingers trailed down her torso, she stopped them before they could dip too low. "Please," she tittered. "Not now." She dropped her smile a bit as she scanned her bedroom. "Not here."

"Why not?" he breathed into her hair, beginning to slip the robe from her shoulders and planting a kiss on the skin he exposed, inch by inch. "I want you here, under his roof."

Lottie grabbed her lapels before the silk could fall. "What?" she half-laughed.

"I want you in this house, where he can hear."

Eyes widening, she snatched both her robe and herself out of his grasp, her smile altogether gone. She adjusted the garment back in place.

"Why would you say that?"

Noble's thin moustache curled with his lip, and he crept toward her. "Because I want him to know you're mine, Lottie."

To avoid backing into the bed, she shifted toward the vanity. "He knows that."

He stepped forward. "*Only* mine."

She stepped backward. "I was never anyone else's."

He sneered, maintaining his pursuit until Lottie was sitting on her vanity table with her back against the mirror. Wedging himself between her knees, he took her chin between his thumb and index finger and raised it to him just like Ransom had earlier.

"Do you…mean…to tell me," he said with dark amusement in his voice, "that nothing's ever happened?" Rotating his wrist, he pressed his finger against her lips, then trailed it down her chin and throat. "A young woman, come of age." His fingertip traced past her clavicle to where her lapels crossed over her breasts. "Right down the hall from a bitter wife. Do you expect me to believe—" his finger split the silk down to her sash "—that never once did Daddy—" he leaned in to press his lips to her ear and eased his palm under the robe and around her bare waist "—tuck you in at night?"

She yanked his arm away with one hand and slapped him with the other. His face turned away with the impact.

"Oh, that's right," Noble said as he slowly faced her again. He then gripped her jaw so roughly she felt it could snap. "He's *not* your daddy. So if he hasn't already lain with you the way a man does with a woman, then he ought to know he never will."

Though the effort hurt in his clutch, she replied through clenched teeth, "You've acted in too many dramas."

He snorted. "You could do with the experience."

"Like all your quiffs on the side?"

"Better than flirts like you with no follow-through. You think you'd be anybody without me? Go ahead, give it a try. Break your contract instead of bluffin' it all the time. You're all talk."

"And you're all washed up. You need *me* now."

He pressed her head back, arching her neck over the mirror as the tip of its wooden oval frame dug between her shoulder blades. "Need you? I *made* you, and I'll—"

"You'll *what?*"

His nostrils flared. "I'll destroy you. My lovely little creation's lovely little reputation, damaged beyond repair once the papers learn she's been makin' nookie with the esteemed Colonel Warne all along." He nodded repeatedly. "That's right. I'll bring that big cheese down with ya."

A warm breeze tickled Lottie's scalp from behind. She narrowed her eyes and straightened her spine as best she could. "Go chase yourself."

He tightened his hold on her jaw enough that she couldn't speak any further. She aimed to spit instead, but before she tried, his gaze softened, if only with mock contrition. Gently, he kissed her forehead and then her lips.

"Better turn off that water, baby." He jerked his head toward the bathroom. "Wouldn't want to drown. Would we."

He slid his hand from her jaw and gripped her throat for a few seconds before releasing her and leaving the room.

Easing off the vanity, Lottie dragged her bare feet across the floor. She entered the bathroom and sat at the tub's edge. Her heart punched against her breastbone while she reached to twist the tap. Dropping her hand from the faucet, she raked the water with her trembling fingertips, zoning out at the ripples she created.

And wanting to see Noble's bloated, breathless face beneath them.

Pairings

to enhance the dining experience

6

"Ransom, would you mind please—oh!" Edith froze where she stood in the doorway.

Lottie, in Ransom's bedroom, sitting at the edge of his chaise lounge in a silvery robe and pearls like a portrait of some Ziegfeld girl. She turned and stood at once on seeing Edith.

"I, I didn't mean to barge in," Edith stammered. "I only wanted help with my..." Numb, she vaguely gestured to her side.

Lottie glided over the oriental rug with a deep flush that belied her composure. "Let me."

"No, no, it's all right." Edith backed out the door. "I can easily manage."

Clutching the side of her gown, she swiftly retreated across the hall. Once she'd closed her own bedroom door behind her, Edith blinked rapidly and willed herself to breathe again. Stiffly walking toward her full-length mirror, she turned her side to it and, after flickering her fingers like a pianist warming up at the bench, set to work. One by one, she fastened the hook-and-eye closures of her dress.

Her lady's maid had been out all week, tending to her ill mother, and Edith wanted all other assistance devoted to the evening's entertainment. Born to more modest wealth than she'd married into, she wasn't so precious that she couldn't dress herself, after all, and usually did except for special occasions. Just as well, then, that her girl wasn't available; Edith wouldn't regard anything that happened tonight as particularly *special*.

"Fool," she whispered over her shoulder to her reflection. Her twisted neck folded her skin unattractively. Yes, she'd been a fool for even trying to tempt her husband with this task. Obviously, it was too late.

But, being a lady of manners, she would not create a scene this weekend. What was happening under her very roof was the concern of only a few, and not all of her guests should be troubled. Be merry they should, so make merry she would.

Feeling almost arthritic, though, Edith fumbled with the last hook. She let out a small yelp and cupped a hand over her mouth, refusing to shed a tear. Still, she heaved with a sob and just stood there a moment, breathing in and out through the space between her fingers.

Eventually, she released her hand. She managed to slide the last hook into place with more ease and even took a moment to admire her slim silhouette. The cascading champagne silk favored her complexion, and the gold beading dazzled in a way that made the finger waves of her oiled chestnut hair gleam that much more. The flutter of chiffon draping behind her bare arms retained some modesty and elegance, as did her hemline's bias cut, which allowed her slender ankles to peek out.

No, she did not wish to ruin this evening. *Have fun*, she told herself again as she crossed to her armoire and swung open its doors.

She retrieved a brown glass bottle from the lower drawer of her wardrobe and took a sip straight from its neck. Along the inside of the armoire, dancing skeletons crossed fleshless finger bones over their nonexistent hearts and swore to die all over again.

The "skeletons in her closet." She huffed a single note of laughter at her private joke. Really, they were only etchings on decorative paper that lined the wardrobe's interior, a pattern of cartoonish, bony figures that was less morbid than silly. She'd commissioned the print from an artist friend just to be clever. But perhaps there was truth in this jest, more that she could add tonight, too. *Have fun.* She concealed the elixir back in her drawer of treasures.

Edith crossed the room and paused at her door, opening it slowly, quietly. Just a crack. And in enough time to see Ransom embrace Lottie in his room across the way.

He held her close, so close. Then, as he leaned back and held Lottie's chin, he kissed the tip of her nose, and she left. Edith watched him standing there alone, clenching and unclenching his fists during a deep exhale. A frustrated man given a little and left wanting more. Once she heard the door to Lottie's room close down the hall, Ransom, too, walked out of sight.

Edith returned to her armoire for another fortifying sip from the bottle. The skeletons danced and laughed at her until she shut the door on them. Then she straightened her jewelry, smoothed her hair, and exited her room to join the others downstairs.

The party of six assembled and sat for dinner.

The Colonel presided from his usual chair at the head of the dining room table, with Edith sitting dull-eyed and far away at its opposite end. Lottie opted to sit nearer to Ransom, of course, with Noble to her right, nearer to Edith. Helen insisted on sitting across from the actor so she could stare into his dreamy eyes — or so Helen had said, and clearly joked, but Noble ate up the attention anyway. That left Rex sitting across from Lottie. She slid the silver candelabra over a little to enjoy a less-obstructed view.

Lottie liked watching him in the low light, how the flickering flames made his ocean-wave eyes dance. The rich cerulean mural wrapping around the room — another of Edith's East

Asian acquisitions—brought out the deep red in his hair, as did his midnight-blue apparel. She would've thought a tuxedo too stuffy for his style, but how she did enjoy the way he wore one. His jacket was the newer double-breasted sort, worn without a vest, which she adored if it meant one less layer of clothing on a man. The only other time she'd seen Rex this way had been in Los Angeles.

For as little coverage as her fine shoulder straps provided, Lottie's décolletage could sure heat up fast. Enough with that memory.

Ransom, at any rate, seemed fixated on Rex, too; he was very knowledgeable of the athlete's record and inquisitive about his experiences on the field. He did not ask about his Hollywood exploits, however. Neither did Lottie. Happy to let Ransom monopolize the conversation for a while, she simply sliced and ate her meal with dainty etiquette, stealing glances at both gentlemen and swallowing what she could into her fluttering stomach.

She did feel calmer, though, after speaking with Ransom in the privacy of his bedroom. She hadn't gone into all the details with him, the threats and accusations Noble had spat at her, but Ransom had assured her he'd snuff out any designs the actor had, no matter what it took. She never doubted he *would* be there for her when desperately needed, but what she hadn't expected was the Colonel's gift of pearls, the ones kissing at her collarbone this evening. A wedding gift, it seemed, for the wedding that wouldn't happen. Delighted by the treasure and warmed by his embrace, Lottie's heart couldn't have felt fuller. Her eyes were still a bit hungry, though, so she let them feast on the man across the table.

Noble, meanwhile, had Helen in stitches at the other end. Even Edith appeared to snap out of her daze a little as her body rocked with quiet laughter.

"So then he says, 'I see that, but where's the cow?'"

Helen hooted. "That's it." She threw her cloth napkin onto the table. "I'm quitting my job and running away with your circus."

"How is work anyway?" Lottie asked her, to diffuse Noble's energy. "We won't find ourselves in next week's society column, will we?"

"Can't blame me if you do! This material writes itself." Helen smiled.

"Hm." Noble grinned back. "We might need to settle this over a doubles match tomorrow afternoon. Though Lottie tells me you're a force to reckon with, Miss Conroy."

"The Gliding Ghost, they called her in school," Lottie said. "Just a streak of white on the court. You could barely see her footsteps."

"You have me confused with Helen *Wills*, I think."

"No confusion there, my dear," Noble said above the rim of his wine glass. "Wills wouldn't look like *that* in an evening gown."

Someone's silverware clinked against a plate.

Picking her napkin back up, Helen dabbed the corners of her lips before clutching the cloth to her chest, concealing the deep V of her dress. "Gown or no gown," she said, "I'd take a Wimbledon championship any day. She was marvelous. I can't wait for the Open."

"No gown, given the choice," Lottie heard Noble murmur into his glass as he swigged more of his red wine.

She cleared her throat loudly. "What was that, darling? More wine? Chauncey, if you could please." Mortification prickled at Lottie's cheeks and down her arms as she reluctantly watched the butler refill Noble's glass. In her urgency, she might have just chosen the worse of two evils.

She looked on in continued dismay at how the actor had foregone black-tie attire for an ascot and burgundy smoking jacket. Not a crime, certainly, for a private party at home, but Ransom did like his formalities and, as host, set the tone with his tailcoat. Either way, the men must've all been so warm on this summer night. Yet if they were, they masked it well. Too wealthy to sweat.

While Noble occupied his mouth with re-emptying his glass, Ransom asked, "Follow sporting events closely, do you, Helen?"

"Yes, sir. Very much to my mother's chagrin," she said with a proud smile.

"Only tennis?"

"Baseball, and I suppose I know a trifle about football, too." She scrunched her nose at Rex.

"She's being modest again, sir," he said. "You should've heard her talk on the way here. Halas could recruit *her*."

"Ever write about it?" Lottie asked.

"In letters and dreams," Helen answered wistfully, playing at the chiffon embellishment on her shoulder strap. "Otherwise, unless it's about the feminine experience at the parks or who wore what where, my editor has no interest." She bowed her head to Ransom. "With all due respect to your staff, sir. I know it's not my department."

"Mm-hm." He narrowed his eyes, and his lower cheek bulged out as he appeared to remove something from his teeth with his tongue. "Well, I make it a rule not to discuss business at the dinner table—" he raised his brow at Lottie, who'd brought up Helen's column in the first place "—and I don't want to mix it with your pleasure this weekend, but—" he looked down at his plate and nonchalantly cut his beef "—if Mr. Rainger here would consent to your interviewing him, I'd like to see that article on my desk Monday morning. And from there…we'll see."

Helen, who'd resumed eating, stopped chewing and stared at Ransom with her fork held in midair. She looked at Rex, who smiled and nodded his agreement, and then back at Ransom. Her mouth freshly stuffed with green beans, she just nodded excitedly until she could swallow. "Oh, that'd be swell, Colonel. Assignment accepted." She flashed a giddy smile at Lottie.

"*Rrrr*ed Fox," Noble growled from across the table. Slumped down and leaning back in his chair, he tapped his fingers on his wine glass. "Gee, that *is* swell. But don't neglect your society column just yet, Miss Conroy. This weekend'll serve you another exclusive, right on a platter." He looked at Lottie out of the corner of his eye and smirked before rolling his gaze at Rex. "After the *fox* hunt." Raising his fist, he extended his index finger and thumb. "*P-kew*," he said as his "discharged" finger pistol pointed from Rex to the ceiling.

"Your dinner's getting cold, darling," Lottie said with a tight grin. If it weren't for Ransom's assurances that he'd help her deal with Noble, she didn't think she could stomach any of this much longer.

Cocking his head away from her, Noble grasped his stemware instead of the silver. He rotated it side to side on the tablecloth.

Ransom ignored him to instead ask Rex, "Will this be your first time chasing your namesake?"

"Yes, sir. My father took us deer hunting as boys, and he's shot all sorts of game, but chasing with hounds is new for both of us."

"Mm." Ransom swallowed another mouthful. "Yes. Lewis told me about the bow-hunting he did up in Wisconsin."

"In his lumberjack days." Rex smiled. "Before he hunted people by trade."

Lottie widened her eyes.

"Oh, I mean," he was quick to say, "well, you know what I mean. Catching, not…killing."

She bit her lip and curled her shoulders with a silent giggle, which he reciprocated out loud.

"Speaking of lumber," Ransom said, "does your father stay in touch with the Ashbys?"

"Too low in the ranks for that, I think."

"Ah-ha, well, I've begun a collaboration with the elder son, Lloyd," Ransom said. "We're funding a lab out in Geneva."

"Lab, sir?" Rex asked.

"Cryptanalysis training. For army students."

"Gosh, you don't say?"

"He's a decorated soldier, you know," Ransom said as he sawed his steak, "now looking to advance military intelligence. Though he still manages the family lumberyards, of course."

"Such a shame about the brother," Helen said.

"Ashby." Lottie squinted as the name took hold in her memory. "Oh, you must mean Alonzo," she said to Helen. "Yes, that was dreadful. Though I didn't know him personally."

"I'd see him now and then at family galas," Helen said. "Lon was a real good-time guy, but harmless."

Something seemed to click for Rex, too, as he slowly tipped his head back. "The one who jumped. Was that just last year?"

"A not-so-happy New Year," Helen said. Both she and Lottie nodded sympathetically.

A long whistle brought their attention to Noble. Carrying his pitch from high to low, he raised his hand and nose-dived it into the tabletop. "Jumped? Or was he pushed…"

As he slurred his *shh*, Lottie shook her head at him.

"My apologies, darling," he said to her. "You were obviously close." He looked around the table. "This has all been very uplifting, really, but if I might have a word with you, Ransom? In private?"

"Now?" the Colonel asked with food in his mouth, his one eyebrow arched.

"Well, perhaps when the others have their dessert," Noble amended.

Chewing thoughtfully, the Colonel stared at the table ahead of him. Once he'd swallowed, he said, "Certainly. But it can wait until we've all had our cake."

"Oh, I have all the sugar I need right here." Noble pinched Lottie's cheek. "And I'm afraid I can hardly *wait* a minute longer."

Lottie firmed her fist around her knife but gave everyone a polite smile.

Ransom placed a bite-sized bit of beef into his mouth and tested the actor's patience with another period of prolonged mastication. Lottie watched Helen's eyes dart from one man to the other as if she were watching a tennis match.

"Well, you see," Ransom finally said, "I can't do without *my* sweetness." Wiping his lips with his napkin, he looked over his shoulder. "Chauncey, when the time comes, Mr. Howard and I will take our cake in the library." Lottie was close enough to hear him add under his breath, "Give the devil his food."

"Sir?" Chauncey asked.

Ransom grinned at Noble. "It's devil's food."

"Mm," Noble grunted jovially.

"Ice cream, Mr. Howard?" the butler asked.

"Please."

The table returned to its clanking sounds. Lottie thought she heard Rex shift in his chair, and she looked up, hoping to meet his eye. He appeared in serious contemplation of his meal, however, so she trailed her gaze around the rest of the table, stopping at the hostess, whose eyes had glazed over again. "You're quiet tonight, Edith."

"Mm?" She glanced up from her plate. "Oh, just taking in everyone's conversation. Congratulations, dear," she said to Helen belatedly with a nod.

"Well, *I* am taking in your beauty, Mrs. Warne," Noble chimed in before Helen could share any gratitude. "You look exquisite tonight." The man practically sharpened his razor teeth on the words: *Missuzzz...exquizzzite.*

That revived Edith somewhat. Flushing from her cheeks to her chest as she tittered, she reached for her own wine. "Oh, Mr. Howard. How you flirt."

Lottie groaned in her mind but realized too late that her face had betrayed her sentiments. Hearing a light snort across the table, she saw Rex was watching her now; he fought to suppress a smile. She shrugged and smiled, too, then glanced at Ransom for some sort of reprimand. The Colonel merely shook his head and carried on feasting.

"This room is exquisite, too, Mrs. Warne," Helen said, gazing around at the wall mural. "You brought this entire landscape all the way from China? It's remarkable."

Edith sipped her wine and smiled at Noble as if he'd paid the compliment himself. "Hand-painted."

He shook his head in marvel. "Exquisite," he repeated, looking only at her and not the artwork they spoke of. Lottie would have thought Helen was ignored entirely if her friend didn't suddenly jerk with a small squeak, then scoot back a smidge and straighten in her seat with a feverish blush. No doubt the table was narrow enough for Noble's long leg to stretch across quite cozily. Lottie had seen it all before. Growing hot herself, she was only grateful for Helen's grace.

"Are you still painting, Mrs. Warne?" Helen asked.

"A portrait of *yourself*, I hope." Once again, Noble directed his words to the lady of the house, who admonished the innuendo in his tone with a flutter of her hand and shake of her head. Although, clearly, she loved it. "Those fetching green eyes of yours, dear."

Lottie dropped her shoulders and sighed. "I thought I saw the beginnings of an equestrian scene in your bedroom, Edith. I noticed it through the doorway."

Edith swiveled her head loosely on her neck with an odd grin before she looked at Lottie. "Oh, from Ransom's room?"

Lottie furrowed her brow. "From the hallway."

"So," Helen spoke up again, "speaking of China, what do you all make of this dispute over the Manchurian railway?"

Not even Noble could spin that subject into something suggestive, and so the dinner conversation successfully shifted to the Soviets and onward to domestic affairs—from the Prohibition Bureau's latest measures against Al Capone in the wake of last Valentine's Day to the Graf Zeppelin, which was expected to fly over Chicago next weekend as it completed its trip around the world (with Hearst's backing, Ransom added grudgingly).

"Speaking of," Lottie said to Ransom, "isn't it marvelous that Charles has taught Anne to fly?"

"You don't mean the Lindberghs?" Rex asked.

"Yes," Ransom answered happily. "She's a quiet one but ambitious."

"I think it's lovely they can share the sky," Lottie said. "And how they managed to marry in private." Only when it was out of her mouth did Lottie wish she'd been less open with her thoughts.

"We won't stand a chance at that, will we?" Noble said as if on cue, laughing into the glass that Chauncey had just refilled.

"You won't...*when?*" Helen asked, her stunned eyes bouncing between the couple. "Have you two—"

"He means we already don't," Lottie said quickly, glancing at Noble only to see his gaze fixed on Helen's low neckline as it had been for half the meal. "With all the publicity around our pictures and—but speaking of the Lindberghs, you know, I couldn't convince Noble to extend our holiday to New York so we could try Charles's new service back to California."

"Mm, yes," Rex acknowledged between bites. "The TAT."

"Which is what again?" Helen asked.

Ransom sliced the remaining bit of his meat. "Transcontinental Air Transport."

"*Air* transport," Noble scoffed, finally drawing his eyes away from Helen's chest to look up at the ceiling with his chin raised. "Rather misleading, don't you think? I wouldn't trust anything that new anyway."

Ransom wiped his mouth. "Charles put extensive planning into that route. Safety's the very reason it *doesn't* transport by air the entire way."

Noble held his hands up. "All due respect. But hopping on and off a plane every day to ride a train overnight sounds like an awful lotta hassle. I'll take the extra ten hours on the *Chief* if it means continuous comfort in a Pullman car. TAT *really* means 'Take a Train,' didn't you know?" He cackled.

"Well," Lottie said, "I think it sounds like a grand adventure. Something different."

"Less private." Noble leaned toward her with a deceptively debonair smile; she didn't smile back, only squinted one eye. "And while on the topic of moving things along…Mr. Warne, if we may?"

The Colonel fixed his dark eyes on the actor. In one swift move, he clapped his palms on the upholstered arms of his chair and scooted it back to stand. Stretching to full height, he stiffly extended his open hand toward the dining room door in invitation for his guest to leave first. Hands in pockets, Noble strolled through the doorway and blessedly out of Lottie's sight.

"Through to the Liberty Library, please," Ransom directed Noble as he approached the door himself. Before crossing its threshold, he turned back to Chauncey and lowered his voice as he said, "No dessert for us, thank you."

Only just deserts, Lottie hoped. She, for one, enjoyed seeing her almost-fiancé not get to have his cake and eat it, too. And if all went to plan, she'd have even more privacy on that Pullman train back to Los Angeles, less one passenger.

7

"Thank you, Chauncey," Helen said as she, then Rex, passed the butler on their way out of the dining room and into the foyer.

Across the way, the drawing room's buttery cream walls received them within a lighter atmosphere than the dim blue dining room, yet gilded sconce light illuminated the pale walls with a warm, golden glow. There, they joined Lottie, with Edith trailing behind. No one had seen Ransom or Noble since the men had excused themselves from the dinner table to have "a word." Nor had anyone had much appetite for dessert, simply poking at their spongy cake slices before abandoning them soon after.

Helen strode to the fireplace, where Lottie leaned her elbow on the mantel. "They, uh, in there?" She nodded toward the wall, referring to the east-wing library on its opposite side. The fireplace where they stood was flanked by two sets of solid French doors. Painted the same neutral shade as the rest of the room, each doorway led to the library.

Lottie pursed her lips and picked at her nails. "Mm-hm."

"And, uh—" Helen stepped closer and dropped her volume "—they talking about what I think they are?"

Lottie looked over Helen's shoulder to where Rex and Edith stood at the southern end of the room, admiring Edith's self-portrait on the adjacent wall. She gave a slow nod.

"I see. And—" Helen glanced over her back at the others, too, before she sidled even closer, spoke even lower "—is this the same topic that you wished to discuss with me?"

Lottie looked sideways and bit her lip. "Desperately," she whispered.

He's a snake, Lottie, Helen wanted to say. *Don't let him sink those ivory fangs any deeper.* Instead, she glided her finger down Lottie's soft cheek to dry a tear's trail.

Her friend took her hand just then, those watery eyes never so imploring. "But I can't—"

She stopped as Rex approached. Whistling a peppy tune, he sat on one of the two amber-colored sofas mirroring each other on either side of the coffee table. The women looked at him from the fireplace and smiled.

"Ladies," he said, "please don't let me interrupt."

"Not at all, dear boy. I was only questioning Lottie's motives for bringing up my column in front of the Colonel." Helen raised her brow at the actress with a pointed look.

"Technically, you mentioned your job first." When Helen started to protest that lame defense, Lottie pressed on. "And so what if I did! Are you going to fault a girl for helping a friend?"

"For someone so reluctant to accept favors for herself, you sure have mastered the art of nepotism, dear."

Hands at her hips, Lottie thrust her jaw forward. "The *Chronicle* hiring you had nothing to do with me, and you know it! And all right, maybe I'm nudging your opportunities there a little further now, but you don't have the position *yet*—and he won't give it to you just because I ask. It's up to you to deserve it."

"Of course you'll get it," Rex said. "I don't know why you haven't vied for it sooner."

"How do you know I haven't?"

Rex shrugged. "Because you'd already have the job."

"How you figure?"

He lifted his shoulders again. "You're obviously qualified."

"Aw." Helen cocked her head and stacked her hands on her heart. "You're a gem, Rex, pretending as if all the stories about you aren't written by men."

The halfback laughed along with her as a courtesy, she could tell, but Helen was content that at least Lottie got it as she smiled, too.

"Now c'mon," Lottie said, "give us a twirl so we can see how pretty you are. The detailing on this is marvelous."

Well, maybe Lottie only partially got it. All the same, Helen let her friend lavish attention on her gown; it wasn't every day or for just anyone that a Hollywood starlet would do that. And so she laughed as Lottie fondled the cluster of chiffon bows that adorned her slim-fitting black dress from its dropped waist to its T-length hem. In kind, she flicked the fringe that hung in tiers from Lottie's belted waist to her ankles.

"I'm surprised Edith hasn't told us yet that we look like women in mourning," Lottie said loudly enough for Mrs. Warne to hear. "Black still too macabre?"

It could've just been the echo of Lottie's raised words reverberating through the porcelain vases on the mantelpiece, but Helen thought she'd heard the baritone of a man's voice through the wall — also raised.

Edith remained in front of her portrait, but her face now turned toward the nearest pair of French doors. Toward the library.

"Edith?" Lottie asked, but when she still received no response, Rex was on his feet and crossing the room.

"Mrs. Warne?" Standing beside her, he laid his hands gently on Edith's arms.

She started at his contact. Looking back and forth from him to the library doors, Edith led him back to the center of the room.

"Goodness, what kind of hosts are we," she finally said, laughing weakly, "throwing a party with no cocktails?"

As if on cue, Chauncey entered the drawing room, rolling in the bar cart of replenished spirits. He parked it in the corner next to a mahogany Victrola cabinet.

"Lovely," Edith said. "Lottie, why don't you put on some music already? You know how Ransom loves to show off his automatic orthophonic."

Ortho-what? Rex mouthed to Helen. She nodded toward the Victrola and revolved her index finger around like a turntable.

"There should already be some records in the changer," Edith continued. At the same time, she shuffled to block Chauncey's pathway to the library. "The Colonel and Mr. Howard prefer not to be disturbed," she told him, "but thank you."

"Anything else I can bring for you, madame, or the others?" He scanned the room.

"No, thank you, Chauncey. You know how I like to manage things after dark." Again that feeble laugh before she sent him to supervise the kitchen downstairs. "Please let the staff know when everything is straightened there and in the dining room, you can all retire."

The silver-haired man knit his bushy brow, not for the first time that night. "Madame?"

"Go on," she sang. "All of you. Enjoy a summer evening outside this stuffy old place."

"Are you quite sure—"

"You *must* have private matters to tend to, same as us." She tipped her head back with a toothy smile. "In fact, I don't want to see a single one of you back here until morning."

"But, madame—"

"Privacy," she stage-whispered. Helen heard the hiss from the fireplace and knew the others had, too, from the bemused expressions the trio exchanged.

And this time, she didn't mistake another sound—again, the vibration of a deep voice through the wall.

"As you wish." Chauncey gave a stiff half-bow before he pivoted on his heel and exited to the foyer.

Wringing her hands at her waist, Edith smiled as she turned to the rest. She opened her mouth to speak but seemed to hesitate on what exactly she wanted to say. "Ice," she stated eventually. "I'll just fetch more ice." Stepping sideways toward the library's north doorway, she said, "Lottie, the music," before disappearing through it.

Helen exchanged looks with Lottie and Rex again, wondering if Edith had heard the voices in the other room, too, and was actually dismissing herself to investigate. In their silence, a ticking pendulum drew Helen's eyes to the grandfather clock in the corner. Twelve past eight.

"She went to the library for *ice?*" Rex asked.

Lottie spread her hands out to her sides and shook her head. "Chauncey could simply bring cubes from the kitchen, but Edith still likes to chip her own off the block. As if it makes the drink taste any better."

Noting that Rex looked even more confused, Helen added, "There's a bar in there. Hidden in the wall."

"Hidden?" He raised his brows and nodded. "Nice touch."

"This house is full of secrets," Helen joked.

Lottie shrugged a shoulder. "Ransom left no detail unturned when he added that extension. Even the firewood has its own elevator in there, like the dumbwaiter in the pantry. When it comes to modern marvels, he spares no expense."

"Boys and their toys," Helen played along with a chuckle. But everyone had seemed on edge since she and Rex first arrived, and she wanted to get to the bottom of it. She could only trust that Lottie would tell her when she was ready. And hopefully before it was too late.

In the meantime, just as her friend had done her one good turn that night, Helen would return the favor, starting with leaving Lottie and Rex to sit together on the sofa while she tended to the electric phonograph. There were indeed some records already loaded in the changer, but Helen searched the cabinet for more.

"This one will do," she said to herself and slid Paul Specht and his orchestra's "Sing a Little Love Song" out of its sleeve to place it on the turntable. Once she'd positioned the needle, she looked over her shoulder at the young couple talking quietly and laughing in each other's company.

Yes, Helen thought, *this one should do just fine.*

The music played on, but when Edith still didn't return by the next song, Rex offered to go assist her. Lottie wouldn't hear of it.

"Probably got waylaid by more of Noble's compliments," she said, walking to the cocktail cart. "Besides, we don't need ice for what I'm fixing you."

"I thought you couldn't mix a drink to save your precious little soul." Remaining at her station at the Victrola, Helen now shimmied to Fats Waller's "Ain't Misbehavin'."

"I can't," Lottie said brightly. "So I'm not." After clinking some of the cart's contents around, she stood straight and circled two crystal brandy snifters in her hands. She held one out to Helen, who grimaced.

"No, thanks. I can't take that stuff straight. I'll wait for the ice and Edith's magic."

"More for me and the Red Fox, then," Lottie sang on her way back to the sofa.

Rex was amusing them with a story from his college days when Ransom burst through the library's south doors.

Without so much as a word or eye contact with anyone, he charged out into the foyer, his footsteps echoing past the main staircase and down the west hall. The air was sucked right out of the room after him.

"Was…" Helen began. "Was that a rifle in his hand?"

Lottie, who'd just been taking a sip when he'd exploded his way through, now sat motionless as brandy dripped from her chin.

Rex took her glass and set it with his on the coffee table. He yanked the handkerchief from his pocket and gently wiped her lips. "Now I *am* going to see what that was all about."

Lottie was on her feet and holding out her hands before he could budge from the sofa. "No, no," she said, leaning down to press his forearms. "Noble's been on a toot since we got here.

You know that. Best leave him to drink himself to the floor and let Ransom calm."

"But Mrs. Warne's in there. If she—"

"I'll go."

Lottie straightened with conviction, yet Helen watched her waver in place for a moment. Then, instead of heading to the library, Lottie strode the opposite way out of the drawing room, shuffling down the long hallway after Ransom.

Rex twisted around and laid his arm on the sofa back, drumming his fingers against it. Helen still bopped in place beside the phonograph—for lack of knowing what else to do—but she met his concerned expression.

"Damn what Lottie says," he insisted. "I think I should check on Mrs. Warne."

"That woman can fend for herself, I assure you. She's probably the one who sent the Colonel out to cool off."

"Well, then I'm going to see about Noble and what upset the Colonel to begin with."

Helen dropped her arms to her sides and finally stood still. "And do what, make matters worse?"

"How could I—"

"That man is in no state to hear reason. Especially not from you."

"Me?"

"All he'll see is the dashing young gent his fiancée was making googly eyes at all dinner."

"Fiancée?" That froze Rex on the spot, looking more like a startled deer than a stealthy fox. "You mean to say they're...?"

"No. Not yet, anyway."

"Then what did you mean by—and 'googly eyes.' She wasn't—at me." If he resembled a fox at all now, it was through his crimson face.

She cocked her hip. "Rex, you really *are* adorable. But you can't be this oblivious."

Huffing out an exhale, he turned his head to the floor. Then he swept up his brandy and stood. "Apparently, I'm a perfect fool." He paced around the coffee table and took a swig from his glass.

"Oh, you sweet boy. All right, I'll level with you." She loaded another record as she spoke. "Lottie hasn't said so much, but I bet dollars to doughnuts Noble plans to propose this weekend, if he hasn't already, and that's why he wanted to speak to the Colonel."

"Asking his permission?"

"In a father's place, yes."

"Didn't go so swell, from the looks of it." He squinted at the oriental rug at his feet as his thumb caressed his glass. "Seems rather old-fashioned for a guy like Noble, don't you think? A little too…proper?"

Helen shrugged. "It'll make him the darling of the media if they can report a sentimental engagement story. He'd be the man every woman in the audience dreams he is."

"Is he what Lottie wants?" Rex didn't meet her eye, only took another, deeper sip of his tawny drink before sinking down on the sofa that faced her.

Twisting her fingers, Helen stared off to her side. "Truthfully? No. I wouldn't think so." With a wry smile, she directed a chuckle toward the floor. "I…see her with someone like you, actually."

When he didn't respond, she looked up to see him pressing his lips together.

"But," she said, "I've been surprised before. No one really knows what happens behind closed doors, right? There could be something there we're not seeing." Walking up to the low bookshelf behind the nearest sofa, she smoothed her palm over its marble surface before leaning against it. "She had something to tell me, though. Something urgent that couldn't wait. So, I don't know."

"Well…" With elbows resting on his spread knees, Rex swilled his brandy. "I guess we have to trust she can make her own decisions."

Helen moved her hand to the velvety sofa back. She smiled, tracing the upholstery's elaborate brocade design with her finger. "That she can." Then she held her hand out to him. "Come on, you. I've got a dance card with your name on it."

Rex grinned and placed his drink down carefully, then stood to join Helen for some simple ragtime footwork. They kept the Baltimore Buzz a-buzzing through the room for a few lively numbers, dancing, talking, and laughing all the while.

He thought he heard the vibration of voices in the next room, and at one point a dull thud and slam, but Rex danced on, spinning Helen around and only missing a step when he heard a motor rev outside the open front windows. Gliding her toward them, he slowed to a stop and peered out.

"What is it?" she asked.

He held a curtain aside. "A car, in the front drive." It wasn't quite dark outside after the long summer's day, but he still couldn't discern anyone inside the automobile.

"Has someone arrived?"

"Or someone's leaving. You don't think it's Lottie, do you?"

"She doesn't know how to drive."

"The Colonel, then?"

"I can't imagine so. Though I do wonder what's keeping Mrs. Warne. You don't suppose *she'd* take an evening drive?"

Edith hadn't crossed back through the drawing room, but that wasn't to say she couldn't have exited via the library's Jefferson porch.

"I don't know. But why would she? Why would any of them—"

"Oh, no," Helen said. "Noble wouldn't—"

"That's it, I'm—"

"Darlings!" Lottie breezed into the room from the foyer with such volume and verve, it made both Rex and Helen start. "I'm dreadfully sorry to have left you for so long!" Her eyes were glassy and red, her skin flushed. She laid a hand on each friend's arm, and Rex could feel her tremble.

"Who is that out there?" Helen asked.

"Hm?" she replied distractedly.

"Is the Colonel going somewhere?"

"Ransom?" Lottie leaned between Rex and Helen to also investigate the auto idling out front.

"Yes?" the man himself said, entering from the foyer just as Lottie had.

Helen spun around to face him while Rex just looked from the Colonel to the driveway.

"Someone's here," Lottie said, pressing her fingertips to the window screen, "but that's your car, isn't it?"

Ransom backtracked to the foyer.

As Rex sidled close to Lottie, Helen walked to the other window, and they all watched the Colonel step out onto the front patio, then descend the stone steps to ground level. He appeared to lean down into the car's passenger-side window and speak to the driver before he stood again, saluted, and soon returned inside to the drawing room.

As he entered, Ransom wore a smile on his reddened face, and Rex first noticed the handkerchief wrapped around his hand when he swept it across his glistening forehead.

"This is rather awkward, but…it seems the staff will be enjoying a night off tonight." Ransom chuckled in spite of his hardened brow. "Evidently Mrs. Warne dismissed them until breakfast."

"So we heard her say to Chauncey," Helen said. "But where are they going?"

"Home to family or off to see what they haven't missed yet at the cinema."

As he said it, the car curled around the circular drive, revealing itself beyond full capacity.

"Where did they all leave from?" Rex asked, positive he hadn't seen or heard anyone in the front foyer.

"Servant access door, out the west wing," he said. "We have all sorts of nooks and crannies to keep their daily drudgery discreet, you see."

When Rex frowned, Lottie was quick to add, "Oh, he's kidding. Ransom treats his staff like family." She laughed, then turned to the Colonel. "Thompson's driving them all?"

He nodded. "Davis and the whole gang. He only pulled around front so Chauncey could check the new porch bulbs."

"Thompson is the chauffeur, and Davis is Ransom's valet," Lottie explained to Rex. "Then there's Hutchins, our cook, and Neely and Botkin, who assist in the kitchen and with the housework, and—oh, applesauce! I guess we're tidying after ourselves tonight." She giggled, nervously it seemed. "If Noble were here, I'm sure he'd have something to say about us having to undress ourselves, too."

"Noble *is* still here, right?" Helen asked. "Or have we driven him out with torches and pitchforks?"

Lottie gave another tremulous laugh. "Wh-Why would you say that?"

The room fell quiet as the last record ran its course. The clock chimed half-past eight.

Ransom dragged his wrapped hand up and down the back of his neck.

"Are you injured?" Rex felt at liberty—or at least inebriated—enough to say. He pointed his chin at Ransom's makeshift bandage.

"Oh, this." Ransom looked at his hand, then rubbed it with the other. "Slipped chipping some ice behind the bar. Stung more than pierced." He hastened to unravel the handkerchief before holding out his palm and flexing his fingers. His hand quivered as he did so. "See? No bother. Lottie shouldn't have worried." He smiled at her.

"Speaking of ice, where *is* our hostess?" Helen asked.

"Yes." Ransom twisted around to view the empty expanse behind them. "She's not here with you?"

"She went to the library bar for ice," Helen said. "Didn't you see her?"

"The library." He squinted. "No." A trace of unease stretched the word across two syllables.

"Well, that's where she went," Helen said, sounding as amused as perplexed. "She might run away with your man if you don't watch them closely enough, Lottie."

The actress snorted and shook her head. "With my blessings." But with a glance to Ransom, her face sobered. She rocked on her feet and inhaled as if waking from a daze. "All right. Time to fetch those two."

"I still think I ought—"

"No." She laid her hand on Ransom's arm. "I told you, I'll be fine."

With a half-hearted smile, she crossed the room so she could fetch her abandoned brandy from the table. She took a gulp before disappearing through the southern French doors.

Everyone watched Lottie's departure for a moment. Privately, Helen wished her great luck.

Rex broke the silence. "So, both doors go to the library?" He tilted his head and stared at Ransom expectantly, though didn't seem to catch the man's attention. "Sir?"

Twiddling the fingers of his injured hand after he'd re-wrapped it, Ransom finally appeared to register the question and looked from the south doors where Lottie had exited to the north doors right behind Rex. "Oh…yes. That's right." He tucked his chin to his chest and cleared his throat with a low rumble. "I'll have to tour you through the new addition later. You must see the Gold Theatre."

"Theatre? You weren't kidding about this place," Rex said to Helen.

She nodded at him excitedly. "Boy, it's a treat."

"I'd hoped to show you one of Lottie's pictures this evening, in fact," Ransom said, "if our schedule hadn't gotten rather… interrupted. I usually entertain with films on Fridays, you see, but tomorrow will work just as well. If everyone's not too fatigued from the early rise, that is. You ever hunted, Miss Conroy?"

"Only for a good scoop, sir."

He chortled, then appeared to notice their empty hands for the first time. "You two look thirsty! What'll you have?" He rubbed his palms together, dislodging the cloth around his hand.

Helen shook her head. She enjoyed her cocktails but didn't desire one at Ransom's hands just now. "I'm fine, thanks."

"I still have one there." As if to prove it, Rex strode to the coffee table and lifted his snifter in toast to his host.

"Ah. Good. I'll just…fix something for myself from Chauncey's inventory." At that, Ransom ventured out and disappeared into the west wing.

Rex looked to Helen and gestured to the full bar cart, but she could give him no better explanation than, "Public people. Private lives." That's the only way she'd known the Warnes to be. "And so, it appears our numbers have diminished again!"

Rex swirled his brandy in his glass. "Chauncey a big drinker, then?"

"What?" Helen asked, then laughed. "Oh. The 'inventory' isn't his personal stash. As butler, he manages it for the house."

"Oh." Rex looked to his feet.

She'd probably made him feel like a bumpkin, no matter what his current success. Helen knew the type. Old money and new money were two different worlds, and despite Rex's status, he was still a world apart from both. Even Helen's *nouveau riche*, north-Chicagoan family only partially ingratiated her to the upper milieu, which helped a great deal with her work in the lower echelons of journalism, covering what society events she could secure invitations to. She did what she did to at least earn a modest living on her own, were she to break from her parents' support—which she aimed to do. Not out of any conflict with them, but for the thrill of independence.

She approached Rex. "I only know from my assignments. They get me into a lot of the big houses." She stepped closer and laid a hand on his arm. "This stuff, it doesn't matter to her, you know. She gets dazzled like everyone else sometimes, but she still knows the difference. What's real and what's not."

Rex sipped his drink, then nodded at the rug. He didn't ask what she meant by that, and Helen suspected he didn't need to. He perhaps knew Lottie as well as Helen did, and something unspoken was clearly going on between the two of them. Already *had* happened, perhaps, while they were both in Los Angeles last spring. There was a story there, but Helen couldn't read anything past the headline forming in her head: *"Red Fox Raids French Hen's Coop."*

"What's so funny?" Rex asked.

"Hm?" Helen felt the silly smile on her face. "Oh, I'm sorry. Just thinking."

She rolled her eyes to laugh it off but couldn't help but worry that instead of a chicken coop, they'd just sent Lottie into the lion's den.

She straightened her face to address him in earnest. "Look at me, Rex."

He did.

"I do trust Lottie to make her own decisions. And I know she's strong, but those two…" She cocked her head toward the library doors.

"Lottie and Noble?"

"*Edith* and Noble. They're awful to her, aren't they?"

His eyes narrowed.

"Oh, hang public people and their private lives," Helen said. "You *should* go. Go to *her*."

Looking to the southern French doors where Lottie had just disappeared, he rolled his shoulders back and swayed on his feet as if indeed raring to go. Yet he'd only taken a step before already turning back to Helen.

"*Go*, all-star." She glanced over his shoulder to consult the timepiece in the corner. Eight thirty-five. "Plenty of minutes left on the clock for an interception. Just don't fumble it." She winked.

Blushing, but grinning ear to ear, he advanced his yards into the end zone.

Rex's heart was in his throat as he twisted the doorknob, and he found himself in a small hallway. This obviously wasn't the library he'd expected, but a few yards farther was another door that delivered him to the goal line.

Except no one was there. Not a soul. Not Lottie, not Noble or Edith.

Yet he felt eyes on him from all around. As he strolled to the center of the startlingly spacious room, they had him surrounded—portraits of Ransom and his ancestry on every wall, all-seeing, all-knowing, and judging from on high.

The air was stagnant but cool. Rex could smell the veneer on the new addition's wood-paneled walls, the same butternut color as the polished wooden floorboards beneath him. Amber-and-blue draperies covered tall windows; between a few of them was an encased collection of rifles, and hanging from its thick ribbon in one special display was the *Croix de Guerre*, France's illustrious military decoration.

Beneath the lofty ceiling that stretched at least twenty feet overhead, Rex felt puny for the first time in his life. The Colonel's Liberty Library, where a blue-blooded man could certainly roam free for hours: expanding his intellect with the books shelved along the walls, warming his spirit beside either of the immense fireplaces at each end, or filling the air with business and pleasure from the pale green sofas and ebony grand piano. The mirrored panels in the hallway doors only enhanced the room's sense of depth, and American flags boasted its patriotism.

But where was the bar?

Then Rex remembered — "hidden," Helen had said. If he had to guess, it was concealed behind the plain wooden panels between the north and south hallways. Rex ran his hand along the smooth wood and over the moldings, but he couldn't find access. Nothing for him here, then. He was just about to leave through the northern hallway when Lottie opened its mirrored door from the other side.

"Oh!" As before, she was breathing quickly and blushing. "Uh." She looked behind her, then quickly ducked into the room and leaned against the door to close it. Bringing her hand to her heart, she laughed. "You frightened me."

"Caught ya red-handed."

She raised her palms to play along with the gag. "Outfoxed by the Red Fox. You got me."

He noticed her snifter was gone but had a more pressing question. "Where are Mrs. Warne and Mr. Howard?"

Returning her hands to the doorknob behind her, she leaned back and flapped her elbows out as she shrugged. Perhaps Edith and Noble had returned to the drawing room at the same time Rex had entered the library. Yet, since he obviously hadn't passed them in the south hall, Lottie should've seen them herself on her way in from the north.

Still, she said nothing, only pouted, her eyes searching the floor beyond him. Then she slapped a hand to her red cheek and smiled as she shook her head.

"That brandy's got me all balled up. Come on." She took his hand. "Let's sit for a spell."

He followed her to one of the velvet sofas facing each other over a long coffee table, like in the drawing room.

"Oh, that feels nice." She sighed as she released his hand and plopped down on a cushion. "I was getting dizzy."

After taking a seat beside her, he found himself staring at those bare panels again.

He pointed. "Is that the bar?"

"Clever, isn't it? You'd never know. When I find my feet again, I'll show you." Consciously or not, when she spoke of her feet, she began swinging them. So much like the little girl with the golden ringlets, dangling her legs from the back of the ice truck.

"You seem in a better mood."

"Uh-huh." She smiled at him sweetly.

"I'm glad."

Snatching his glass away, Lottie set it on the table, then took both his hands in hers.

"Rex," she said, her doll eyes beseeching. "About Los Angeles..."

He pressed his thumbs against the fine bones of her hands. "Not another word about it, Lottie. You did nothing wrong."

Looking to her lap, she bit her lip. "But I did. I put you in an awfully tight spot, and it wasn't...it wasn't very ladylike." She looked into his eyes. "Or what a friend would do."

"You *are* my friend, Lottie. A very good one, no matter what." He ran his thumbs excitedly over her knuckles. "I can't tell you how happy I am to have you back in my life. At least, to the extent you're willing, of course. I mean —" *fumbling, fumbling* "— it's just good to see you. And that, through it all, you're still the same."

She snorted good-humoredly. "The same? I didn't act like that when we were kids."

He firmed his grip on her fingers. "You know what I mean. It's people like you who keep me grounded."

Her eyes drooped and her lips parted for a few silent breaths, her complexion cooling to its normal color. "Me? But..." She lowered her voice to a hush. "But how can you *know* that? After all these years, and—in that short time, in that false place." A little crease formed at the center of her forehead.

He released a hand to run it through her satin hair. His fingers lingered behind her ear, and the pad of his thumb swept across her cheekbone. "Because I do. I know you. Even after all these years." He stroked her hair again. "I do because you've never done anything to hide it, and I've always known where to look for it."

She swallowed and pursed her lips.

He tilted her chin up. "You wear your heart pinned right to that sleeve, if you haven't noticed. Always have." He traced his finger along her bare forearm.

"Some actress I am."

"Some woman you are. Lottie...what happened in LA, it wasn't like that. Not to me."

"I was zozzled on free champagne and cornered you. I took you away from your party."

"You took me to a quieter place where we could talk. And we did."

"Talk? Maybe, about my silly movies."

"About your profession. About Belleau. Your horses. You also asked me about my career and interests. My family. We covered a lot of ground, Lottie. We couldn't have done that otherwise."

Her eyes never left his. "I tried to kiss you."

"Yeah?" he said softly. "And where's the crime in that?"

"Well, Noble..."

"I didn't see any handcuff on you." He looked down and lifted her left hand, running his thumb over her ring finger. "Still don't."

Lottie's lips parted again as her delicate clavicle heaved up and down. "You won't," she said, barely above a whisper.

"No?" Rex brushed her finger ever more gently.

Slowly, she swiveled her head side to side. "Not for him."

"Je pense que je t'ai toujours aimé, mon cheri," she'd said that night, heady on champagne and gin fizz. *I think I have always loved you, my darling*—Rex's first real lesson in the language of love, no matter how much French she'd taught him in the back of that ice truck.

"But," she continued, and Rex's heart sank. She looked down at her lap. "When I tried to, you didn't…"

"Not because I didn't want to, Lottie. And not because you were acting in any way out of line. I just had to know you wouldn't regret it. It would've killed me if you did."

"And if I didn't? Regret it, I mean? If I…wouldn't?" She looked up at him hesitantly.

Clear as anything, Rex saw it. A window opening where he'd feared a door had closed. Looking back at Lottie's left hand, he wanted to bring it to his lips and press a kiss on that bare ring finger. Instead, he raised his gaze to her.

Propriety be damned, Rex wouldn't mix his messages any further. Not when this could be his last chance. Desiring that Lottie make no mistake where his heart was, he played the strategy in his head—how he would lean closer to her, see if she did the same. He anticipated how her petal-soft lips would mold to his, her long lashes fluttering against his cheeks. Their noses brushing, and then—

Lottie turned her face away. Staring at the wall that concealed the bar, she held her breath as if she'd heard something and listened for more.

"I'm sorry, Rex." She got to her feet, stepped away and circled around the opposite couch. "I can't—be here now." Wringing her hands, she paced behind the sofa, then stopped to stare off toward the bar again.

Rex stood and cautiously approached her. His shoe skidded a little as he did so, and he looked down to see little puddles and a few chips of ice dotting the floor's wood grain. Had someone spilled a cocktail? Or maybe it was the bucket of ice water that Lottie's abrupt change of heart had just dumped on him.

"Everyone must be back in there now." She straightened the fringe just below her waist and gave him a half-smile. "We should probably rescue Helen."

Rex offered her his hand.

She stepped closer and accepted it, then brought his knuckles to her breastbone, where he could feel her heart race, too. "We'll talk later?" she said.

Reading her eyes, he knew she meant it. Still, he could only nod like an idiot.

"Should we bring some ice?" he finally asked, for lack of anything else to say. "You know, in case Mrs. Warne did get waylaid by Noble's charms and forgot?"

When he smiled, she returned a vague giggle but tugged him toward the door. "Oh, Chauncey can bring more if we need it."

"But he left with the others, remember?"

"Oh. Right." Lottie shook her head. "So odd that Ransom and Edith would allow everyone to leave in the middle of a party."

"Perhaps the party's over. Might be best if we all just call it a night and catch extra winks for the morning."

"Oh, but…" She looked over her shoulder, then slumped a little. "You're right. I do wish tomorrow would come quickly." She stroked his arm with her other hand, smiling at him slightly. "Though I hate for tonight to end. I wish I hadn't—Maybe we *should* talk now, only, somewhere else? Where we can really be alone."

Rex wanted nothing more than to follow that direction, but Lottie's first instinct had been the right one; nothing could happen tonight while that man was in this house. In her life. Letting go of her, he stepped back and slid his hand along the wooden wall panels, trying to find the bar once more for distraction.

"Morning'll come fast. We should sleep." It took real effort to relax his voice. "Though I, for one, won't rest till I know how this contraption works." He grinned as casually as he could muster.

She seized his arm again. "Oh, nonsense. Come, I know the perfect—"

"No, really, show me."

"Tomorrow." Stepping between him and the wall, she gazed up at him more seriously, almost stricken. "Please. I didn't mean to —"

"May as well now that we're here." He stepped around her and continued feeling along the wall for the sweet spot, determined to keep his focus and get the blood rushing back to his head. "Tomorrow, we'll talk — somewhere else."

He winked at her playfully, only to see her stare back through dimmed eyes. She didn't try to stop him anymore, but she didn't help either. From the way her irises shifted side to side, a torrent of thought appeared to sweep behind them. For once, he couldn't read her.

After a while, her frame deflated, and she looked to the wall, resigned. With seeming sleight of hand — albeit a shaky one — she managed to unlatch one panel, revealing it to be a large door that opened to the left half of the bar. The mirrored and silvery interior beamed out at them like some mystical Art Deco ice cavern.

"Boy, that's nifty," Rex said, still trying to cut the tension and return her spirits to where they'd been — to return *them* to where they'd been, if only as friends.

He was just about to compliment the decorative etchings on the glass, too, when he saw a side pane had shattered. The mirror was splintered from a central impact point radiating outward like a sinister web. He met Lottie's eyes in their reflection across the way and could tell she'd seen it, too.

A light tapping drew their attention, its source out of sight.

The countertop was set back a few feet, so Lottie was able to step inside the hidden room. Leaning over the bar, she peered behind it. When she stood back up, she glanced over to her right, into the other half of the nook still concealed from Rex's view. Then she did a double-take, this time gazing down at the floor near her feet at the front of the bar.

She froze.

From somewhere in the room, a clock tolled a quarter to nine one heartbeat before the actress screamed.

On the Rocks

to chill the spirit

Helen and Ransom burst into the library through separate doors.

The Colonel had only just returned to the drawing room, apologizing for his rudeness in leaving in the first place. He'd been pacing by Edith's portrait as Helen restarted the Victrola when they'd both heard the scream and looked at each other from opposite sides of the room. Wasting no time, they'd bolted to their nearest door.

Lottie stood shaking and crying into Rex's chest. With his arms wrapped tightly around her, he gaped at the others in speechless horror.

"What's happened?" Helen asked, eyes darting from one to the other.

Lottie's hands muffled her sobs while Rex swept his gaze from Helen to Ransom and then to the bar. From the direction of his pained stare, Helen chanced a glance but saw nothing.

Until Ransom drew the second panel open to expose the full bar — and the body lying within it.

Helen gasped, mirroring Lottie as she brought her own fingers to her lips. Ransom looked toward the floor and uttered nothing, all color leaving his face.

Rex murmured something into Lottie's hair, to which she nodded in response, and he applied a soft kiss to her forehead before handing her over to Helen's care so he could stand at Ransom's side. Helen caught her breath and turned to rest both palms on Lottie's shoulders.

"Are you all right?"

Lottie didn't uncover her mouth but nodded yes. Then she shook something dreadful on another sob.

"R-Rex and I were just talk — talking, and then we fo-hound, in here, like this —"

"Lottie, breathe or you'll hyperventilate."

Though her friend stood rigid, Helen managed to guide her to the farthest end of a sofa to sit. She monitored her there for a few cautious seconds, then crept back to observe the two men kneeling over Noble.

At the front of the bar, the actor was sitting up but slumped over, with his lower back to the side wall and his lolling head and right shoulder leaning against the counter's base. The left side of his face looked a bit swollen, Helen thought, but perhaps the other side was, too, from all the alcohol he'd consumed. He — the entire bar, really — reeked of it. Above him, a jagged block of ice dripped as it melted.

Rex removed the actor's disheveled ascot and felt his neck for a pulse while Ransom stood and stared dumbly over them both.

"Has he…passed out?" Helen asked before noticing the red stain in the center of Noble's white shirt, as deep crimson as his smoking jacket.

Rex's lips pressed into a grim line. The movement was slight, but he shook his head. He reached to take Noble's wrist next. His efforts at finding a pulse there appeared futile, too, from the way he dropped the actor's hand to the tile and slumped back onto his heels. Noble's coat appeared sodden in patches and also unbuttoned. Gingerly, Rex pulled the velvet lapels apart to reveal more stains below his shoulder.

Helen spun away and covered her eyes, relying on one of the open bar doors to bear her weight. *Drip, drip, drip*, she heard in the men's silence. That awful silence.

Mostly out of view of the body, Lottie had recovered her calm and now clasped her hands on her lap as she stared off in front of her. Wiping her hand down her face, Helen turned back to the men.

Ransom removed his tailcoat. "Should we," he half-asked Rex as, bending down, he presumably wanted to lay it over Noble.

"We probably shouldn't touch anything more than we have."

Languidly, Ransom stood tall again and slid his arms back through his coat sleeves. His dazed stoicism was unnerving to no end. All he did was chance a tentative glance at Lottie across the way.

She turned her face to him, her expression equally vacant, and shook her head.

"Wh-Where's Mrs. Warne?" Helen finally had the presence of mind to think, though it only came out as a whisper.

"Whoever did this could've harmed her, too," Rex said.

Still suspended in the discovery, Ransom remained in place for a few beats. But at last, the spark of realization entered his eyes, and he fled into the north hall. They heard the drawing room door violently slam behind him.

Rex got to his feet.

"Is it safe for him to go alone?" Helen asked.

"I don't know. But I'm not leaving you two alone, either. Let's give him a few minutes."

Helen crept around to kneel beside Noble. "It's dreadful," she said, "how the water drips on him." Coldly anointing, as if in forgiveness of what sin could've caused this.

Rex slid the ice a little farther back on the bar top and mopped the meltwater with his sleeve. For a moment, he rested his elbows on the counter and hung his head. But suddenly, he stood and backed up.

"What is it?" Helen asked.

"We should make sure we're safe in here." He ducked out into the north hall where Ransom had disappeared, returning a moment later with assurances that no glass had been broken in its ground-floor window and that the lock was secure. "Let's check that these are sound, too."

Lottie still appeared numb but slightly more alert. She rose to her feet and nodded.

They divided and conquered, Rex heading north while the ladies ventured south, pulling back the curtains and testing each window frame and pane. Though windows were open elsewhere throughout the house to let it breathe in the summer air, these were all closed.

Meeting in the middle, at the door leading out onto the Jefferson porch, the trio overlapped each other's efforts by continuing around the room so that every window had been checked twice and by all three pairs of eyes.

They then looked at each other from their reversed positions on either side of the library and agreed that every piece of glass remained unbroken and every sash was locked airtight. The door to the porch was further reinforced with bolts locked from the inside, and for good measure, they glanced underneath tables, behind chairs, and in the great hearths.

When she crossed in front of the bar, Helen's own reflection in the mirrored walls gave her a fright until she recognized it; she looked down to see no one but Noble's gruesome figure. Snake or not, he didn't deserve this.

Striding to a grand floor globe in the corner, she gave it a frustrated spin and took in the whole room from this vantage. She watched Rex peer into the empty, oversized firewood rack in a last-ditch effort, but she'd already checked it herself and knew there wasn't so much as a stick of wood in there, just some depressing dirt and dry grass. Rex shook his head, and Helen dropped her eyes in exasperation. That's when she noticed the dark stains on the wooden floor, just outside the bar. She held her breath in her chest, stepping closer and exhaling only when she realized it wasn't blood but damp spots.

"What's this?"

"What?" Rex and Lottie asked in unison.

"Did something spill here?"

"I noticed that, too," Rex said, "just before we found him."

"Your brandy?" she asked Lottie, pointing to the snifter on the coffee table.

"No, I…" Lottie looked down at the table and then around at the room. "I must've misplaced it."

"That one's mine," Rex explained, "and I didn't spill it."

"Noble might've tipped his drink," Lottie muttered with a broken voice. "He was so unsteady all evening."

"That could explain why his jacket's so wet. Smells of gin."

"Or he spilled it when he was attacked," Helen said gently, knowing it wasn't what Lottie wanted to hear but worth considering if it meant piecing together even one sliver of the puzzle.

Rex knelt, and after pressing his hand on the floorboards, he brought his fingertips to his nose. "I don't think it's alcohol. Just water."

"I don't see any…blood," Lottie said quietly. "If he *were* attacked out here."

They all fell silent.

Seeing her friend stand there, sniffing back tears while sleuthing her own almost-fiancé's death, Helen's heart swelled, and she saw Rex gaze at the little woman with the same sympathetic pride.

God, did Helen pray Lottie had nothing to do with this. But if she didn't, then — who?

"Do you suppose the Warnes are all right?" she asked. "Neither has come back."

"It's such a large house," Rex said, "and I bet he's covering every inch of it." He crossed over to where Lottie had resituated herself on the sofa and sat at her side. "All these entryways and passages. It sure becomes a funhouse when you look at this like this."

Lottie raised her reddened eyes to him. "Don't make fun, Rex. He's so proud."

"I know." He clasped her hand and rubbed it. "This place impresses me, too. It's just a devil to find your way around, and we've got to figure out how someone might've gotten in and out. How they'd get past us."

If they did, Helen mused, observing the other two on the sofa. She recalled their closeness when she'd first found them in the library, the way Rex had held Lottie and murmured into her hair, had kissed her head. Even in the short time they'd been alone together, something between them was more electric than before. And now there they were, a pair of possible lovers, seated a few yards from the only obstacle that had stood in their way...

She hated herself the instant that thought crept out. She herself had only encouraged Rex to leap that hurdle.

"I'll wait with you here until the Colonel gets back," Rex said, "but then—"

Lottie feverishly shook her head. "Can't we wait in the other room?" Her eyes fixed on the scene across the way, her lips shuddering.

The cold silver of the bar's interior—and what lay within—made Helen shiver a bit herself, and the library's open, imperial space offered little comfort. "I wouldn't mind that."

"It probably *is* best that we don't track over any possible evidence in here. Although, I hesitate to leave now that we can trust we're secure on this end."

"Trapped, more like," Lottie said, "if someone were to come back."

"Or never left."

"Which is why we're likely safer in this room," Rex said. "We could always escape out onto the porch. But we don't know who might still be in the rest of the house."

"Oh, Ransom," Lottie whispered.

"What if we closed the bar doors again," he said, "just like it was before we found him."

"It'll never be like it was."

There was a stony finality to Lottie's tone, and Helen noticed Rex's face fall a little. The negative edge overtaking her friend dismayed Helen, too, who became all the more convinced that something *had* already happened between Lottie and Rex tonight, and now this disaster threatened to unravel it all. Noble triumphing in death.

Not if Helen could do anything about it. Damn her speculations. Trivial as affairs of the heart might seem at such a time, *something* bright and good had to rise from these ashes. Because if Noble didn't deserve this, Lottie certainly didn't either.

"What if we only go as far as the drawing room?" Helen suggested. "That way we know it's safe on this side and could better hear if the Warnes need our help on the other."

It wasn't much, but apparently enough to win over Rex. Standing, he took Lottie's arm to escort her, and Helen trailed behind. As they stepped through the drawing room door, Louis Armstrong was playing "Muggles" on the Victrola.

And there stood Ransom, staring back at them like a cornered animal.

Rex lost his tender hold on Lottie as she ran across the drawing room to the Colonel.

"Where's Edith?" she asked, breathless.

"Mrs. Warne is fine," Ransom announced rather formally. "A little shaken, now that I've alerted her to the situation, but fine." He appeared unsettled himself.

"What happened?" Helen asked. "Where'd you find her?"

"Her bedroom," he said stiffly. "She'd been feeling faint, but she'll be right down."

"We never even noticed her leave the library," Rex had begun to say when Lottie exclaimed, "You're all wet!"

At first Rex thought she was questioning Ransom's honesty—*You're all wet*, as in, *You're full of it*—but then he realized she wasn't speaking slang but quite literally: The Colonel's tailcoat remained unbuttoned from when he'd removed it earlier, and, with his wingtip collar now detached, his bib-front shirt indeed appeared damp and rumpled.

"I was simply assisting Mrs. Warne with…and…" His eyes wandered the room as he seemed to have no idea how to finish his sentence. "She'll be right down," he repeated.

"If you'll stay with the ladies here, sir," Rex said before he abruptly walked out the door and into the foyer.

"Where are you going?" Lottie asked.

"To telephone the police."

Snapping to attention, Ransom briskly followed him out, catching Rex right before he entered the study. "No, no. That won't do."

"But we have to. There's no —"

"Now, Rex, my boy, the last thing we need is a scandal on our hands. If we —"

"Our *bloody* hands, until the law finds the real culprit. That's how it'll look, anyway."

"But that's just it," Ransom said. "They'll presume us guilty before we can be proven innocent. Even then, our reputations will remain mired in the guilt and, and — suspicion. No, son, I can't let word of this get out. Too many people would too eagerly take us to task."

"A man is dead!"

Rex heard Lottie mewl at his words in the drawing room. Ransom puffed his chest but only breathed deeply through his nose while he twiddled his fingers at his sides.

"Colonel Warne," Rex insisted, "not reporting this would only make us look guiltier."

Helen scurried up behind them. "But we *aren't* guilty."

"That's what I'm trying to tell you," Ransom cried, in a desperate flurry that Rex would have never expected from him. "It's the *reporting* that will make us look guilty. In the papers. Not mine, God willing," he said pointedly to Helen, "but…"

Rex just shook his head.

"If none of us *is* guilty, though," Helen said, even though Ransom technically hadn't denied it, "then there's nothing to worry about."

The Colonel leveled her with stern eyes.

"I only mean that the police will confirm our innocence, so then—"

"This is my house, my responsibility." Very slowly, he emphasized, "I said no."

"Yes, sir, this is your property," Rex said, "but the situation is the law's jurisdiction. We can't—"

Ransom wheeled around on him. "I *can*. We must."

Rex met Helen's eyes across the foyer, with hers waterlogged in the same bewilderment that he felt. Glancing behind her through the drawing room door, he wished he could shield Lottie from this awkward exchange.

Surely before long, the Colonel would come to and see reason, be the leader they knew and respected. The man who had seen the world—and world *war*, from the sidelines to the trenches as a correspondent in the Great War.

Though a noncombatant, Ransom had joined the Marines in France during the Battle of Belleau Wood, wearing the same uniform and traversing the same fields at the same risk, if not greater. Armed with nothing but his pencil and paper going in, he'd come back out with bullets in his side and a soldier hanging on his arm. But thanks to Ransom's quick reflexes, they'd both survived a near-fatal blow, and the United States likewise reigned victorious.

He'd since renamed his family estate Belleau and wore it like a tremendous badge of honor—along with his actual medals. Along with his honorary title as Colonel, which the state had awarded him for his contributions to the National Guard before the war and Ashby's cryptology efforts after. Along with the countless wars of words he'd waged and won with his *Chronicle*.

Rex wasn't certain into what foxhole *that* Ransom Warne had just jumped, but he knew the man was there and prayed he'd emerge soon.

"At least let me phone my father," Rex offered quietly.

"I can't involve Lewis in this," the Colonel whispered to the floor. "He's retired, deserves a break from—"

"He's also a friend. And he'd be fair."

"Son, I—"

"My father is the only person we know who's remotely qualified to investigate this and would keep it private as long as possible." He stood taller. "Unless you don't trust him."

"Of course I do!" Ransom bellowed.

A sob sounded from the other room, followed by footsteps. The music stopped with a shatter just before Lottie appeared in the foyer.

"Stop it!" she cried. "Please stop and *do* something!"

Ransom's entire bearing drooped. "Do what, Karlotta?"

She flopped her arms at her sides and looked up and around as if the answer were written somewhere along the winding staircase. "Well, we can't just stand here, worrying about reputation when Noble's...when he's...*lying* there and—" She clasped one hand over her mouth and wrapped the other over her stomach, hiccupping on another sob.

Helen moved to place her arm around her friend's weeping frame.

"Please, sir," Rex said. "We need to have the house searched and the body inspected. There's no reason we can't have this investigated properly without drawing public attention to it."

"Well, that's where the Colonel does have a point," Helen said, looking up from Lottie. "A death famous as this could hardly remain under wraps for long."

Even as she'd said the word *death* so pragmatically, Rex couldn't believe this was real. Obviously, none of them could; they were all like talking automatons going through the motions, trying to move forward while their emotions remained fixed in time and space, hovering helplessly above the body on the floor.

Ransom covered his eyes with his hand and leaned back on a console table, knocking over one of a pair of porcelain Chinese foo dogs. "I-I'm sorry. I know I'm not making sense." He rubbed his temples with his thumb and middle finger. "Of course we need to notify the authorities. If you'll agree, I *would* like to consult your father first, Rex, unofficially.

"But before that, please…I do ask that we look into this as far as we can on our own. We haven't even had a conversation among ourselves, and Mrs. Warne isn't fit for such scrutiny yet. If we could…sort the sequence of events, get our alibis straight…I think, or I at least hope, the culprit can be determined before any of this has a chance to make headlines."

"Are the headlines what matter?" Helen asked.

Ransom scrubbed his hand down his face and squared his jaw, looking at no one in particular. "That man broke her heart enough while he was alive. I won't let him take anything from her in death, too."

Within Helen's arms, Lottie had gone still. Her downcast eyes were less tumultuous, almost serene, but also clouded with God knew what emotion.

Soft yet resolute, Rex said, "We don't need to discuss that right now."

Helen glanced from Lottie to the men. "Right now, I think we need to discuss everything."

As if coming out of a trance, Ransom's eyes sharpened, and he swung around into his study, where Rex hoped he'd change his mind and phone the police after all. But all he heard was a drawer open and close and then the jangle of metal before the Colonel stepped back out.

"Ladies, if you'll excuse us," he said, "I'd like to see Mr. Rainger in the library. Only briefly, and we can lock the doors around you. You should be safe here." He gestured to the drawing room door much like he'd escorted Noble out of the dining room earlier. Silently, they all complied.

Once past the threshold, Rex paused at the phonograph, where Lottie must have ripped the record from its turntable and broken it against the cabinet's hard edge. Helen brought her to a sofa while Rex switched off the appliance and knelt to collect the jagged onyx pieces. Standing again, he placed the fragments inside the cabinet before turning back to close and lock the door they'd just entered through.

"Leave it, Rex," Helen said. "For Mrs. Warne. We'll keep a close eye. Don't worry about us."

Nodding reluctantly, he took two steps toward the library door before hesitating again. Things hadn't worked out so well for the last man to accompany Ransom into that room.

But, of course, this was nonsense. Just the shock of the moment. Rex had nothing to fear about being alone with his host.

He removed his tuxedo jacket and laid it on the nearest bookcase with one last look of concern at Lottie. He couldn't imagine what she felt right now and chastised himself for sensing even the remotest bit of relief that Noble would no longer factor in her future. *Their* future, the one he'd dared to glimpse at, if there was any longer a chance at one together. Perhaps Noble's absence would end up affecting everyone more adversely than his presence.

The Colonel was right in his concern for Lottie's welfare in that respect, but they couldn't worry about it now. A man was dead and his killer's identity and whereabouts unknown. Rex set off after Ransom straight away.

He reentered the grand library, where Ransom had stopped immediately beside the doorway. He stared at Rex intensely for a moment before digging into his tailcoat. Retrieving the set of keys from an inner pocket, he turned to the wall and unlocked one of his gun cases. He first pulled out a revolver and then a small pistol, laying each one on the nearest table. The sound of heavy metal on polished wood — there was something so sharp and final about it. Feeling underneath the table, Ransom next removed a box of cartridges from a hidden compartment there and proceeded to load each weapon. He closed the glass display door quietly when finished, tucked the keys in a trouser pocket, and handed the pistol to Rex.

Rex accepted it and scanned the room. "How could someone get in, sir? We just checked every window and door. All closed and locked from the inside. No sign of breaking in."

"Your father always cautioned me about the rise in burglaries out here. I made security utmost priority when adding this wing.

Everything's reinforced." Ransom's gaze rose all the way to the tall ceiling and roamed its perimeter.

Pride had reentered his voice, and Rex could see it in his eyes—the satisfaction and solace this man took from Belleau, the home that had stood on this hill for three generations. When he looked at Rex again, Ransom gave a tight grin that, though brisk, somehow managed to soften his face with an almost boyish innocence.

Rex merely nodded and stuck the barrel of his pistol into his waistband. "Were the windows ever opened today?"

"I know *I* didn't touch them, and I doubt Mrs. Warne or staff would have. We avoid that on hot days. Walls are thick, you see, lined with clay tile to prevent the spread of fire." Clearly keen for an opportunity to expound on another of his home's features, he went on to explain the added insulating effect that kept the room cool so long as the draperies were closed along with the windows.

Resting his hands on his hips, Rex shook his head. "I imagine that even if a window or door were open for someone to get through, he couldn't lock it from the outside after he left."

Ransom tossed his jacket onto the table. "No."

"Which could mean he's still inside."

"Yes," Ransom replied, frowning.

"But no one could've passed through the drawing room without one of us seeing him. Although…"

"What is it?"

"Well, sir, we had the music playing, and Helen and I danced for a time. Distracting ourselves. But—well, even then, I don't see how anyone could've snuck past. We even noticed the car outside, sir, when your staff was leaving. That was right before you and Lottie came back to us."

"And before then, was someone always in there?"

"Helen and I were, ever since dinner. And when I wasn't, I was in here. Lottie, too. Except—well, yeah, Lottie was in here, too."

He'd caught his tongue just before relating how he'd actually been *alone* in the library at first. He'd expected to find Lottie in there and couldn't account for her whereabouts at that time — although Helen probably could.

Yes, if Rex asked, Helen would surely say that Lottie had come back to the drawing room from the north hall at precisely the same time he'd left through the south hall — in which case, no doubt Helen had redirected her friend back to the library, being so transparent about getting the couple alone together. It was a funny tale of timing that they could laugh about later. Whenever anyone was ready to laugh again, that was. And besides, if Lottie hadn't been in the library when he'd first entered, then she couldn't have been in the bar either. Right?

Rex rubbed his hand over his mouth, staring at the floor. "Now, *I* entered from the south hall, and Lottie came from the north. And after she screamed, you and Helen entered from both halls, too. So, no one could've been hiding in one of them or we'd have seen him, I would think." Rolling his sleeves to his elbows, he brought his hands back to his hips. "Damn," he added after a spell.

"Don't sound so disappointed we didn't cross a killer's path."

Rex bit his upper lip and heaved a loud exhale. "But I don't understand, sir. If the only way in and out of this library is through those halls to the drawing room, then how did Mrs. Warne get past us, too? Did she go out on the porch and reenter from another door? But why would she do that? And *how* could she, if the porch door was still bolted from the inside after she left?"

Ransom tapped the tip of his revolver against the table, his eyes closed as though scanning mental blueprints of his property or the ever more complex labyrinth of his wife's reasoning. When he offered no answers, Rex looked at the two wide wooden panels standing open in front of the bar. He walked over to squat next to Noble again.

"I don't think you should," Ransom started to warn, like Rex had before, but his curiosity evidently won out as he stepped to the athlete's side.

"I *know* I shouldn't," Rex said as he delicately pulled Noble's jacket farther open, "but if you won't allow outside help yet…"

The soiled dress shirt's top buttons were already unfastened, and Rex noticed for the first time small tears in the silk where the stains were their deepest. Pinching the collar with just his fingertips, he pulled it from beneath Noble's chin and parted it enough to see the undershirt was partially unbuttoned as well. Slowly, he peeled the fabric across Noble's skin, meeting slight resistance where drying blood had already clotted to the fibers.

Ransom crouched closer. "You shouldn't have to see this, son."

"Too late for that, I'm afraid." Rex swallowed, unable to remove his eyes from the ghastly sight. Dotting the actor's chest were several puncture marks, circular holes more than gashes. "A knife would leave a longer cut."

"A bullet wouldn't," Ransom said on inspecting the wounds from close range. "Small-caliber. Twenty-two, if I had to guess."

Rex thought of the rifle in Ransom's hand earlier but couldn't ascertain what ammunition it took. And couldn't bring himself to ask.

Laying his hands on Noble's shoulders, Ransom gently pushed the man forward, only a couple of inches or so. Scanning his back and then raising the bottom flap of the actor's jacket as far as he could to see underneath it, he shook his head. "Doesn't look like anything exited out his other side. Shots must've lodged inside him."

Resting Noble as he was when they'd found him, the two men stood to examine the bar next.

"Mirror's broken," Rex said, "but I don't see any bullet holes." Observing Ransom while the man didn't notice, Rex took in his large, strong build and the revolver in his hand. With some relief, he recalled, "I didn't hear any gunshots either."

"Neither did I. Though these walls are fairly soundproof with that extra lining."

Rex wasn't sure whether to feel better or worse that Ransom wasn't helping his case as the only person witnessed with a gun earlier that night. Though, ultimately, he had to believe that a guilty man would point the finger as far away from himself as possible. He had to believe that *this* man wasn't guilty, period. But damn if he wasn't acting odd.

Rex knelt beside Noble again and scanned around his body for any other clues. Finding nothing, he returned to his feet and leaned over the counter, which, it occurred to him, stretched from wall to wall.

"How do you get back there?"

Ransom stared at him for a moment as if the question were rhetorical. Then, turning on his heel, he stepped out of the bar and exited the library via the north hall. Rex watched in confusion but stayed with the body at the front of the counter. Soon enough, he saw the Colonel enter the rear of the bar through a slim door. It blended so well with the bar's back wall that Rex hadn't noticed it before.

So, in addition to the two wood-paneled doors that opened to the front of the bar on the library's side, the Colonel had snuck in yet another hidden door at the back.

A hidden door that he'd accessed from the north hall. The same hall from which Lottie had entered the library.

The hall had access to the bar…the bar that Lottie had looked at so anxiously before opening its door…

Something crunched behind the counter as the Colonel stepped inside.

"Careful," Rex said. "The glass from the mirror."

"Broken bottle, too. It's wet. I can smell the gin. There's some blood as well. And—" He reached down and stood with a soggy hardcover book in his hand.

"What is it?"

"Lindbergh's autobiography. Signed it for me, you see." With that faint, boyish grin again, Ransom leafed through to the title page and held the book out as if Rex needed to see it to believe it.

"Very nice, sir. But what's it doing back there?"

After admiring the signature himself, Ransom flipped to where several pages of the book were severely warped. He regarded them mournfully, then touched the pad of his middle finger to one. On examining a glittering speck that his fingertip lifted from the paper, he looked back down at the floor and his face hardened. His eyes then rose to scan the bar top and the interior below it. Clapping the cover shut, he slammed the book on the counter and charged out the rear door.

"Sir?"

Ransom didn't return to the library, yet Rex heard his footsteps.

He ventured into the north hall, only to see Ransom wasn't there. All Rex saw was a new door gaping open in the middle of what had been a paneled wall moments before.

Through this doorway, he saw a second one to the left—a slim one, the one Ransom had used to enter the bar. But what the Colonel hadn't disclosed was that this hidden hallway door *also* opened to a stairwell.

Rex hesitated to abandon the women on the ground floor—still marveling that Ransom had done so with Edith upstairs—yet he felt no choice but to pursue him.

All the same, he checked in with the ladies in the drawing room first, which met with a confident nod from Helen. From beside the sofa arm, she raised the iron fireplace poker, and Lottie feebly lifted the porcelain vase she'd been clutching to her stomach. Unusual accessories with their cocktail attire, but Rex gave a smile of kudos before retreating to the hall and slowly descending.

With walls papered in a silver calla lily print, the hidden stairwell spiraled down. Along the way, Rex thought he heard a clang, and, for certain, a door slammed somewhere below.

He picked up his pace until he reached what could only be the Gold Theatre. With its entire ceiling gilded in gold leaf, the space boasted burnt-orange walls and portions built of glass blocks. From the silver fluted columns to the chrome trim along curving cabinets, everything looked utterly sleek and state-of-the-art—not least of which was the large movie screen just to his left and the projection booth in back.

He saw another door across the way, where Ransom was jiggling the knob.

"Where does that lead?" Rex asked.

"Pantry and kitchen. Also stairs to the dining room and upper-floors."

"In the west wing?"

"That's right."

Pointing behind him, Rex verified, "And is that the only stairwell to the east?"

"Yes. I'm a fool for not thinking of it sooner."

Rex didn't comment, only tested the doorknob to the west wing himself.

"I've locked it," Ransom said.

"It wasn't before?"

When Ransom shook his head, Rex looked back at the individual chairs lined up in rows before the screen. "Your security measures," he said, "do they apply to internal doors, too?"

"To a degree, to contain fire, though they're not as reinforced."

He reached out as Rex handed him one chair before going back for another.

"Help me blockade this?" Rex asked when he returned to the door and wedged the other chair beneath the knob.

"Oh, I hardly think it necessary," Ransom protested while Rex set another chair against the door and went back to fetch yet another.

"We should take every precaution, wouldn't you agree, sir?"

When Ransom didn't reply, only stared at him through a paralytic mist, Rex took the chair from his hands and stacked it before the door for him. He also took the opportunity to notice that the handkerchief was no longer wrapped around Ransom's right hand, the knuckles of which appeared a little swollen.

Quickly, Rex checked the projection booth to see no one inside it. Then he walked along the theatre's eastern wall, reaching a hall midway. He mentally mapped out the layout aboveground.

"This hall leads out to the pool?"

"Yes, from underneath the porch."

Rex had noticed this basement entrance earlier from outside, when he'd stood by the pool after helping the ladies out of it. The door was situated in the middle of where the Jefferson porch's imperial staircase split off on either side. It was also lower than ground level, with its own set of stairs leading down to it.

"What else is down here?" Rex felt around for a door, finding one on his left and another on his right. He tried both knobs, but they were locked.

"Utility rooms," Ransom said from behind him. "For storage and such."

Shakily, the Colonel withdrew the keys from his trouser pocket, which came out along with a bunched-up ball of white cloth. Transferring the keys to his left hand, he hastily wrapped the handkerchief around his right knuckles before opening each door and confirming with Rex that no one was hiding behind any of them.

Rex mostly saw a hodgepodge of equipment. In one room, a low stack of dank logs sat beside an odd mechanism with a pulley system. Another room seemed devoted to laundry. Everything looked coated with dust, disused, the floor freckled with dried crumbles, skid marks of dirt, and oil spots.

In, out, and around they stepped, yet their search was a hasty one. Discovering this alternative entrance to the east wing had Rex alarmed more than ever for the women's safety upstairs. Fast as he could muster, he checked that the door to outside was also locked and secure before running back up the silver staircase to protect Lottie and Helen.

Just who to protect them from, however, remained one horrid question of many.

"Any sign of anyone?" Rex asked after he'd dashed into the drawing room just ahead of Ransom, gasping. "Mrs. Warne?"

Lottie hadn't moved from the sofa, but Helen had taken to pacing the room minutes ago. To see a seasoned athlete like Rex try to catch his breath was more than a little unnerving. As was the handgun tucked in his waistband and the one in Ransom's hand.

"No," Helen said, "but what's happened?"

Before giving any response, Rex closed the French door behind him and locked its crémone bolt into place before doing the same to the other set of doors. He marched through the room, inspecting all openings and latches with an almost primal urgency while Ransom darted glances at him like a reluctant schoolboy awaiting instruction.

"Has something happened?" Helen repeated.

"The Colonel just acquainted me with his secret stairwell to the basement."

He'd said it evenly enough, yet couldn't mask that he found the feature indulgent. Ransom said nothing, but, with raised chin, clearly bridled at the unspoken critique.

Both women's eyes went wide.

"The theatre." Helen shook her head. "It's beneath the library, isn't it?"

"Oh, how didn't I think of it?" Lottie covered her face in her hands. "He could've been anywhere."

"Still could be." As could Edith by now, whatever the *deuce* was keeping her. How peculiar that Ransom would've left her on her own; Helen could only pray he hadn't made a fatal error.

"That's why I hurried back to you," Rex told Lottie gently. "We've all just had the shock of our lives, but we have to concentrate now. And *remember*. But first—" he looked at Ransom "—I think Mrs. Warne should be here. It isn't safe to leave her alone, and we need to know what she knows."

Ransom fiddled with his fingers, his chin still elevated, but, after a moment, he nodded and exited to the main staircase in the foyer.

Rex took his seat beside Lottie, and Helen sat across from them. The three avoided eye contact during a long silence, Rex crisscrossing his palms as Lottie sagged in place at the edge of her seat. Helen lounged sideways against the sofa arm, picking at her lower lip.

"That's it," Rex said after a time. He slapped his thighs and stood. "The longer we wait to have someone inspect the body, the more we could lose answers. I'm phoning my father."

Lottie leaped to her feet. "But—"

"I understand what the Colonel wants," he said, taking her hands, "but this is life and death. It's not like in the movies. We can't write whatever ending we want."

She snatched her hands away. "Well, what a pretty little fool I must be if I can't tell the difference." The whites of her eyes were tinged pink but dry, and her expression firm.

Helen stopped playing with her lip and watched dejection overcome Rex once more.

"No, no," he scrambled. "I wasn't, I mean—"

"That's not what he said, Lottie, and you know it."

"Well, it's what you're all implying, all of the time!" Lottie sauntered to the bar cart and over-served herself another brandy in a new glass. "*Bien alors*, do you mind if your little fool has a drink?"

"I don't know if that's—"

Helen pushed her palm toward Rex to quiet him. She recognized that critical moment when her friend would cross from sadness to sulking, and there wasn't much to be done at that point. Pressing her would turn the sulk into a show, as Lottie lashed out at anyone in earshot. Rex needed to learn how to manage her moods, too, and what better time than the present.

He was a good pupil, it turned out. He simply sat back and said they could all probably do with a drink to calm their nerves. *And get us talking*, Helen thought. *Certainly a little truth serum could help here.* But because Lottie had poured herself such an absurd amount of brandy, Rex wisely qualified that he'd just take a few sips from her glass to make it easy.

On Lottie's way back to the sofa, she handed Helen a shallowly-filled snifter of her own, which she couldn't refuse this time. Helen swirled her glass before raising its false promises of relief to her lips. Lottie then let Rex take the first sip from hers. He made it a deep one, whereas Lottie, seeming to come back to her senses—or at least good graces—took only a small taste. She grimaced slightly but followed it with a contented exhale.

The brandy had just begun to blaze in Helen's belly when Lottie spoke.

"I'm sorry. Both of you, I…This is all so shocking beyond words."

"We understand," Rex said. "Of *course* we do. Not to the extent you must feel it as—as someone who knew him well, but to be sure, it's got us all rattled."

Helen had never seen the Colonel so disconcerted, that was certain. Naturally, he would feel responsible for this happening on his property and must have been frantic for Edith when she'd disappeared. Yet, again, *why* would he have left her alone once he'd found her? Did he not care, or did he know she was safe, that the situation was already contained? Could Edith be involved, and Ransom's strange behavior just a knee-jerk effort to protect her? Or was he protecting himself?

Helen didn't dare vocalize such speculations now, but in the horrific event this was an inside job, those two had spent the most time with Noble around his hour of death.

"I do hope Edith is all right," Lottie said. "That Noble didn't…frighten her."

Rex raised his brows. "Or hurt her, even before our culprit could've had the chance."

"Oh, this is a mess." Helen slumped farther down in her seat and took another modest sip of her brandy. "It's been a complete farce of people walking in and out of doors all night. Once those two come back, none of us ought to leave this room."

"I agree." Rex took Lottie's hand. "And no matter what happens, we're in this together."

The athlete's little pep talk was enough to encourage the trio to smile weakly at one another, and they continued to cozy up with their brandy—and each other, in Rex and Lottie's case. Little by little, she nudged closer to him on the cushion, and he wrapped his arm around her bare shoulders.

The warmth of alcohol seemed to spread and put everyone more at ease. Yet just when Helen opened her mouth to ask if she could bring Lottie anything else of comfort, the main staircase creaked with heavy footsteps.

Helen heard Rex cock his gun.

Edith entered the drawing room just ahead of Ransom with a vacuous expression. Her pale skin flushed on making eye contact with the rest, but she offered a dull smile and nodded as Ransom assisted her to Helen's sofa with uncharacteristic delicacy.

She appeared unharmed, but her chestnut hair was darker—damp, it seemed, and loosely pulled up with two hair pins of silver and intricately carved jade. Stray tendrils framed and softened her face, which bore little trace of makeup now. She had changed out of her evening gown as well, now robed in a two-piece silk *crêpe de chine* pajama set with a Mandarin collar, waist tie, and wide-legged trousers. Casual, yet terribly chic and of a light cream and rust color that suited her beautifully. If Edith didn't look so disoriented and fragile, Helen would think this was the most stunning the woman had ever looked. She half-wished she had her *Chronicle* photographer there to capture the moment.

In fact, they could use photos of the crime scene as well. Helen wondered if Chief Rainger would bring any such equipment or if they'd have to wait for the local authority. Perhaps the Warnes had something on hand in the meantime?

But she couldn't stand to delay their talk any longer, and Noble very well wasn't going anywhere.

"Are you all right, Mrs. Warne?" Rex asked.

Lottie eyed her warily. "We didn't notice you slip upstairs."

"I crossed through the basement," Edith said, somewhat hoarse. "But I apologize for my rudeness. I simply…didn't feel quite myself." She glanced at Ransom out of the corner of her eye. "I thought a bath might revive me."

"You saw Noble, then," Helen said, "while he was still alive?"

Edith's lips fell, and her earlier color left her complexion. "Yes." She swallowed and looked to the hands that she worried in her lap. "He was still alive when I left him."

"Which means he was still alive when *you* left him," Lottie said to Ransom with some light back in her eyes.

"Of course he was!"

"Don't get defensive, Ransom," Edith said faintly.

"We're only trying to understand the sequence of events, as you suggested," Rex said. "No one's accusing anyone here."

"Well, I should say not," the Colonel huffed and, noticing the snifters in the others' hands, went to the bar cart to help himself as well.

Edith and Lottie both sighed.

"We can't necessarily accuse someone *not* here, though," Helen said. "Right?" She felt their astonished gazes burn into her. "I'm not claiming one of us is guilty, only that the likelihood of someone else is worth questioning, don't you think?"

"Easy to say when *you* were never alone with him." The crystal stopper in Ransom's wrapped hand rattled against the neck of its decanter as he tried to replace it. "Or were you? Something you should tell us?"

Lottie jumped up from the sofa. "Ransom!"

"Miss Conroy never left my sight until I left hers," Rex insisted, "which was to go into the library only minutes before we found Noble. So *her* alibi is solid. The only one we know of so far."

Lottie looked down at him and sank back onto the cushion.

"And she's right," he said. "We just ate dinner with the victim. We're all suspects until we can be ruled out and someone else proven to have had a motive and the means."

With his back to them, Ransom's chin fell to his chest; he bent to rest his hands on the cart. "Forgive me, please," he said without turning around. "This is all so distressing, and I don't know what…"

Heartened by the apology and her friends' defense, Helen pressed her point. "We know now that the library looks secure from the outside and that the only probable way someone could've snuck past us is through the basement. But with Mrs. Warne herself passing through there and the staff in the west wing while we were here in the east—this is a grand home, but surely we *all* couldn't have missed something?"

Lottie sucked in a light gasp. "You don't think the servants had anything to do with it?"

"What motive would any of them have?" Rex asked.

She snapped her head to him. "What motive have we?"

"I didn't say we did."

"Which isn't to say we don't." Helen raised her hands when all heads snapped to her in turn. "Even if none of us did it, that doesn't mean we wouldn't have had reason to."

"What?" Lottie asked. "Why would any of us do such a thing?"

"You need to talk about it?" Helen had asked Lottie in the study, after they'd come in from the pool. *"Tonight,"* Lottie had said, nodding, *"if I can. There's something I might need to take care of first."* Something she'd had to take care of first...

"It's not whether we *would* but if we'd *want* to."

Lottie huffed as Ransom had done earlier and rapidly shook her head. "Yes, I imagine it *is* easier to say when your own alibi's proven. Leave the rest of us holding the bag." A queer defensive smile curled the corners of her lips, and she snatched the brandy snifter from Rex's hand before drinking twice her average sip. This time, she didn't flinch as much from its potency, and she did not hand the glass back.

"Lottie, you act as if I'm accusing you!" Helen said. "Fine, then. If it means you'll understand my point, I'll out with it. I'll gladly be the first to admit I'm not sorry to see him gone. I never wished him dead, of course—" she looked around at each speechless face "—but he didn't treat you well, Lottie. You all but told me you weren't happy with him."

Lips tight, Lottie glared at Helen with watering eyes. "That was in confidence."

"I know," Helen replied with remorse, "and only now did you confirm that I'm right about that. But, my dear, this is no longer the time to play coy with our feelings. I wished that man gone out of love, and I suspect I'm not the only one."

Rex weighed Helen with a concentrated stare before looking to his lap.

"It's true, Lottie," he said. "Don't think any one of us wouldn't defend your virtue if necessary."

"My virtue?" She croaked out a cynical laugh. "Yes, I saw Edith defending my *honor* all day, didn't I?"

That brought some color back to Edith's pallor, though she met Lottie's frown without a word.

Ransom stepped to his wife's side and laid his injured hand on her shoulder. The lighting was too dim to tell for certain—perhaps it was a shadow—but Helen thought she spied a dark smudge on his bandage that hadn't been there before. Perhaps he'd dirtied it while inspecting Noble or the other rooms.

"Now, Karlotta," he said, "that's not—"

"Oh?" Lottie persisted. "She's not even going to deny it?"

Helen swapped a glance with Rex, feeling one of them should say something, yet terribly curious how this would play out. Words needed to be said in this household even if Noble were still alive. Rex seemed to reach the same understanding in the way he shifted forward and parted his lips only to shut them and ease back again in his seat.

"You both were so very humorous, weren't you?" Lottie said, her voice tremulous. "A real comedy duo with me as the punch line. Planning to take that act on the road?"

Ransom shifted an uneasy look down at Edith and squeezed her shoulder. Beneath his large hand, she shrank a little while Lottie swigged another sip.

"And that shameless flirtation," she carried on. "Really, a woman of your age and status. It's most unbecoming."

"And what of him," Edith at last bit back, lurching forward in her seat and out of Ransom's grasp, "who was equally old and almost engaged to be married?"

"Noble got paid for his charm, so don't fancy his flattery was serious. Or is it because you knew it *wasn't* that you, that you—" Lottie's voice had grown shrill, and she choked on her last words just as everyone else finally protested in alarm.

She was sobbing now, her drink held topsy-turvy on her fringed lap and swaying with her tremors. Rex tried to take it from her but resorted to cupping his hand around hers to at least help hold the glass steady.

"Well?" she cried. "What am I supposed to think when you didn't come back from the library with Ransom? When you *stayed* in there with Noble? Intoxicating him with more of your potions if not with yourself, I'm sure."

Edith's stick-straight spine, still angled forward, now wavered from her waist like a weathervane in shifting winds. "What was *I* to think, when…" she uttered, barely above a whisper.

"When what?" Lottie asked. "When responding to his attentions, you realized you couldn't steal him from me, so you stole his life? Anything to ruin my happiness, anything to take away what I've achieved! What *I've* achieved!" She beat her palm on her chest with the last two words while the others looked on, stupefied as the train drove off the rails and ground into the dirt, slowed but not stopping. With her cheeks mottled from the brandy and the feverish pitch she'd worked herself up to, Lottie quavered side to side as if about to swoon. "You were the last to see him alive," she wept. "You were the last!"

"He *was* still alive, wasn't he?" Helen dared to ask.

"She's already said he was!" Ransom shouted with surprising might, his clear impatience with the journalist's questions rekindled.

The outburst fiercely startled Edith, who crumpled into her lap with her forehead cupped in her palm. Pressing her other hand to her stomach, she began rocking.

Helen reached a tentative hand toward Edith's back; laying it there a moment, she started rubbing up and down in light, consoling strokes. She could have chipped at the tension with an icepick after that, the atmosphere thick with all their unspoken words.

Eventually, Rex did say, "Motive or not, it'll look strange to the police that your entire staff left around that same time."

"They left because I ordered them to," Edith said.

"But why?" Helen asked. "With guests here for the weekend?"

"We only needed the dining room and dishes clean for breakfast in the morning. They could've sorted everything else during the hunt." Edith looked up wearily. "They'd already worked so hard to make this weekend up to Lottie's standards."

"*My* standards?"

"When did you last see them, Mrs. Warne?" Rex asked before more came out of Lottie's indignant mouth.

Dropping her hand to fold into her other one, Edith still leaned on her lap but looked up. "After I left the library and crossed the basement, I witnessed them all busy at work in the kitchen. Even the men were lending their hands if it meant getting their dinner faster, I'm sure."

"Did you speak with anyone?" Helen asked.

"No, I — didn't wish to delay them any further. They'd been slaving all day," she insisted, "so I took advantage that they didn't seem to notice me and hurried past to let them get on with their evening."

"But to leave until morning," Lottie said tersely. "Even the ones who live here?"

Edith swallowed. "They've wanted time off to visit family for a while now. I'm not surprised I didn't have to ask twice."

"But why *now*, Mrs. Warne?"

At Helen's question, Ransom shifted on his feet.

"Yes, why?" Lottie echoed. "They've worked much larger occasions before, with much less going on in between. Why so concerned with their well-being tonight?"

"Because I think we all knew this night wouldn't end favorably."

Helen cocked her head. "Why do you say that?"

"Because that, that —" Edith's volume began to rise, but she quickly reclaimed it. Squeezing her eyes closed, she seemed to concentrate on her next words. "Because you're right, Miss Conroy, that I am also glad that man is out of our lives."

A long silence followed that remark, with Edith's eyes fixed on the floor, Ransom's on her, and Rex's on Lottie. Helen, too, looked to see how her friend would react. It was perhaps what Lottie *didn't* do that made the biggest impression. She did not start crying again, nor did she flare in defensive anger. Instead, her eyes also looked to the floor as, expressionless, she took a slow sip of her brandy. Once ready, she spoke in a muted, measured voice to Rex.

"What would your father do, if he were here right now?"

He perked up a bit but glanced first at Ransom, who nodded his consent to answer.

"Well, I can't say Pop has much firsthand experience with—*this* degree of...But, I think he'd want to hear everyone's accounts of when they last saw Noble alive. So that he could sort out a timeline. We've had a rough start of it, but are you okay to try again?"

Clutching her snifter, Lottie wiped her cheek. "Yes, I think so."

"Are you, Mrs. Warne? Colonel?"

"Call me Edith, dear." She widened her glassy eyes, her head and shoulders vacillating ever so slightly. "I think it's warranted under the circumstances." The last word came out on a vague slur. "Ransom?" She looked up at her husband, who nodded again, as did Helen when Rex consulted her next.

"Good," Rex said. "Then we can get on better footing before he gets here. I think we need to back up to when we can all agree we last saw Noble alive. Together, I mean, before we separated as a group. Correct me if anyone thinks otherwise, but I remember hearing a clock chime beside me while we were all still at the dinner table. The one on the mantel behind the Colonel said eight o'clock. That was moments before he and Mr. Howard excused themselves to speak in the library, and we all retired in here not long after that."

"Yes, I think that's right," Helen said. "When I first stood here at the fireplace, the clock there"—she pointed at the grand timepiece in the corner—"was approaching quarter-past the hour. The four of us"—she looked around at Rex, Lottie, and Edith—"were all still here."

"Then let's begin," Rex said, "with the first to see Noble alone tonight after dinner."

Pouting, Ransom looked down at the rug and continued to nod his head. He swirled his brandy for several seconds before realizing everyone was staring at him.

"Ah." His eyes shifted as he reddened. "Well, as you know, Mr. Howard asked to speak with me privately after dinner. And so we did."

Additional seconds dragged as he said nothing more.

Catching Lottie's eye, Helen raised her brow, begging for clarification. She didn't want to ask Ransom herself lest she set him off again. Especially now that he was finally talking. Almost.

Lottie coughed into the back of her hand, then looked everywhere but in anyone's eyes as she fiddled with the fringe on her lap. "I doubt it comes to anyone's surprise," she said, "that Noble asked Ransom for my hand in marriage tonight. That was the purpose of our visit."

Glances were exchanged all around, except for Lottie, who wouldn't look up from the coffee table.

"And so he did," was all the elaboration Ransom offered to the stone-silent group. Drawing an armchair closer to the coffee table, he sat, switching his glass to his left hand and intermittently clutching and relaxing his right.

"Feel any better?" Rex asked.

His question would've seemed random if it hadn't sounded rather pointed, Helen thought, as Rex closely watched Ransom's fist.

"Oh." The Colonel spread his fingers and looked down at the back, then palm, of his right hand. A tremor ran through it, and he clenched it again. "Yes. Though somewhat stiff."

"You said you cut yourself?" Rex said.

"Slipped chipping some ice," he'd said. Helen remembered the ice block, could still see how Rex had pushed it back to stop it from dripping on Noble.

Drawing in a slow, steady breath, Ransom shifted his weight in his chair. After a pensive sip of his drink, he said, "No, didn't cut."

"I wrapped his hand myself," Lottie said, "only against the swelling."

"It 'stung more than pierced,'" Helen recalled aloud of his earlier claim. But thinking of the stained handkerchief, its patch of rusty pigment now out of her sight, she wondered if his injury bled after all.

Glancing at his bandaged knuckles, Ransom leaned forward to set his drink on the coffee table. He discreetly slid the handkerchief off, bunching it tightly in his other hand before stuffing it into his trouser pocket.

"Sure stung all right."

He smoothed his moustache with his thumb and index finger. And then he told his story.

Earlier that evening,
just past eight o'clock

"Mr. Warne, if we may?"

Standing, Ransom extended his hand toward the dining room door for Noble to leave first.

"Through to the Liberty Library, please," Ransom said to him before turning back to Chauncey. "No dessert for us, thank you."

Once in the foyer, Noble paused, and Ransom gestured again for him to walk through the eastern door to the drawing room. He made a point to guide him by the bookcase that held an autographed photo of Charles Lindbergh, and when Noble strode by without a glance, Ransom gritted his teeth and quietly snatched up the autographed book Charles had also gifted him. He carried it with him into the library.

Hands in his pockets as he strutted around like a rooster, Noble let out a long whistle. "Sure some place you got here." Cutting past the sofas to the east wall, he stopped before a gun case. "Those real?"

"Some were my father's and grandfather's, others I collected after the war."

Noble pivoted to examine him with real or feigned interest, Ransom couldn't tell. "Yes, of course. You served."

Holding his book in one hand, Ransom rubbed his other fingers together. "I reported," he decided to say modestly. The confounded man full-well knew the Colonel's story already, would've remembered had he ever paid attention to anyone but himself. Fortunately, when it came to the Great War, Ransom didn't mind an opportunity to repeat himself. Now just wasn't the time.

"Fascinating." Noble strolled over to where the Colonel stood. "I don't suppose you got anything to drink in here? The occasion calls for a toast, I think."

"That so?"

"Without doubt."

"Well, in *that* case," Ransom said with just as little sincerity.

But he was still pleased for an excuse to reveal his special secret. With what he considered a smooth move of bravado, he released the hidden doors to his bar and beamed at this clever trick up his sleeve. If only he'd stationed one of his men behind there, standing at the ready to tend bar. But Edith proudly considered cocktails her domain at these smaller soirées.

Noble indulged him with a couple of chuckles. "Man of mystery aren't you, Mr. Warne? Isn't *this* the cat's pajamas." Stepping right up, he leaned over the bar to fish out a bottle of gin from behind it.

"Do help yourself."

"Oh, but I want to help *you*. How do you like it?"

"Allow me." At this point, Ransom only had one neat trick left to show, so he exited to the north hall and revealed to Noble the hidden door at the back of the bar. He entered and, setting his book down on the counter, reached underneath for a glass — but only the one.

"You aren't joining me, sport?" Noble smirked with a glint of mistrust before instructing Ransom how to make his preferred martini.

Almost as soon as the Colonel started going through the motions of bartending, he stopped. The bottle clanked against the bar top as he firmly set it down.

"No, Mr. Howard. I don't think I will." Leaving the bar and hall doors open behind him, he walked back around into the library to confront Noble. Man to man. "Lottie won't be joining you either, I'm afraid."

"What?" Noble laughed.

The Colonel laid a hand on the other man's shoulder.

"It's our pleasure to have you here, Mr. Howard, truly an honor. Mrs. Warne and I appreciate the opportunities our dear girl has enjoyed with you, both professionally and personally." Forming the rest of his words in his mind, Ransom pressed his lips together and tapped his thumb against Noble's velvety shoulder a couple of times.

"Why, thank you," the actor said with a chipper grin. "And you're welcome."

After beginning to tap his fingertips on Noble's shoulder as well, Ransom removed his hand altogether to twiddle it at his side.

"Yes, well." His gaze began to waver, but with a reaffirming sigh, he fixed Noble back in his crosshairs. "Lottie has apprised me of your intentions, you see."

"Mm," Noble acknowledged through tight lips.

"I regret to say, however, that I can't give you my approval."

Noble broadened his smile as if he'd heard him wrong.

"We do appreciate your willingness to extend this offer to her," Ransom continued, both to fill the awkward silence and stress his point. "But there will be no marriage as long as I have any say."

"As long as *you* have say." Noble appeared to mull over the statement as he snatched up the gin bottle, opened it, and dumped its contents into the martini glass without replacing the cork afterward. Still wearing a smile on his face, he nodded and sipped his drink, then nodded and sipped it again. "So, tell me, what does 'our dear girl' have to say about it? That she won't marry me unless you approve?"

Ransom's heart squeezed in his chest, but he kept his bearing tall and face firm. "That she won't marry you regardless."

Noble's chin cocked back into his neck. "Really," he exclaimed dramatically. "And why's that, all of a sudden?"

Puffing his chest, Ransom looked down at the movie star and firmed his fists with an equally raised voice. "I think you know."

"I'm sure that I don't! Lottie and I are in love. She *will* marry me."

"You think so."

Noble shrugged. "I know so!" He took another swig of gin. "Aw, what're you afraid of, ol' man? Having me as a son-in-law? That isn't so bad, is it?"

"She doesn't love you."

Noble's brows pinched together for a fleeting moment. But he held his confident stance, and his teeth clicked against the glass as he took another hearty sip. "Sure, she does," he then said at a lower volume.

"No."

Furrowing his brow more deeply this time, Noble gave a light huff. "Oh, so she confides in you, does she?"

Ransom straightened to his full height. "Yes."

Noble nodded as he appeared to consider this. A soberness entered his eyes, encouraging Ransom that this might go better than expected.

Until Noble said, "Tickles when she whispers in your ear, don't it?" He lurched his head back with a stiff smirk.

"What are you —" Ransom nearly shouted before he reined it in, closing his eyes and then opening them into a narrowed gaze. He rubbed his palms together. Slowly, methodically. With forced calm, he said, "I believe we both know that Lottie doesn't love you any more than you love her. That all this has ever been about is publicity."

Noble *tsk*ed. "So cynical."

"So sin*cere*. And I ask that you please be the same with me."

Noble exhaled loudly through his nose and watched his glass as he swirled it. He still wore a vague grin, but his manner had noticeably deflated.

"I *am* sorry," Ransom said, still trying to temper his tone. "I know this business is between you two. But it *is* just business. Between you. In expressing the facts on Lottie's behalf, I don't mean to be hurtful."

Noble's head snapped up, a new sharpness in his gaze. "You can't hurt me."

"And neither can she, I wager." Ransom returned his hard stare.

But the actor faltered first, his wounded eyes fluttering side to side before looking to the floor. Noble stared absently at the wooden boards as he pursed his lips and stood silent a moment.

"Was she...ever planning to tell me this herself?" he eventually asked. "Or —" he gestured around "— is this it?" He then cleared his throat and swallowed. "I assume I'm being dealt with here? My bags are all packed in a car out front?" His stare grew sullen as he bit the inside of his mouth and continued to look away.

The change in attitude caught Ransom unawares, and he couldn't help but second-guess his own judgment. Not in rejecting Noble, of course. But always so quick to rush to Lottie's aid, perhaps this time he should've let her sort this mess for herself, the one she'd gotten herself into, after all. No doubt Edith would admonish him for coddling once again, as if Lottie were still his charge. Yet when the girl had fluttered into his bedroom before dinner, panicked and not even yet dressed, there was so much her eyes yearned to tell that her tongue wouldn't. He saw it; he knew it. How could he not seek to protect her?

Extending an arm, he patted Noble on his shoulder. "Now, now, my boy. She surely intends to speak with you. You can only imagine how hard it is for her, too." When the drooping blue eyes raised to his, Ransom felt compelled to add, "She does care," however unconvincingly.

Noble tapped a finger against his glass, making fidgety adjustments to his posture while he frowned. "Dare I ask—" he cast a forlorn look around the library "—that if she doesn't love me, there's somebody else?"

On the last words, he met Ransom's gaze.

"I couldn't say."

"No?" Noble's lips cocked into a more characteristic side grin as he looked into his glass. "You haven't someone else in mind for her?" Tilting his head, he fixed his host with a speculative eye.

Ransom shifted on his feet as an image of Lottie appeared—little Karlotta, a child running across Belleau's garden and into his waiting arms. Then a budding woman, practicing jumps on horseback under his instruction. Then a starlet descending his stairs with such grace. Such verve for life. A grown woman, aging but not so much as he'd aged.

Now in his mind, they were walking between the trees again. Along the allée, arm in arm, like he was escorting her down the aisle as the adoptive father he'd promised to be. He'd promised. But as her apparition looked up to him through tear-rimmed eyes, how he hoped she would see him for the man he really was, the true relationship they could have. One he couldn't put off any longer for fear of what others would think.

Just then, he saw a younger man in his place, one in uniform, crossing a field with his men and valiantly dodging the blows. A hero in his own right. Ah, that Lottie would love that man, for everything he'd been, still was, and would be. For her.

"I'm right, aren't I?" Noble asked after a prolonged silence of wallowing and swallowing the rest of his gin. Looking out the corner of his eye, into the bar, something made him smile. "And I've gotten in the way?"

His visions ripped from him, Ransom returned to the unpleasant reality he had yet to conquer. "What? No. That is, I—"

"You fancy you could offer Lottie more than me."

"Well, now, I *do* think—"

"You can't stand the idea of me gettin' the goods for myself."

"I wouldn't say—but, pardon? *Goods?* What do you mean by—"

"And she *is* good." Noble swayed back and forth a bit. "Or so I imagine. But you already know that, don't you? I'm not stoppin' ya from *those* sweet rewards. Got it backwards, if anything." His head jerked back again with a croaking sound, something between a laugh and a hiccup.

As Noble continued to teeter on his feet, Ransom squinted at him, unsure of what the younger man was saying and even less sure how to respond.

"So, yeah...no," Noble said. "I bet I know what's *really* got your goat."

Ransom raised an eyebrow. "Oh?"

"You bet. No, *I* bet, I'd bet anything...that you, you're afraid"—he jabbed his glass at Ransom's chest each time he said *you* —"that I'm gonna inherit it all. Everything you've worked for."

Ah. Ransom followed him quite clearly now. Clenching his jaw, he let the scorned suitor keep digging his own grave.

"Everything you've built," Noble rambled on. "Until the walls come crumbling down." He scanned the library. "Starting with these, I think."

"I won't stand for it," Ransom said barely above a whisper.

"I should think you won't be standing at all, ol' man! Resting your pretty head for eternity, right? So don't worry it now."

"I'm not so old, you know."

"I know. But I've got time to wait."

"Insurance for when your own fortune runs out?"

Noble laughed through his nose. "You know what I'm worth?"

"I know what you're not. And that doesn't tend to earn interest over time."

"Oh, I've got interest. Just ask around."

"So I've heard. Your carousing doesn't escape *all* the gossip rags, however deeply you have Hearst in your pocket."

Easing a hand into his actual pocket, Noble bit his lower lip before he began rocking on his feet once more with that smug grin.

"Hearst." During a slow nod, he finally lost his smile. "Now *that's* a man with some say. Important. Rich, you know? You oughtta see the parties *he* throws. What his pleasure palaces provide." His lips continued to make soft *puh-puh-puh* sounds. "Oh, not that your quaint little homestead here isn't just swell, sir."

He looked down at his glass with a laugh as he swirled nothing but air inside it, then set it down with a heavy clink. Still swaying back and forth on his feet, he raised his brows and nodded.

"And wait till you getta load of the story I've got for him next…"

13

The present hour

Ransom stopped speaking, only stared with hardened, glassy eyes to the floor. He felt a hand on his arm.

"Colonel?" Helen said. She released him and leaned back in her seat on the sofa. "What happened then?"

His lips trembled around his gritted teeth, and a pain shot through his injured hand as he clenched it into a fist. "He—" Pressing his lips, Ransom shook his head. He refused to look up, but he heard Rex's voice next.

"Did Noble claim to have a story on you, sir? Something he threatened you with?"

When Lottie gave a little gasp, Ransom darted a glance at her fearful eyes. She opened her mouth as if to speak, but her breath caught in her throat again. Her small body actually lurched with the intake of air, like she'd hiccupped, but he knew it wasn't the brandy that widened her eyes with a terrified alertness.

She knew.

She knew what Noble had deduced, yet she'd never said anything of the sort to Ransom. Only where her true feelings lay. The ones he'd tried to impress upon Noble. Nothing further. Until Ransom had made his own admission to her afterwards…

"He didn't, did he?" Lottie said in a hoarse voice. Her eyes filled with tears as she shook her head against the inevitable truth.

Edith's expression firmed as she watched her. Ransom slackened his jaw and let it hover open.

"What happened next, sir?" Helen prodded when he remained silent.

"Well, he…" Ransom rolled his gaze around the room but focused on nothing as he saw Noble instead, standing before him in front of the bar with that wretched smile. "I remember he held his hands up."

"Did he strike you?" Lottie half-whispered.

"No, he only held them like this, you see." He raised his outward-facing palms, wishing he could use them to push away the memory.

"In defense?" Helen asked warily.

Ransom screwed his face as he looked down and shook his head again. "In gesture, while he spoke…"

Holding his hands up at eye level, Noble pulsed them from his left to his right with every next word as if seeing the headlines now: "'Married Magnate Makes Merry with Mistress.' What do ya think of that? Or how about, 'Warne and His Ward: From Daddy to Sugar Daddy.' Got a ring to it, don't it?"

"What are you saying?" Ransom growled, his fingernails nearly cutting into his palm while Noble turned away to refill his glass.

"What did he say, Colonel?" Rex asked.

Ransom's lips and tongue refused to form the words as he looked from Rex to Lottie, wishing he could deafen himself to the awful sound of Noble's voice.

After taking a swig of his freshly poured gin, Noble rolled his head on his neck to sneer over his shoulder. A lock of greased hair broke away to fall over his forehead. "Oh, I think you hear me fine. The truth will out, good man." He gulped the rest of the gin, slamming the glass down on the counter before turning and leaning his back against the bar. "And when the world learns you two've been bar-ney-mugging, just think what it'll do for your little ward's reputation. For your own, Mr. Warne."

"That's Colonel."

Ransom scrubbed his hand down his face. "He fabricated a lie." Meeting Lottie's desperate gaze, he emphasized, "A damned lie. To ruin my reputation. After all but admitting his designs on my fortune, and—and he was so insolent, the way he refused to call me Colonel."

"Colonel." Noble snorted. He pushed off the bar and paced around his host. "When you haven't seen a minute of combat."

Ransom rotated his head to follow his moving target. "I've seen it, all right."

"Just didn't participate."

Staring at the Colonel's busted hand again, Rex asked, "So you hit him?"

"Oh, Ransom," Edith said coolly, "so petty."

"I saved a man's life." Ransom firmed his fist, his furious gaze trying to bore a hole into Noble's head. "God knows who'll save you."

"Not Lottie, certainly." Noble stopped walking and giggled al-most coquettishly. His forehead glistened, and his skin had flushed a shade closer to his burgundy jacket. "God knows she hasn't even saved herself for me. Not when she's nursing her wounded soldier, huh?"

As Noble's head fought for balance on his neck, he narrowed his eyes and licked his lower lip with a lecherous sneer.

"Nursing him," he repeated. *"I'll bet she is. Or has she already weaned you off those ripe little—"*

CRACK.

Ransom didn't even register the pain in his hand, the way it felt like every bone had splintered against Noble's skull, until the actor had spun one hundred eighty degrees and dropped onto his knee, one hand splayed against the bar to keep from falling farther.

"Petty. Yes," Ransom murmured, keeping Noble's awful accusation to himself. "Though you know how at…certain times, I… can't seem to mind my temper."

Through a lens of red, Ransom watched the hunched form in front of him shake, hissing with laughter. While Noble uncoiled and struggled to his feet, the Colonel marched to the north wall and seized his hunting rifle from above the mantel. It wasn't loaded, but Noble didn't need to know that as he stood and then stared down the barrel pointed at his brow. Or was the gun loaded, after all? In that instant, not even Ransom was so sure.

But he held his aim steady as his chest heaved, pumping air in and out through his nose. For a long moment, he heard nothing but his own fierce breaths and the blood surging in his head. Smelled nothing but a weak man's fear. Until a blast echoed in his ears and warm drops spattered on his face, imposed a metallic taste on his tongue. His fingers fossilized around the trigger. His lungs captured but would not release his breath. Again and again, the blasts sounded around him, ripped through him. He buckled.

Bent at the waist, he peered up to see Noble frozen before him, the invisible explosions around them gone quiet as the actor held up his hands in surrender. Before Ransom could process anything else, he gripped his gun sideways, used it to shove the enemy back, and went AWOL.

"That's when we saw you cross through here, still holding the gun," Rex said after Ransom related everything that had followed the punch. The Colonel had refused to share any of Noble's specific words, though, looking fatigued from his storytelling whereas Lottie just looked relieved.

"And you followed him," Helen said to her. "But where did you both go?"

The Colonel stared down at his lap, rubbing his sore hand. Lottie watched him and quietly said, "I found him in his sitting room. I knew I would."

"And where's that?" Rex asked.

She motioned with her chin to the foyer. "Down the long hall there."

"My personal library," Ransom finally said, though his eyes were vacant. He lowered his volume. "It's where I often go to think."

"And you knew to find him there," Rex said to Lottie, noticing Edith bow her head in the corner of his eye.

"Funny," Edith said without looking up, "how you always know where to find him." Her voice was still cold and now quavering.

Lottie knit her brow, which mirrored Rex's confusion — until he recalled her same quizzical expression at the dinner table, in response to Edith's same tone. When Lottie had mentioned Mrs. Warne's newest painting, Edith had asked if she'd viewed it from Ransom's room.

Surely Edith wasn't implying…

Surely *Lottie* wasn't…

Not with Ransom…

Surely?

Rex inspected the actress's eyes, hoping for answers within them.

What he did see was realization. Almost as instantly as Lottie had scrunched her features, she smoothed them. But whatever her thoughts were, she didn't state them.

Just as well. Rex didn't want to get sidetracked again. In the interest of the investigation, they needed to stick to the timeline. He also had to wonder if he should stick to the *side*lines where this girl was concerned. "So, Lottie, when you found the Colonel in his sitting room…"

"He was seated at his chair, polishing his rifle. He seemed in a fog, the way he just kept stroking it."

"Lend a hand, did you?"

"Mrs. Warne," Helen admonished.

Edith almost as immediately bit her lip and looked down at her folded hands. She closed her eyes and shook her head.

Ransom appeared to ignore what she'd said—more so what she'd *implied*—but Helen's sternness had snapped him to attention. He sat up straighter.

"I went to my sitting room," he said, as if Lottie hadn't already. "The gun was in my hand. I didn't know why. Or what had just…I don't, that is, this doesn't normally—" Pressing his lips, he lowered his head. "But it does, as I said. Sometimes."

Her eyes still closed, Edith wore a pained expression. But when she raised her lids, she simply nodded and gazed at her husband with quiet understanding. Lottie did the same. Meeting Rex's eye, Helen mouthed the words that had just dawned on him, too.

Shell shock. No wonder they hadn't seen the Colonel in top form this evening. Never mind that he wasn't actually a trained soldier who'd been promoted up the ranks; not even the most skilled combatant was immune to the effects of battle. With all he'd seen, all he'd narrowly lived through—when covering a story had become covering a body with his own to shield it from shellfire—no wonder the man was so lost tonight. Admitting that alone took such courage. Rex felt even guiltier for doubting him, at least in that regard.

"You remember everything now, sir," Rex said. "That's what counts." He nodded at Lottie, who took the cue to continue on Ransom's behalf.

"When I first found him, he said he was readying the gun for tomorrow's hunt. But of course, I knew better."

"Because we wouldn't use guns for a fox chase," Rex said.

"He doesn't hunt with them regardless," Edith added softly. "Not anymore."

Not since the war, probably. Rex bobbed his head with solemn realization. The Colonel might collect his weapons, even rely on his revolver now for protection, but, very likely, he no longer saw much sport in shooting to kill.

Lottie stared at Ransom while she told the others, "I saw he was hurt, too. I gave him no choice but to tell me what happened."

"The memory came slowly," he admitted, "but clearly enough."

"Same as he told all of us now," Lottie said, "and I wrapped his hand while he spoke."

"You should probably put ice on that," Rex said.

"I'll be fine, son, but thank you."

Helen looked across the table at Rex with a soft smile. He reciprocated before asking, "Is there anything else, before you both joined Helen and me in here?"

Lottie and Ransom looked to each other. Their eyes spoke volumes that their closed mouths didn't, and Edith's demeanor hardened once again as she glanced between the two of them.

Rex, to his own shame, responded the same way. Pretending to adjust for comfort and give his muscles a stretch after sitting for so long, he scooted an inch or so away from Lottie on the couch. Their intimate conversation in the library suddenly seemed like he'd only viewed it onscreen.

"Anything relevant to Noble and his death," Helen qualified, in the spirit of Rex's earlier focus.

Lottie smiled and dabbed a fingertip to the inner corners of her glassy eyes before she sniffed and said, "No, that was all." Fanning herself with her hand, she added, "I'm sorry. It's been such an emotional evening."

"Of course," Helen said.

Yet Rex saw how closely Helen watched Lottie take a deep sip of her brandy. Maybe she wasn't so sure about her friend after all. Or maybe Rex was reading too much into every word and action.

No doubt, something was off between the Colonel and Mrs. Warne, as well as between Mrs. Warne and Lottie—that much had been apparent ever since Rex had arrived that day. What he only just began to see between Lottie and the Colonel, however, was more unnerving, harder to shake.

He could see, now, how their closeness might be viewed through Edith's eyes. Interpreted as something more than just a guardian and his ward. Had Noble thought so, too? Is that what he'd threatened in the library? To expose the Colonel for an affair? If this accusation were true, then Rex didn't know quite what to feel. Who in this house hadn't fallen under the actress's spell? Would Lottie be running away with Chauncey next, for God's sake?

Know your onions, he warned himself. It wasn't like him to jump to conclusions, to seek drama where it might not exist. Only on the football field did he let his aggression out; in life, he didn't antagonize people. He sought the best, not worst, in them. But where *murder* was concerned…

What if it was all related? If the guilty parties of one offense were guilty of the other? What might forbidden love drive people to do? That Alonzo Ashby who'd jumped to his death in Chicago last year—rumor had it he could no longer carry on an unacceptable tryst. If one lover was willing to take his own life, what prevented another from taking someone else's?

A guardian and his ward…

Maybe it wasn't as easy as ending a marriage or engagement. Perhaps Edith would never give Ransom a divorce, or Noble would blackmail him just as he might've threatened. Perhaps the headlines would disgrace Belleau in scandal, and the fame and fortune would flee. Maybe it *was* better to carry on in secrecy. And if Edith knew, too…maybe she'd also resigned herself to live with it. And agreed Noble must die for it.

Rex cleared his throat, determined to stay on course. Stick with hard-and-fast facts. "So, in the interest of the timeline." But he found he had no further to go with that.

To the rescue, Helen said, "Well, again, I remember it was around eight fifteen when the rest of us were still in here. That's about the time you left for the library," she said to Edith.

Wringing her hands in her lap, Edith started a little when the attention was brought to her. She looked at each of them blankly, shaking her head. "I left to get ice." On the last word, her eyes widened and zoned into something unseen before her.

Wrinkling her brow, Helen added, "I also remember thinking I'd heard voices. Raised ones, coming from the library through the wall."

Rex nodded. "I heard them, too, which makes sense now that we know the Colonel and Noble were, in fact, arguing."

"Was that the real reason you left the room, Mrs. Warne?" Helen asked, gentle but assertive. "Were you concerned?"

"I left to get ice," Edith repeated, staring into nothing.

Helen met Rex's eye across the table.

"Well," he said, "I also remember hearing another noise when we were dancing, Helen."

In the corner of his eye, he saw Lottie's face turn to him, but when he looked at her, her gaze moved to Helen. With all she'd just given him to mull over, fair enough if she was jealous of his attentions to another woman.

"I thought I'd heard a loud bump or slam," Rex explained. "That was right about when I noticed the servants leaving out front. After Mrs. Warne had left for…ice, but also after the Colonel and Lottie went to his sitting room. And then you both came back here," he said to Ransom and Lottie, "while Helen and I were looking out the window at the driveway."

"The music had stopped by then," Helen added, squinting as if sharpening the sight and sound of the memory. "And then the clock chimed, but only briefly."

"Eight thirty, likely," Rex said. "So then, we've just accounted for everyone at that time. Except…"

All heads turned to Edith. She didn't acknowledge anyone in the room until the silence eventually cued her to rejoin the conversation.

"Well, yes, as you've established, the servants left, while you two," she said to Rex and Helen, "were in here and those two," she said without looking at Ransom or Lottie, "were in the sitting room."

"Leaving *you* two in the library," Helen said carefully. "Or had you left Noble by then? What *happened*, Mrs. Warne?"

Smoothing the creamy silk over her narrow thighs, Edith replied, "Dear, I already told you."

"You left for ice," Helen sighed.

The lady of the house gave a sad smile and shook her head. "No, I told you to call me Edith."

14

Earlier that evening,
twelve past eight o'clock

"Ice," Edith said to the others in the drawing room. "I'll just fetch more ice." Reminding Lottie to play some music, Edith then stepped into the north hallway, closing the solid French door behind her.

She stared down the dark corridor, hearing the buzz of deep voices beyond.

"You can't hurt me."

"And neither can she, I wager."

Laying a hand on the wood-paneled wall to her right, Edith edged closer to it as she crept forward. The hidden hallway door to the stairwell was open, and she used it to shield her presence so that the men could continue uninterrupted.

After a silence, she heard Noble say, "Was she...ever planning to tell me this herself? Or is this it? I assume I'm being dealt with here?"

Edith curled her fingers at her chest and clawed at the beading there, sympathetic to the despondency in his voice. Poor

Noble, invited here only to get ganged up on. Why would Lottie subject him to such a ruse if she knew where her heart really lay? The prize she'd win without a fight since the opponent knew all was already lost.

Of course, Noble's pathos now could all be an act, performed by a master of his trade. But didn't Edith understand the ache of unrequited affection? Even if Noble didn't love Lottie, he'd want to feel loved himself.

"Now, now, my boy," she heard Ransom say kindly, as though channeling her sensitivity. "She surely intends to speak with you. You can only imagine how hard it is for her, too. She does care."

"Dare I ask…that if she doesn't love me, there's somebody else?"

Edith's chest inflated beneath her fingers; she stopped playing with her beads as her entire body froze on the gasp she couldn't contain. *Somebody else.* What a fool she'd been to imply so much to Noble on the porch, as they'd watched their respective lovers walk away on the lawn. *Oh, God, Ransom, don't answer.*

"I couldn't say," he said.

Drawing her eyes closed, Edith gradually released the air trapped in her lungs through her mouth, but it caught again in her throat when Noble persisted, "No? You haven't someone else in mind for her?"

Her heart bouncing off her breastbone, she couldn't bear the silence that followed. Risking a glance for some clue of what could come next, she peeked with one eye past the stairwell door to see the slim one to the back of the bar also stood open — no wonder she could hear the men so well. Peering across the bar into the library, she couldn't see Ransom from that angle, but over the countertop, Noble stood in view. He swallowed the rest of the drink he held.

"I'm right, aren't I?" he asked. "And I've gotten in the way?"

"What? No. Well, that is, I —"

"You fancy you could offer Lottie more than me."

Edith ducked back behind the stairwell door, pressing her back to the wall and trying to still her breath as Ransom stammered through his replies.

"She *is* good," Noble said. "Or so I imagine. But you already know that, don't you?"

Edith didn't focus on the rest as she squeezed her eyes closed against the visions his words conjured. A heavy clink against the countertop broke the dark spell, but woke her to an even worse reality.

"And wait till you getta load of the story I've got for him next," she heard Noble say. "'Married Magnate Makes Merry with Mistress.' What do ya think of that? Or how about, 'Warne and His Ward: From Daddy to Sugar Daddy.' Got a ring to it, don't it?"

"What are you saying?"

What are you *saying, Ransom, in not denying it?*

"Oh, I think you hear me fine," Noble said. "The truth will out, good man."

Edith flinched when a glass slammed down on the bar again.

"And when the world learns you two've been barney-mugging…"

Her mouth hovered open with shallow breaths as her heart and stomach clenched like two fists pummeling her from the inside. She folded her arms over her waist and bent over, dropping her head loosely from her neck to breathe deeply in and out. Concentrating on the lively music in the drawing room, she lost herself in its rhythm until—

CRACK.

Edith threw her head up and stumbled against the door; she grasped at it to catch herself. At the same time, she heard a weight fall against the bar. Squatting, she couldn't move a single limb to straighten herself to standing again, only listened to the mocking laughter, the heavy footsteps, the cocking of a gun hammer, and then only the hissing of breath against the muffled musical backdrop of "Ain't Misbehavin'."

How could she cower like this? Why didn't she do something? Why wasn't she on her feet and running into the library to save that man from her husband!

Nothing felt tangible anymore. The haze she'd drifted through during dinner had already set a surreal scene, and though the men's argument had brought her into sharper focus, shock seemed to again coat her in a downy daze.

More footsteps and a door slam, but no one entered her hallway. Then another door slam and Helen's voice: "Was that a rifle in his hand?" Yet no one had fired a shot.

Edith eased herself up the wall, bracing her hands behind her on the polished wood. Then she laid a palm against the stairwell door, intending to shut it and bury that spectacle forever.

"Edith?"

The door had only creaked closed an inch when she stopped and held her breath.

"I'm right, aren't I? That you're there?"

She wavered in place as she willed her legs to move. Which direction they should go, though, she wasn't sure.

"No? Yes?" Noble asked before she could decide. "All right. I'll come to you."

With a jovial chuckle, he opened the library door to the hall. Slick with perspiration and pomade, he bowed with one hand on the doorknob and the other across his waist. Like the perfect gentleman. When she hesitated to respond, he smiled more deeply and staggered over.

With slightly more finesse, he placed a hand at the small of her back and guided her into the bar through its rear door. Once inside, she realized he'd shut the library-side doors before making his way to her, closing them in.

"I'm sorry, dear, for whatever you've just heard. The ol' boy needs to cool off, and so do we."

Grinning, he carried out the literal meaning of his words as he snatched up the silver icepick from the counter and began chipping away at the ice block. He made a satisfied-sounding exhale as he set the utensil down and tugged a handkerchief from his coat pocket. Snapping the cloth to unfurl it, he then wrapped it around the loose chunks of ice and held the bundle to his jaw. He leaned against the counter and smiled at Edith.

"Does it hurt badly?" she asked.

He cocked his head side to side. "Not my first time. I'll live."

One side of his upper lip raised to bare a canine tooth. He squeezed his improvised ice bag, then set it directly on the Lindbergh book resting on the counter. Edith inwardly rolled her eyes; Ransom was so proud of that autographed copy and had no doubt brought it in there in a futile attempt to impress the movie star. She should really remove that handkerchief from it before the ice melted through the cover.

Or perhaps she should leave it right where it was.

In tune with her thoughts, Noble stepped toward her and gently grasped her arm. Running his thumb across the delicate skin of her inner elbow, he turned her question back on her. "Does it hurt badly for you?"

Edith's gaze swept the floor, becoming blurrier as the tears pooled. Her lip trembled as she feebly denied, "It isn't true."

"No? Oh, tell it to Sweeney, my dear." He raised his other hand to her cheek, tipped her head back to look at him. "You know it's true, and I think you've known for a while." When she didn't reply, only stared at him through her watering eyes, he clasped her face in both hands. Wiping her tears with his thumbs, he said, "I think I've known, too, only didn't want to believe it."

With a sob, Edith sank her head into his hands, prompting him to bring her face to his shoulder as he held her closer, an arm wrapped around her back while his other hand hotly gripped behind her neck. His fingers massaged at the nape while he kissed and breathed into the hair above her forehead.

She'd been dangling her arms loosely at her sides, but at the contact, Edith let herself bring them to his waist. When he tightened his hold, she did, too. Though she hadn't once seen him with a cigarette, his jacket smelled of sweet tobacco. The soft velvet was a comfort. As was the firm chest beneath her chin and the strong arms around her.

Noble continued his massage down her neck, and the thumb at her lower back began kneading up her spine as well, loosening her tension. She relaxed under his touch, yielded her muscles to his healing, and as she elongated her posture with a deep breath, she brought her face level with his throat. Her lips were within such close distance to the smooth skin above his silk ascot, her nostrils infused with the civet musk of his cologne. Extracted from an actual wildcat, the oil's scent would've been off-putting if not for the primal lure of it. Edith could've licked it from his neck.

Perhaps sensing this, Noble removed his lips from her hair to look down into her eyes. His own were reddened, glazed, and the left side of his face had already begun to swell from the blow Ransom must've doled him. She felt him swell elsewhere, too.

He slid his hand from her neck to her jaw and brushed her lips with the pad of his thumb, silencing the *No, we shouldn't, we can't* that could have escaped them. Could have if Edith had wanted the words to. But she didn't.

Instead, she let him silence her further with his mouth against hers, rough from the start. But she liked it that way, having felt so numb for so long and pent up with the same frustration he was releasing on her.

Almost wildly, they clung to each other, Noble's hands groping her head, her waist, her rear, as she raked tracks down the velvet of his back. His roving fingers loosened her hair from its pins, ruffled the chiffon at her arms and scraped over her beaded form. She didn't dream of ruining this moment for a second with words until he fisted the fabric of her dress and began pulling it over her knees, up to her hips.

"No, Noble," she panted against his lips.

"Oh, but my dear," he murmured across her jaw to her earlobe and down her neck, "isn't this what we both want?"

When he returned to her ear to suckle at the lobe once more, she breathed, "Yes," and ran her fingers through his hair. "But we mustn't get carried away. We've already gone too far."

Unrelenting, his hand released her dress only to cup her breast over the silk while he spoke between kisses. "How can that be when you're enjoying it so much? When's the last time you've felt joy, Edith? After what they've done to us?"

"But—" At the thought of *they*, the memory of Lottie in Ransom's room, naked beneath her robe, Edith fumbled. *"Married Magnate Makes Merry with Mistress'...And when the world learns you two've been barney-mugging…"* Try as she might to restore her defenses, the ones that had fallen so easily, she only pressed harder against him and gripped his waist to hers.

She actually moaned in protest when he suddenly pulled back.

Noble laid his finger on her lips. "Pardon this brief intermission," he whispered as he slipped away, catlike, to close the hallway door and then the bar's slim door to the stairwell. The room was now concealed on all sides, camouflaged within walls.

Sauntering back to where he'd left her, he unbuttoned his coat and backed her up against the mirrored wall. "And now, my love, for the second act."

Edith sighed as his lips returned to her neck and his hands to her curves. She closed her eyes and tried to revel in it, but his short departure had created a cooling effect. Her eyes drifted open, glancing past the shining face in front of her. The first thing they fell on was the book on the bar top. She found herself unable to look away.

Could she follow this through, with the others in the next room? Should she take Noble through the basement instead, to the west stairs and up to her bedroom? Could she chance it?

She stared at the cloth-bound ice resting on the Lindbergh book, almost saw it melting and seeping into the hardcover's fibers.

The others…right in the next room. The man she married—and the woman *this* man sought to marry, the child she had raised…her child, only child…

"Ohh," she groaned within Noble's all-consuming embrace. "Oh, God, no, Noble, we cannot do this." She moved her palms to his chest to press him away.

He kept up his efforts, remaining sealed to her. "But why? Why punish ourselves when they've done it enough? This is *their* fault, darling, not ours."

When he leaned to kiss her lips, she turned her head to the side. The stale alcohol on his breath had overtaken any other intoxicating scents.

"Yes, I blame them, Noble, but we can't punish them either. There's no winning, you see, not this way."

He backed off slightly, though still stood close. "Winning? Do you think I'm only playing a game with Lottie? With you? Do none of you take me seriously?" A childlike dejection entered his features as he held her hands.

She threaded her fingers through his and gave a gentle squeeze. "We do, dear. *I* do. I heard you speak some ugly threats tonight, but I do believe they only come from great hurt. And I'm sorry for that, for the pain my family's caused you. I'm fond of you and do want to comfort you if I can."

"Truly?" He gave a soft smile, lit with new hope, Edith thought. That pleased her, until he said, "Good."

Seizing her hands tighter, he brought them over her head and against the mirror. Holding them there, he pushed his mouth onto hers. She received him again, nearly melted into him again, but the mirror behind her was too hard, too cold, his force too strong. Now pinioning both of her hands with only one of his, he once more worked her dress up with his other.

"No," she gasped as she struggled, to which he let go of her frock to seize her throat instead, holding her to the wall.

Staring into his crazed eyes, she tried to soften hers, to hide her fresh fear as best she could. Trembling, she hoped to pass it off as breathy lust as she offered him a sultry smile — also as best as she could. Surely nothing compared to Lottie's practiced smile, but it seemed to work, as Noble smiled, too, then plunged his tongue between her lips again while he eased his hand from her throat back down to her breast. She relaxed her arms and writhed into his caresses until he loosened his grip on her wrists, too. Then she yanked her hands from his clasp, ducked beneath his arm, and lunged for the door.

He caught her by the waist just before she could grasp the doorknob. Pulling her back to him, he ripped her dress at the side seam where the hook-and-eye closures gave way. She flailed an arm and seized the liquor bottle on the counter, swinging it around at him. But he ducked, and momentum pulled the bottle from her fingers, propelling it against the side mirror, which shattered along with her weapon as it hit the floor.

"Don't make so much noise, baby," he coaxed, "and don't let them make such fools of us. C'mon, we'll show 'em. We'll show 'em."

Noble continued his assault and bent her backwards over the counter, pinning her to its edge with his body as his hands feverishly groped at both her hem and his trousers.

The bar's edge digging into her spine, she stopped pushing his shoulders away and felt around her instead. Her hand bumped into Ransom's book, which she snatched up by its front cover and whipped at Noble's head. He flinched from the impact but carried on. She went to throw his martini glass next, but he grabbed her wrist in time to deflect her aim, continuing his below-waist pursuits singlehandedly.

Thus occupied, he didn't notice her free hand move to the ice block. Didn't heed how it felt around until finding the object of Edith's deepest affection at the moment.

She curled her long fingers around the icepick and brought it down into Noble's chest.

15

The present hour

"Oh, Edith," Ransom breathed while his wife wept into her hands.

"I was so eager to get away," she cried, "I didn't realize I'd left him there to die."

When she finally looked up, she saw the expressions she could only expect: the Colonel resting his forehead on his hand, clenching his jaw, Helen's mouth agape beneath watery eyes, Rex's brow pinched above a grave frown, and the muscles beneath Lottie's face continuously rearranging between horror and fury.

Of course, Edith had also seen these reactions over the entire course of her story, along with the audible ones as the details grew worse and worse—starting with the particulars Ransom *hadn't* shared of his conversation with Noble.

As she'd relayed the sequence of events, Rex's and Helen's cries had been out of alarm, out of concern for her wellbeing, whereas Lottie's and Ransom's sounds of worry were mixed with protest as well. At each outburst, though — even his own — Rex had insisted everyone remain calm and let Mrs. Warne tell her story, while Helen assured her she needn't answer any of their questions until she was finished. After a time, the interruptions did fall off until the whole sordid affair had stunned them all into silence.

They sat this way for a few minutes. Normally cursing time for flying too fast, Edith never knew it could pass so slowly, each minute taking an age to follow the other on the clock. She took the opportunity to measure her breathing, like she'd done in the hallway, encouraging her racing heart to keep time with the slow seconds. Still tremulous with tears, she did remain still and quiet. Just bit her lip as she stared off toward the oriental carpet. The dreaded telling of it all, at least, had brought her back into focus.

"I heard it," Rex eventually said. "I heard the noise. But then, the servants were outside. I thought, maybe, it was only the car."

"I played the music too loudly," Helen lamented.

"I never screamed for help," Edith said to absolve them of any guilt. "I always thought it would be like in the movies, when a woman screams like that." She chanced a glance at Lottie, hoping she wouldn't bristle at the comparison, but it was difficult to read insult in the range of emotions already swarming the actress's face. "In the actual moment, though, I...had no voice at all." She brought a hand to her throat, stroking it in memory of the brutish way Noble had grabbed it. "As though my vocal chords were paralyzed. Thank goodness my body wasn't."

"No, it wasn't," Lottie bit out.

No one spoke until an odd sound escaped Ransom's throat.

"I don't understand," he said from beneath his hand, sounding about to cry himself, "why you, *he*, thought that of us." He raised his head. "How could you think it?"

Edith met everyone's eyes around the table, stopping at Lottie, whose crumpled face stared back through tears as her shoulders shook. Rex didn't reach out to comfort his old friend as he had before, Edith noticed. He just rested his elbows onto his spread knees like Ransom, his somber gaze fallen to the floor.

Her nose too stuffed from her crying jag, Edith breathed softly through her mouth. She couldn't summon the venom she had before. She'd wanted to blame Ransom for bringing deceit into their lives, wanted to blame Lottie for bringing that man into this house. But now that it was out there, had reverberated off their eardrums and dispersed throughout the room, freed from festering inside her broken, jealous heart, Edith didn't have the energy to blame anyone for anything anymore.

She did blame Noble for what had happened behind the bar. But she blamed herself, too. Not for doing anything to encourage the attack, but betraying her husband had been wrong — and petting with her adoptive daughter's betrothed downright reprehensible. So, she blamed herself for sinking to that vindictive, vile infidelity. And now the law must blame her for murder.

"I," she began weakly. "We — we saw how affectionate you two are. The way you look at each other. There's s-such love, and —"

"A father's love," Ransom said quietly.

"Yes." She looked to her lap. "I know that's how you felt. As you should have. But she's a woman now, Ransom." Edith gazed back at him. "Not bound to you in that way. As your ward, a child. As an adult, she's —"

"My daughter."

A squeak broke from Lottie as she slumped with heavier sobs. The piercing sound brought Rex back to sitting tall, and this time, without hesitation, he slid to her side and held her in his arms. Helen sat mutely, pensively, dragging her gaze between Lottie and Ransom. Then she, too, sat a little taller.

The Colonel watched Lottie with his usual tenderness, then aimed it at his wife.

"All right, Ransom," Edith said. "I understand it doesn't take blood to be family, but —"

"But she is," he said. "My blood." With quivering lips, he gave a surprising laugh as if the weight of the world was lifting off him, brick by brick.

Edith squinted. "Your blood? But—"

She glanced at Lottie, saw her still crying but now smiling at Ransom. Edith then looked at Rex, who raised an eyebrow at Helen, who in turn covered her mouth with her hand.

Edith's breath held in her chest. Until she spoke the truth for herself.

"You're her father."

He nodded.

She looked away at the fireplace, pressing her fist to her mouth. Eyes widened, she looked over every molding, every tile, every rug thread in her view before centering on the ashes in the hearth. Everything she'd thought, everything she'd known... everything she'd *thought* she'd known, burnt to cinders. She squeezed her eyes shut.

"Why, Ransom?" she whispered against her curled fingers. "Why wouldn't you tell me?"

He wasn't quick to answer. In that silent space, she turned to Lottie.

Languidly shaking her head at the unasked question, Lottie's voice trembled when she spoke. "He told me tonight in the sitting room. I was wrapping his hand, and he just...said it. That he's my natural father." She sniffled against Rex's shoulder as she leaned into him. "I'm still trying to get my head around it. But I think I'm ready to hear more details," she added with a glance at her father. "I didn't mean to keep it secret, too, Edith. Only agreed to wait for a better time to share it with you." She laughed humorlessly at her lap and smeared a palm across her wet cheek. "Leave it to Noble of all people to bring this out."

When Ransom still didn't speak, Edith ran a mental calculation.

Turning twenty-one this year, Lottie had been born in 1908—several years before Edith had met Ransom. The young couple's fondness had grown out of something so ordinary as a garden party, and as the courtship continued, Edith fell deeply in love with the young journalist, celebrating his successes and mourning their separations for three years while he covered the Great War. On his narrow escape with his life, they married without further delay in 1918, shortly after he'd received the *Croix de Guerre* for his heroics. But Edith wasn't the only one to whom Ransom had made vows that year; he'd sworn to protect the child of a friend he'd made but couldn't save in France.

And so, barely a bride, Edith had become a mother as well. To someone else's child, when it wasn't even in the cards to have one of her own. And at ten years old, Lottie'd been more like a pesky little sister, whose language Edith couldn't understand, no less. Having to share her new husband's attentions so soon after moving under his roof also hadn't encouraged her maternal instincts any.

"But your friend from the war," she continued when Ransom wouldn't. "The soldier."

"A nurse," he said at last.

"Nurse?" Hadn't he always said Lottie's father was a soldier?

No. Not now that Edith really thought about it. She couldn't recall him ever specifically saying the word *soldier* or *father*. It was always "an old friend," who'd died in France during the war and left behind a child. The topic was so emotionally loaded, the orphan so vulnerable, no one thought to question the situation any further than what Ransom had said it was. Edith marveled to think of that now. She'd loved him with eyes wide open yet trusted him blindly. At least on that point, she had.

A nurse. 1908. France.

Ransom had spent quite a lot of time overseas as a younger man, writing for London's *Daily Telegraph* in addition to the *Chronicle*, which he knew he'd inherit soon enough. So, in the meantime, he'd wanted to sow his oats, and his father's influence opened many doors. There was nothing about those early adventures he hadn't shared with Edith, she'd thought. But of course, she couldn't possibly know everything he'd done, or when or where or — with *whom*. Still, she fit the pieces together until she could see the full front-page spread.

Beginning with 1907. "After you covered the French campaign in Morocco," she said, "you went to Paris."

He nodded. "Salpetrière." Looking from Helen to Rex, he explained, "A national school of nursing, a new one at the time. I'd heard they trained for military hospitals, so I traveled there hoping to cover a story on women and war."

Staring down at his hands as he rubbed them back and forth, he paused until his eyes seemed to catch sight of what his mind searched for. "Lottie's mother...was a young nurse in training. Her family had wealth, enough that she wouldn't have had to work a day in her life. But she wanted to contribute to war efforts alongside men, insisted on it."

He looked to Lottie, who visibly hung on his every word. Clearly, he *hadn't* given her all the details earlier.

"I found this so inspiring," he said, "and they allowed me to interview her, you see. She was so very easy to talk to, and we would take these long walks in the hospital gardens. There was a lovely avenue of trees there, like ours, just like we walked through today, Karlotta. And your mother, she was...spirited, proud. Beautiful. I admit I was quite taken with her, and after a time...Well, I suppose it didn't take all that long for us to—"

"Yes," Edith said, raising a hand from her lap. She could imagine the scenario from there. "So you—*befriended* this woman in Paris. When did you learn about Lottie?"

He'd been scanning the floor, but Ransom looked directly in her eyes when he replied, "Not for years." Then he gazed at his daughter just as intently. "I swear I knew nothing until I returned for the war."

"Don't tell me she nursed you after Belleau," Edith said. "That's a happy coincidence, isn't it?"

Ransom dropped his eyes again. "I took leave to visit her. At her home, not a hospital."

Edith settled back on the sofa, smoothing the silk on her lap. Chin down as she watched her strokes, she said, "Ah. So, fate didn't bring you back together. You sought her."

"When I completed my time at Salpetrière, I needed to leave France immediately for my next assignment. I promised Clothilde I would return to her, that I—"

"Wanted a future with her?" Venturing a sidelong glance at him, Edith swallowed.

He met her eye. "I thought so at the time, yes."

"Then why didn't you? Have a future?"

Ransom drew in a deep inhale. "I did contact her many times, but no assignments brought me back to Paris that year. Travel made it difficult to know where to reach me at any given time, so in my letters, I assured her that I, at least, would always know where to find her. She had only to trust that I would.

"Until one day, the hospital notified me she was no longer there. And any letters to her parents' address came back unopened. I couldn't imagine she'd given up nursing, not with the conviction she had, but I wondered if she'd transferred to another institution, if her family had moved. I questioned, too, if her father had disregarded her wishes after all, maybe married her off to some European aristocrat. Whatever the case, I didn't understand why no one would offer me explanation."

"So you gave up?" Lottie asked, sounding spiteful toward him for the first time.

Edith wanted to feel resentful, too — toward Lottie, for wishing her father had ended up with her mother instead. But naturally the girl would've wanted her parents together. Edith had no right to let that sting when she hadn't even known Ransom at the time — when she was, after all, the one who'd gotten to marry him in the end. Even if by default. She'd also gotten to raise Lottie when the girl's own mother couldn't.

Edith had every opportunity to be a happy wife and mother herself, but she hadn't seized it. The regret she'd released after telling her story about Noble returned as a new knot in her throat.

"You simply gave *up* on her?" Lottie repeated. "With your connections, was there no one else you could've contacted?"

"I looked for her until it became clear she didn't want to be found, Karlotta." He sounded so tired. "Whatever choices she may not have had, she did make that one. So, I moved on, as we must do."

"Until a decade later," Edith said thickly when Lottie remained silent.

"Yes," Ransom said. He glanced at Lottie before staring off at no one. "Clothilde never finished her training, of course. How could she, in her condition? An unmarried woman at that. Her family disowned her. She had to leave her entire life behind and didn't want to drag me into her disgrace, even though I was every bit as responsible. Or so I told myself for a while. More likely, it's *because* I was responsible that she didn't want anything to do with me. She would never say.

"Thank goodness for the mercy of others. A farming family outside a small village that she knew as a girl, from summers in the country. They allowed her to live in a little outbuilding on their land, which they made as accommodating as they could for her. She only needed to help with chores. Before long, she became one of them.

"She wrote me from there. It had taken an age to track me through the paper, and she'd had to beseech an old society friend for help, but there it was, a message from her. Only one in all those years. She still said nothing of Karlotta, explained nothing of her circumstances, only asked me to please come to her if and when I could. And so, after recuperating enough from the battle, I did. Not without some difficulty, but I found her. And you, Karlotta."

All while I waited for you here. Edith fought to contain the words to her mind as she navigated her complex emotion. *As I prayed for your life. Longed for you to return to me. Do I owe this woman any gratitude that you did?*

"Clothilde was clearly in her last weeks when I saw her," Ransom said, "if not days. Little Lottie had been playing nursemaid to her. She wanted to care for me, too, once she saw my bandages." He exchanged a bittersweet chuckle with his daughter. "But nearly as soon as I'd arrived there, I was turning around to leave again, to seek the doctor—which I did, though it was already too late. All he could do was try to make her comfortable until she passed on. All *I* could do was care for the child after that.

"Clothilde asked me to look her in the eye and promise, make it mean more than my last one had. And then she asked me to go, to leave her and the girl to the care of the doctor and farmer's wife until someone next contacted me. She had all she'd wanted from me and wished to live her remaining days in the peace of the decent life she'd made for herself. A life I wasn't part of. And only when the necessary time came would Lottie become a part of mine."

The room fell quiet again, save for a few sniffs and fidgets. Edith opened her mouth, but all that came out was a sigh. She deflated with the breath and chose to lay everything she could've said to Ransom — out of spite, love, guilt — to rest. She'd never needed to compete with the young woman sitting across from her. No sense vying against the dead one across the sea.

After a while, Helen said to her friend, "You truly didn't know any of this until tonight?"

Lottie shook her head, then asked her father, "You tried to tell me this afternoon, though, during our walk, didn't you?"

"And countless times before," he sighed.

She stroked the pearls at her neck. "And when you gave me these?" Undoing the clasp, Lottie dangled the necklace from her hand. Staring at it perhaps more closely than she had before, she said, "This isn't new."

Her tone held no complaint, only wonder, and on inspecting it from where she sat, Edith recognized the clasp.

"An heirloom," Edith said automatically. One she'd always thought her husband would gift her. She'd taken offense when he hadn't, took offense now as Lottie handled the jewelry with her own delicate fingers.

"From your mother?" Lottie asked Ransom.

"From yours."

Edith picked at her fingernails as Lottie cradled the pearls in both hands.

How many times need Edith chastise herself this evening? Of course Ransom never offered her that necklace; it wasn't his to give. The only one with any claim on it was in possession of it now.

"She did hold on to some of her old life," Ransom said. "Mostly to pay her way and insure yours. But this must've meant more."

Lottie pursed her lips. "It means everything." She brought the necklace to her heart before fastening it back around her neck.

"You certainly were gay when you returned to us," Helen said to her friend gently, "after you found out. This must be upsetting as well, though. Are you okay?" She glanced from Lottie to Ransom. "I only mean, well, after all this time, sir. It's joyous news, of course. I'm not — angling for a story, if that's what you're worried about."

Lottie seemed to weigh her response, if she could even find any words.

"Ever since I was a little girl," she finally said, her voice small, "I pretended he *was* my father. It didn't take much pretending, really. I believed it, as though somehow I always knew. Even if it wasn't real...it felt real, and that's all that mattered. And that's the only way I loved him. To imagine —" Her gaze flitted up to Edith, who promptly lowered her face. "I don't want to imagine. But I suppose I can see how others might've seen..." Closing her eyes, she shook her head. "It doesn't matter. I'm happy." Nodding, she opened her eyes to Ransom. "I am. More than I can say."

Tears welled in his eyes as he gazed back.

"When I used to pretend, though," Lottie went on, looking at her lap, "when I *believed*, wanted so badly to believe and wanted to ask so many times, I, I guess I also didn't want to. Because if *the* Colonel Warne were really my father, then...then why wouldn't he just tell me so? Why not tell anyone and everyone we knew? He would've had to be so very ashamed of me not to, wouldn't he? He would've had to care so very much what other people thought..."

The Colonel smiled sadly. "My only shame is that I ever did care about that. Never ashamed of you, Karlotta. You must know that I've only been proud, that I've strived every day to even deserve to be—" He became too choked up to finish.

"And what of me?" Edith couldn't help but challenge. She was trying to understand, really trying. But after all these years…"Was I not deserving enough to know?"

Ransom hung his head, his throat still clogged with emotion. "I hated being so dishonest with you. With you both. Have hated *myself* for it, and could've never concealed this for so long if it had only been my own reputation at stake." He looked imploringly at Helen and Rex. "What was everyone to think of Edith, raising my child out of wedlock? What would they think of Lottie? What would that do to her future? And what would you have thought of me," he asked Edith, "knowing the child was mine, when I had barely known myself? And that I'd risked so much to find an old lover before returning to you, my fiancée? What *do* you think?"

With a drawn face, Edith held his stare for a long moment.

"I think," she said, "we've all been such damned, stupid fools."

And then she broke down once more.

Digestif

to help digest

Rex couldn't bear to watch Mrs. Warne cry like this, nor could he fathom her pain. This news about Lottie and the Colonel was really quite wonderful, but he understood why the Colonel's wife might not think so. And how the timing was dreadful after what she'd just confessed.

Because she *had* confessed, hadn't she?

Rex waited out wave after wave of hesitation. There would never be an appropriate chance. This would never feel right. So be it.

"Colonel?" he finally ventured. "May I please phone my father now?"

Edith shook harder, and even Ransom's face broke. But he nodded, and without looking at Lottie as he left her side, Rex strode to the study before anyone could change his mind—including himself.

Earlier, when only a stranger could have carried out this heinous act, Rex had been so adamant, so righteous in handing

Noble's murder over to the law. Now that the perpetrator was truly someone in that room, someone he'd known since childhood…well, Rex still couldn't comprehend it. He was actually relieved not to contact an active-duty officer. Yet.

Waiting for the operator to connect his call, Rex worried his father was perhaps already in bed. If he didn't answer, Rex would go there in person, rap on the door, if not directly enter his childhood home to wake his old man. If the others would trust letting him leave, of course. If he could trust them in his absence. He knew nothing at the moment. Only a dull awareness of a clock ticking somewhere in the dark room. He hadn't even bothered to turn on a light, only felt around for where he'd seen the telephone earlier. Back when he'd beamed and blushed with Lottie as they'd stood there in their soaking clothes. In the waning light of day, when neither of them could've known the real darkness to fall that night.

Rex closed his eyes, pinched the bridge of his nose. The receiver in his other hand started to slip from his ear. Until—

"Lewis Rainger speaking."

"May I speak to you? Just the two of us?" Helen asked Lottie, concerned her friend wasn't coping with all the evening's discoveries as well as she portrayed. "We'll only be a moment," Helen said to the Warnes, "just in the hallway there." She cocked her head toward the French doors behind her.

The couple nodded.

In leaving them, Helen was consoled somewhat that, once she stepped away from her seat, the Colonel took her place on the sofa, beside his wife. She opened the door for Lottie to walk through into the north hall.

Lottie wiped her eyes from their inner to outer corners, and in the same fluid motion brought her hands to Helen's shoulders. She pressed her cheek to her friend's collarbone as Helen wrapped her arms around Lottie's waist and held her close. Their deep breaths rose and fell in sync with one another.

There was Helen's answer. No words necessary. Just a private, quiet sanctuary to process everything that had happened. And to prepare for what would happen next.

"What will happen?" Edith whispered into Ransom's lapel. On sitting next to her, he hadn't expected her to fold into his arms as readily as she had. "I didn't mean to. You know I wouldn't —"

"Shh," he breathed into her hair, which was still slightly wet. "Of course you wouldn't. I know that. We all do. Even Lottie. She only needs time." He cuddled his cheek against her head. "As do you. I hope that, in that time, you can learn to forgive me."

Pressing her fingernails into the seam between her lips, Edith shook her head. "I could never ask *her* forgiveness."

"You won't have to, darling. She'll give it to you. In time. I can't speak for her, but you're her mother —" he added a soft laugh "— whether either of you likes it or not."

"I do love her," Edith said quietly, "in my way."

"I know."

"But I've envied her more. Bright young thing, when I'm so dull. Running to you, never me. Yet for every step she didn't take toward me, I leaped away."

Holding her tighter, Ransom rocked Edith gently. "Paris, you know, that was only a young man's fancy. I love *you*. Always have, from the moment you crossed that lawn." He chuckled to himself again. "Calling off your father's dogs."

"They loved *you*." She laughed, too.

"Yes, rather," he mused. "They soiled my trousers and nearly made me do the same."

"Lucky you were Daddy's size." She giggled more girlishly than he'd heard in some time.

He could still see Edith's determined stride across the grass that faraway day, the sun on her hair, the healthy glow of her skin. She was average height, conservatively dressed like any other respectable gentleman's daughter, and easy to overlook when standing among the other partygoers.

But once she'd broken away from the pack, the athletic grace of her gait from afar and the gleam in her emerald eyes up close—he'd been done for. More so when she'd jovially yet shyly guided him into her family's home and to a private dressing space, blushing when she handed him a fresh pair of slacks through the doorway. He'd been enamored ever since, taking to calling on her frequently, sharing his world travels with her as she shared her artistic and equestrian pursuits with him. She'd taken to his world so naturally, and proved consistently more than met the eye.

But how he loved what his eye beheld as well.

How he wished he *hadn't* beheld her the way he had earlier tonight—upstairs in her bathroom after she'd fled from that monster in the bar. Lying lifeless in her bathtub, nearly submerged to her nose. Those deadened eyes, knowing eyes, filled with loathing as they hardened, though at the time he hadn't known if the disgust was for him or herself.

Yet hadn't she been lifeless before then? Dull, just as she'd said. But not so much dull as *dulled*. The gradual change in her he'd dismissed as boredom, depression, and why wasn't that more cause for concern? He supposed he took for granted she was strong; if she fell off a horse, she picked herself back up. She relied on him but wasn't needy. Independent, her own person, and so he regularly left her on her own to tend to his work. Bolstering his papers while his wife dissolved to pulp.

"You're still the vision I saw that day and so very accomplished yourself," he said, nonetheless. "But you distanced from me, too." He felt her head nod against his chest. "I understand why. I do now. And I'm sorry I did nothing to bring you closer. That I didn't tell you everything you had a right to know."

She shook her head as she looked up at him. "You must be very disgusted with me. That I ever thought—"

"Don't speak of it again." Closing his eyes, he breathed deeply. "Let's not so much as remember."

A pregnant silence followed.

"But," Edith began, then paused. "When Lottie was in your bedroom earlier…" Pressing her hand to his chest for leverage, she sat up a little.

"She came to me expressing her doubts about Noble. More than that. She knew. She knew she'd refuse him."

"There were other women."

He bowed his head. "That, and something must've just happened between them. I don't know what, but she was in a state." Lottie would've never gone to Ransom dressed so indecently otherwise. Still in her robe, too distressed to ready for the evening as if everything were normal. "She needed peace of mind to get through the night, and so I gave it to her."

A crease formed between Edith's brows. "Did she ask you to intervene?"

"She didn't need to. I told her I'd take care of it so she wouldn't have to carry on the charade."

Edith sighed, but to preempt any judgment, Ransom continued.

"I know I shouldn't fight her battles, dear, but whatever occurred between those two had her frightened. She didn't say so, but she shook like a leaf. I feared she was in actual danger." He cupped Edith's jaw in his hand. "We know now I wasn't off the mark."

Her eyelids fluttered closed, and she sank her face into his palm.

Ransom regarded her tenderly. "I should have done more so you would never doubt. And never, *ever* feel you had to turn to —"

"But I stopped, Ransom." Her warm tears slid into his hand. "I turned to him that one time, but I stopped myself."

Stroking her damp tresses, he brought her face to his chest again. His chin nudged against her forehead as he nestled against her. "I'm not speaking of him."

Sniffing, Edith grew still. She didn't move or say anything for a while, only slumped against him with deadening weight.

Ransom could still hear the clack of glass on hard tile, the brown bottle he'd tipped over with his knee when he'd found Edith in the tub and rushed to kneel beside her. Some of the bottle's contents had splashed on the floor, so at least it wasn't empty. *"The skeletons,"* she'd murmured at the rattle.

Ransom had patted her cheek and lifted her face farther from the water, where she'd been barely breathing above it. Straining to lift her shoulders up to the bathtub's edge so her neck could rest against it, he'd then continued to pat her cheek and stroke the wet, ropey strands out of her face, prying open her eyelids to inspect her constricted pupils before feeling the slow pulse in her neck.

"Can't get away," she'd whimpered as she rolled her head against the tub's edge, facing away. *"Won't stop till they dance on my grave."* Only then had Ransom finally registered the pale dress clinging to her shoulders, billowing beneath the water tinged with pink. Thought of it later when he'd discovered its beads on the bar floor, garnishing the mix of blood and gin.

And that's when he'd wondered how she'd done it.

"I thought," Ransom said now, "that you were only to take it for temporary relief. Periodically, in small doses."

"I know."

"And a long while ago. I thought…"

He shook his head at how he'd struggled to pull her dead weight out of the water. How he'd then fetched her favorite pajamas. Uncertain where they were, he'd opened an armoire drawer clacking with glass containers. One by one, he'd picked up the brown bottles inside, reading their labels closely and verifying they all matched the one he'd found beside the tub: *Tincture of opium.*

"But it kept happening, Ransom," she said. "And I suppose after the last time, I needed—*wanted* something stronger."

"And the doctor gave it to you?"

"A friend, at first."

"Who?"

Squeaks rattled in her throat. "She only wanted to help," she said raggedly. Pulling away, Edith cupped her hands in her lap.

"She?"

"In Shanghai. I—"

"Shanghai?" He broke from his melancholy. "That doesn't sound like Winifred to—"

"Not Winnie."

Ransom stared at Edith foggily for a couple of seconds, bemused, until his sight sharpened. "Zellie." He laughed without humor as he looked to his lap. "I should've known."

"That's not fair."

"No? She handled her liquor terrifically, and now I find she's given my wife—"

"We all do what we must."

"Do we? To what?"

"Cope."

"With what? *Too* much money? *Too* many parties?"

He didn't mean to turn on Edith in her time of greatest need, but her choice in allies lately was really leaving something to be desired. In protecting her, he couldn't help but protest, too. And he wasn't speaking of *her* anyway. It was that Zellie. That damned flapper.

"Too little attention," Edith snapped to his surprise. Though could he fault her? On the cusp of making a new start, here he was, pushing old buttons and returning the spite to her voice as she said, "The 'Paris of the Orient' still isn't exactly *Paris*, as you know."

No, surely it wasn't for Zellie, a Parisian socialite who'd married a British businessman. Gil had relocated his bride to China, as had Winifred's husband, a mutual friend of Ransom's from the *Telegraph* in London. Hugh now edited for *North China Daily News*, and during the Warnes' frequent visits to his Shanghai home, while the three gentlemen tended to business and other masculine pursuits, the women had apparently found their own fun.

"When a man's actions change a woman's life," Edith continued, "you don't think that takes its toll? For Winnie, too, not to mention another woman I could name?"

No. She would not veer this back to Clothilde.

"Zellie seemed to get on just fine," he said.

Zellie never even seemed real, that girl. Always in a haze of smoke. Always in motion, always a blur. Ransom imagined that's how she'd seen her shiny new world, too, surrounded by exotic ladies and admiring men, with a constant cocktail in her hand.

"She's not fine," Edith said. "And neither was I. Not without help."

"That's help? Getting you addicted to your own medicine?"

"*Not* medicine," she whispered harshly.

Exhaling, Ransom slumped back against the couch cushion. Remembered the sweet-smelling rosewood box he'd found beside the bottles of tincture in Edith's drawer. With silvery corner fittings, the case was carved with East Asian designs. And behind it, an embellished stick of bamboo. Nearly two feet in length, the tube had green jade and silver casings at each end, and a circular jade knob protruded from its center. It had seemed an exotic flute of sorts, something from antiquity. Just another of Edith's acquisitions that she had yet to showcase, he'd assumed.

He should've known she was too organized to store any unrelated items together.

He no longer regretted how, in his dismay, he'd raised then dropped the bamboo antique unceremoniously back into Edith's drawer, knocking over her little opium bottles and possibly damaging what he now realized was a smoking pipe. Anything necessary to load and light it probably resided in the rosewood box.

"Am I to believe," he said, "that you women roamed the streets of Shanghai for those sordid dens?"

"No," she said firmly. "We didn't go farther than the one in Zellie's home."

"Gil would never—"

"He designed it. Supplied it. Taught her everything she knew, all that she taught me in turn."

"Madness. I never once—"

"Because you see what you want to see, Ransom. But Zellie knew. She saw everything under your nose that you couldn't. Still can't."

Uttering a single note of objection, Ransom knew the folly in it and hung his head instead.

"She knows something about desperation," Edith persisted, voice shaking. "And she recognized the same in me. She knew of my drops, so—"

"She offered you—"

"Something better. To truly ease my pain."

"What pain could that ease?" he nearly yelled. Not *at* her but *for* her, for all she'd been through in the last decade and the pain they both still felt over it. "Did she even understand why you took them? By *doctor's* orders, not feckless whimsy? And that you weren't anymore because you didn't need—"

"But I did. I clearly *do*." She picked at the skin around her thumbnail. "I don't use it here, what she gave me. Transporting it alone was reckless, but—it was a gift. To refuse would've been impolite."

"Impolite." Ransom huffed a bitter laugh. "Yes, you do know your etiquette, don't you."

"I don't use it," she repeated. "I don't have the nerve to on my own. I wouldn't even know where to—" She sighed. "I thought the tincture would be better. Safer. *Lawful.* I've simply increased the dosage."

"And potency. The doctor never prescribed *that.*"

"I know." She worried her hands in the crevice between her silken knees.

He watched her elegant nails and noticed that a couple were chipped. Thought of how they'd scratched at the open armoire door, where she'd stood naked and dripping while he rifled through her drawer. Like a ghost, she'd hovered there beside him, watching his discovery as she slowly peeled the door's paper lining away from its wood, the torn pieces dropping to the floor where her torn dress lay as well. *"No more skeletons,"* she'd murmured in her daze.

"You're right that we see what we want to see," he said. "And I see now that I've turned a blind eye to you in more ways than one."

"I love you," she whispered, reaching for him. "I'm so sorry."

She sniffed again, meekness curving her spine. With her glassy eyes and pale skin, she looked as fragile as a china doll.

Taking her hand from where it gripped his lapel, Ransom pressed a kiss into her palm.

When he returned to the drawing room from the Colonel's study, Rex caught the Warnes in an intimate embrace.

"It's all right, Frederick," Edith said before he could duck back out. "Sit. Please."

"Sorry, I…" He scratched his head. "Er, where are the girls?"

"In the hall there." Ransom gestured to the northern doorway. "Seems we all needed a moment."

Bobbing his head, Rex considered resuming his seat on the sofa, but he hated to be their third wheel again — especially this time, when they seemed to be reconciling, not warring. "I'll just, uh —" He pointed to the door and slipped through it. On its opposite side, he stepped into an empty hall.

"Lottie? Helen?" he asked as he walked down the short corridor to the library. He couldn't imagine they'd return to the scene of the crime, not with the corpse still in there, but he peeked into the expansive space all the same. Nothing. He backtracked to the stairwell and ran down it.

Crossing the Gold Theatre, he stepped through the door on its other side, the one he'd seen Ransom lock shut earlier but which now stood open.

Treading from the theatre's light into blackness, his eyes took a while to adjust, and his sweat cooled in the subterranean stillness — but his ears detected voices just beyond. He felt around toward another doorway and then another until he'd navigated his way into a large room of modern appliances shining even in the dark. The warmer, musty air still held the savory scents of the evening meal. The kitchen. And just beyond, a light glowed out of a doorway. All had fallen silent within.

Creeping past the pantry toward the little corner room, Rex knew it was the ladies he'd heard inside it. But he approached slowly and quietly all the same, not wishing to alarm them any more than he probably had.

"Lottie? Helen?" he asked again. "It's only me."

"Rex?" he heard Lottie call out, and he took momentary comfort in the relief that her voice had wrapped around his name. How he prayed she could still rely on him, that she still knew that for herself.

Her head peered out before he reached the door, and, with a frying pan in her hand, she threw herself into his arms. "Oh," she sighed. "It *is* you."

The pan only added to the puzzle of her being down here in the first place, but Rex held her as long as she would allow. It felt so good to have her this close again, before the night's shock and sadness, anger and mistrust, could pick away at the loose threads of everyone's stories until their relationships unraveled, too.

He rested his chin on her head and let her face nuzzle into his neck. Every muscle in his body relaxed at her touch, and they both sank deeper into the embrace. Not even the stiff handle of the pan jabbing into his back caused discomfort.

After the high alert they'd been on all night, it made sense if she was still fearing an intruder. Again, Rex felt bad if his approaching footsteps had scared her. But his girl had been protecting herself, and now he was here to assume that duty.

"It's me," he murmured into her hair, then pressed a kiss to her scalp. Her hair smelled of coconut oil, and he savored her sweetness.

A loud clamor right behind him startled them apart. Lottie'd already had his heart pumping, but Rex thought it would leap out of his chest at the fright.

It was only the pan.

Lottie had apparently relaxed at his touch, too, to the point of relaxing the handle right out of her fingers. They both giggled uncontrollably, a surprising yet welcome release.

"*Di mi!* What the heck are you two up to?" Helen stood in the doorway with her hands on her hips and a smile on her face. She held her composure all of two seconds before slapping her knees in laughter herself. "Who needs a fire extinguisher to cool things down when you've got a frying pan!"

Lottie kept laughing as she smacked her friend's arm. "Neither's necessary, thank you." She stepped back into the lit room, and Rex followed them both to a round kitchen table.

"This is where the staff dines," Lottie informed him, her face flushed.

Rex noticed a plate of saltine crackers near the table's edge. And a glass of milk, which Lottie tapped with her fingertips after plopping the pan down beside it. Helen sat next to her, and Rex seated himself across the way.

"I needed something to settle my stomach, you know?" Lottie said. "Can I offer you anything?"

He shook his head with a soft smile, and Lottie seemed to channel her nervous energy from her glass to the crackers. Picking one up, she shyly smiled back at him as she bit into it. She crunched her cracker through the awkward silence that followed.

"Sorry we left without telling anyone," Helen said. "We figured it'd be safe enough, now that we know, um — but we still kept our guard up, just in case. And we'll be back for when your dad arrives."

"We have a little while yet," he said.

"Mrs. Warne okay?" she asked.

"I think so. Considering."

Lottie stared straight ahead with a blank expression as she bit down on the cracker again. Closing her eyes as she chewed, she breathed heavily through her nose.

"What about you?" Rex asked.

She raised her lids and took a sip of milk.

"I didn't love him," she said after a time, slowly yet frankly. "Maybe I thought I did, once." Her tongue swam around behind her closed lips, polishing her teeth. "I think I hated him, really." She paused as that seemed to sink in. "Such a fine line…But I'd never wish him dead."

"We know that, honey," Helen said.

"I've imagined it. I *have*. But only the way you do when you're angry, you know?"

As she still held the cracker in her left hand, Rex leaned across to take her right. She looked down at her plate, eyes welling.

"I don't want her to die either." The words cracked, coming out thickly, perhaps more so from the milk, which made her sound heartachingly childlike. A little girl crying over crackers and cream. "I've only just found my father, and I can't—I can't lose another mother."

"We know that, too," Helen said, her own voice a bit broken.

"She's difficult to love." Lottie sighed. "She's made it so. But that doesn't mean…When her guard's down, I still see what everyone else does. All I've wanted is for her to see what others see in me, too. I want her to accept me, to—love me back."

"She does," Helen said. "Lottie, you know as well as anyone that some people have a funny way of showing it. It doesn't excuse how she's treated you, but everything's changed now. You have a new chance to make amends."

Lottie nodded. "Just in time for it to be too late."

Helen shot Rex a despondent glance.

"She was only defending herself," he assured. "My dad will say the same. And he'll make sure she receives justice."

"That's what I'm afraid of."

"I mean the kind that *protects* her. She's not a murderer, Lottie. The law will recognize that."

"I won't let her hang for that man."

"She won't." Rex would have said this no matter what to console her, but it also happened to be the only thing he could say with certainty. Illinois had foregone hanging for electrocution two years ago, but he wasn't about to morbidly point that out for technicality's sake. He could have told her, too, that even the most serious form of murder was rarely penalized by death in this state, and not even that sentence was always carried out. But the Warne family would be educated on the system soon enough. Already, they were undergoing their trial by fire.

"But even if she doesn't—"

Lottie stopped as her gaze darted to the open doorway, in the direction of where Rex had heard a noise, too. A short and then a long creak, or maybe more abrasive than that, like a chair dragging along a floor, but it stopped as soon as it had started. If Lottie hadn't also reacted, Rex would've thought he'd imagined it.

He held a hand out to the women and then pressed a finger to his lips as he stood and reached for his pistol. Sidling up by the door, he leaned his shoulder against the jamb and peered around into the hall.

All was still in the kitchen and scullery. He edged out into the darkness, feeling his way out of the kitchen and back toward the theatre. Stopping in its open doorway, he listened.

All he heard was light tapping and scraping along the floor behind him, before fingers coiled around both his biceps and Helen and Lottie crept on each side.

"Maybe your father's here?" Helen whispered.

"In this old part of the house," Lottie said, "sounds carry from everywhere."

Rex nodded. "We should get back upstairs."

17

The doorknocker sounded like a death knell. More than one person flinched at its sudden clap.

The party of five had reconvened in the drawing room. The Colonel and his wife were still seated on one sofa, comforted in one another's arms. Across the way, Rex and Helen sat on either side of Lottie, each holding one of her hands. Beyond their physical consolation, everyone sat in silence—until the clack of metal on metal echoed into the stillness. Duty calling at the doorstep, not long before midnight.

In the absence of a butler, Ransom hadn't forgotten his role as man of the house. After a kiss to Edith's temple, he rose stiffly to walk out to the foyer. Chancing a soft peck on Lottie's trembling fingers, Rex released her to follow the Colonel to the door.

Ransom reached for the knob, pausing a moment before twisting it. When he dropped his head, Rex laid a palm on his shoulder for whatever support that was worth. To his surprise, Ransom laid his own hand over Rex's, giving it a firm squeeze.

And then he opened the door to Chief Rainger's stern face. A felt fedora shaded piercing eyes.

Lewis struck an imposing silhouette, framed as he was in the doorway. Broad-shouldered and standing at a height of nearly six and a half feet, he was every bit the strong man of his lumberjack days, which had worked greatly to his benefit in enforcing law as well. Not many culprits hadn't gone quietly when the brawny chief read their rights. Never mind that when it came to young offenders, he was known for doling more fatherly advice than punishment.

Lamplight and shadow sharpened the retired officer's expression even more severely, but Rex knew it was only concern that pinched at his father's eyes and lips.

"Colonel," the man said briskly, extending a big hand.

"Chief," Ransom replied with a sturdy handshake.

Then the men's faces broke into smiles, and they tugged each other into a one-armed hug with loud slaps to the back.

"You know better than to call me Chief."

"And I've told *you* not to call me Colonel." Ransom stepped aside and gestured for his visitor to enter. "Please."

Chief Rainger crossed the threshold. "It's good to see you, friend," he said in a low but kind voice as the door closed behind him.

"I'm so grateful, Lewis. I hate bringing you here at this hour."

"I'm just sorry this has happened. To all of you." At this, he looked around at Rex. "Son."

Rex shook his father's hand and exchanged masculine yet affectionate pats on the shoulder. He rarely saw Lewis in a suit coat like this, but true to form, the man didn't wear a tie, instead leaving his shirt neck unbuttoned.

"I appreciate the call, Freddy." Lewis glanced back at Ransom. "I only wish you'd done it sooner. Or better, Chief Thompson."

"I know," Ransom half-whispered toward his feet. "I hope you can understand. That it, we—"

Lewis gripped Ransom's arm. "I do. Though I won't lie. I don't agree. It's not my authority anymore, not to mention the conflict of interest I have here. My own family and friends — suspects. I'll be hard-pressed to explain my presence here."

Rex watched Ransom process his words, accepting the chastisement and swallowing his pride. The Colonel was a large man himself, but beside the chief, he appeared small, humbled, his power diminished in the presence of the one man pretension couldn't impress. The one man Ransom could trust with his life.

"But I do understand." Lewis patted Ransom's shoulder. "And I'll see what I can find. I'm on your side." He chuckled into his chest. "Therein lies the problem. But I am on your side, no matter what."

"The others are just in the other room, Pop," Rex said. "Would you like to speak with them now? Together or one-to-one?"

"I think you'd better show me the body first."

Kneeling in front of the bar at Noble's side, Chief Rainger just stared pensively for a moment with his mouth smashed against his hand. His thumb pushed the meat of his cheek up in a comical way, though he clearly wasn't amused.

When he did drop his hand away, he asked, "You didn't move him, you say? Found him like this?"

"He was like this," Rex said, "but we did move him a little to see where he was hurt."

"That's why the shirt's unbuttoned?"

"No, sir, we found him like that, too," Rex said, "but it helped us see the wounds on his chest."

Lewis tugged Noble's collar apart to view the injuries himself. What Rex now understood were stab wounds.

"We first thought it might've been a twenty-two," he said. "We hadn't considered it could've also been —"

"An icepick," Lewis deduced.

"I also checked for any wounds on his back," Ransom said.

"Find any?"

He shook his head. "Then we moved him right back."

"Mm-hm." Lewis's palm had suctioned to his face again, muffling his next words. "And did that cause the smear, or was that already there?"

"Smear?" Rex asked.

Lewis pointed at the black base of the bar's counter, waving his finger side to side to indicate a short burgundy streak by Noble's head.

"I—" Rex knit his brow. "I don't know, sir."

Lewis looked up at Ransom. "You?"

The Colonel blinked rapidly as he seemed to notice the nearly invisible smudge for the first time, too. "N-No."

Lewis pulled Noble sideways by the shoulders, toward himself, and leaned in to inspect the other side of his dangling head. Yanking a handkerchief from his shirt pocket, he dabbed it against the right side of Noble's skull. He brought it in for a closer look, then held it up for the other men to see. "Something broke the skin. Whether he suffered a blow or fall, I'm not sure. There's swelling, though. Looks to be on his left cheek as well. Any ideas why?" He gazed at Ransom's right hand, which the Colonel had been rubbing, consciously or not.

"I struck him," Ransom replied, his face grim.

"Why? What happened?"

"He'd made accusations. Vulgar."

"He threaten you?"

"Lottie *and* myself."

"Physical harm?"

"Scandal." Ransom hung his head. "I lost my temper, I'm afraid."

"I see."

Leaning around to face the body from the front, Lewis balanced Noble's lopsided face in his hands, minutely swiveling it one way and then the other. Then he stood and motioned his son toward him with two fingers. The hat he'd perched on his knee fell off in the process, and as Rex approached, he quickly stooped to fetch it from the floor. He could still see the darkened water stain on the floorboards, fainter but there.

"Thanks, son," Lewis said. Retrieving the hat, he curled its brim in his grip before cocking his head toward the body. "Ransom, if I can get your help here, too, please?"

When the Colonel stepped around, he seized the body from under the arms while Rex grabbed beneath the knees. Rex noticed how intently Ransom held his eyes open, unblinking, how measured he kept his deep breathing, and Rex had to wonder if the former war correspondent was beating back images of the woods and open fields, the fallen men who would fertilize the soil.

Lewis set his hat on the nearest sofa before returning to the bar and squatting to inspect the tile beneath the lifted body. Rex peered around to see that patch of floor within the bar's boundaries was stained with blood but not pooling in it.

While the men lowered the body down, just as it was, Lewis sat back on his heels. Then, slapping his lap, the chief hoisted himself up, asked how to get behind the counter, and walked out of the library and back into the bar from its rear door. He knelt there, too, out of sight for a minute or so. Rex could hear cabinets and drawers open and close as bottles clinked together. Bottles. Behind the bar. *Behind* the bar, where Edith had alleged she'd stabbed Noble.

Rex stared at the body before him, leaning against the bar's opposite side.

If the counter stretched from wall to wall, how had Noble ended up here in front of it? Edith claimed he'd still been alive when she'd left him, but even in that case, why would the actor have walked out the bar's back door, down the hall, and into the library when so badly wounded? Had he tried to find help, only to find he couldn't go any farther? But then why wouldn't he have tried the drawing room, where the others were more likely to be? Why the library that he already knew was empty? And *then* why enter the bar from the library's side and close himself up behind the wooden panels?

Rex supposed he couldn't enter the mind of a man like Noble, nor imagine the logic in *anyone's* thoughts when staring down death's door. But he also couldn't understand what this might mean for Edith's story. He'd clearly been too stunned to think of it at the time—the others, too, it seemed—so he certainly wanted to raise the point now. But he owed his father a chance to gather the facts on his own first, in his own way.

When Lewis reentered the library, he stepped up to Ransom. "Nice setup you got back there."

"I'm sorry, Lewis," the Colonel said quietly.

Chief Rainger raised his hand against the pink elephant in the room. Rex knew his dad had a no-ask policy where his friends' indulgences were concerned. They committed no crime in buying or consuming alcohol, after all; the law only cared for the source. As far as Lewis wanted to know, his pals had procured legally manufactured hooch before January 17, 1920 and managed to make it last a decade. Sure, that was a stretch. But he knew full well who and what caused the real trouble in his town, and decent folks tickling their noses with champagne bubbles now and then usually wasn't one of them.

"Now, when you hit him," Lewis said, "did you strike him with just your fist?"

The Colonel nodded.

"How many times?"

"Just the one."

"Where?"

"Across the jaw."

"No, I mean where were you?"

"Oh, er, right around here." He gestured to the area right in front of the bar.

Lewis bobbed his head as he appeared to mull this over. "And when you slugged him, did he fall? Slam into the wall, anything like that?"

Ransom's lips formed soundless words as he squinted at the bar. Squeezing his eyes closed, he wrinkled his forehead. "Yes, he, he fell. He s-spun and fell." A deep inhale hissed inside his nose, and Rex could sense the man's fight to remain calm as he perhaps remembered the real along with the imagined, the Colonel's trauma probably worse than Noble's at the time.

"He caught himself, I think. Even laughed, but he might've hit his head against the counter then. I'm not sure."

"I don't think he did," Edith said from — somewhere.

Rex looked through the bar's back doorway and into the hall, where Mrs. Warne stood meekly, as if wanting to join the men but without having to see the body. She wrapped her arms around her waist and leaned against the doorframe while Lewis turned to face her.

"Mrs. Warne?" he called across the bar. "Might you join us in here? 'Nfact, I'd like to see everyone. Bring the girls in with you, would ya please?"

Edith's pallor looked almost grey now. "Oh," she said before swallowing and clutching at her silk collar. She stared into the bar with a creased brow. "Yes, of course."

She retreated from view and entered the library a minute later through the mirrored door, Helen and Lottie in her wake.

Right away, the two younger women crossed to the room's other side. They stood by the Jefferson porch door without looking toward the bar, Helen worrying her dress ruffles in her hands as Lottie folded her arms and stared at the floor. Edith, however, had halted where she was. She seemed reluctant to step in any farther from the hall, where the bar's open paneled door could still block her sight of Noble.

Lewis must've perceived this, too, as he dropped the formalities and said, "Edith, honey, I'm sorry to make you come back in here. But it's my understanding from Freddy you were the last to see this man alive. That right?"

Before she could answer, Rex said to her, "I didn't tell him what happened between you two, only —"

"It's all right, Frederick." She smiled wistfully. "I understand. Yes, I saw him last."

"And that was?" Lewis began.

"As soon as Ransom left the room."

"This room?"

"Yes."

"And what time was that about?"

"We think around quarter past eight," Helen said from across the way. "That's what Rex and I recall, anyway."

Nodding, Rex said, "And it couldn't have been more than half an hour later when Lottie and I found him like this."

"Hm."

Edith's fingers still curled at her throat as she gingerly made her way toward the center of the room. She stepped up to the sofa where Lewis had set his hat and didn't once glance at Noble's body while she sat down with her back to it. Interlocking her hands in her lap, she lowered her head. "Chief Rainger, I confess. I did it."

The formal way she'd addressed him showed her respect for her friend as a one-time official, but also how she must have prepared this canned declaration to just out with it before she lost her nerve.

The chief crossed over and sat opposite her. "That's Lewis, hon'." He leaned in familiarly, resting his elbows on his knees and threading his fingers. "Now, what precisely do ya think you did?"

Ransom stepped around the body and laid an assuring hand on Rex's shoulder when he passed by to sit at Edith's side. Rex himself walked over to the edge of the coffee table but remained standing.

On the sofa, Edith gazed over at her husband and took his uninjured hand.

"Only when you're ready, darling," Ransom said. "I'm here."

She bit at a flake of dried skin on her lip, raising her eyes to the chief. "He attacked me, and I fought back. I didn't mean to do it."

Lewis nodded politely. "Can I ask you to back up just a little? To before the attack? Maybe start from when your husband socked Mr. Howard. Were you here when that happened?"

She squeezed Ransom's hand and related all she'd overheard from the hall.

"So—" the chief steepled his fingers and tapped their tips together "—tempers escalate from there. You knock the victim's lights out, Ransom, and leave the library. Where'd you go then?"

"My sitting room," he said, "just down the hall in the west wing."

"You meet your wife on the way?"

"No, I took the opposite hall. To the south. They run parallel."

"Lead to the same place?"

"Yes, the drawing room."

"But only the northern hall has access to this bar, through that door?"

"Correct."

"I see." The chief closed his eyes with a pinched brow as though picturing it mentally. "So then, in taking the southern passage, Ransom, you still had to cross the drawing room to get to the western wing. You had to pass where Miss Landry and Miss Conroy were with my son."

"Yes."

"You stop to talk to any of them?"

"No."

"Did any of them follow you out?"

"Lottie did."

"What about you, son?"

"Miss Conroy and I stayed where we were, sir."

Lewis laid an arm on the sofa back and twisted around to look at Helen.

She nodded. "That's right, Chief."

"Doing what?"

"Talking," Rex said.

"Dancing," she added.

"Weren't you worried about the others?" Lewis asked his son. "What with everyone leavin' and not comin' back?"

"Yes, sir. It sure was odd, sir." His cheeks burned. "But we had no way to know what was wrong and no reason to think it was serious. Didn't feel it was my place to ask anyway. And soon as Miss Landry and the Colonel did come back, everything seemed right as rain."

"They returned to the drawing room?"

"Yes," Rex said.

"Together?"

Rex nodded.

"Miss Landry and the Colonel. What about Mrs. Warne or Mr. Howard?"

"No, sir."

"And you didn't find that strange?"

"Well, sir—"

"We thought that—" Helen appeared to lose conviction once everyone looked at her. "Well, *I* thought maybe Mrs. Warne was just comforting Noble—Mr. Howard. They got on so well before that, and…" Her words faltered again when she looked at Lottie, who screwed her lips. "Well, she's such a gracious hostess. She wouldn't want anyone uncomfortable in her home."

Lottie murmured something as her eyes scanned the ceiling.

Still sideways on the sofa, Lewis angled his head and narrowed an eye at the actress before looking back at Rex. "So, let me get this straight. At one point, the four of you were all together in the drawing room at once, while, Edith, you were where? Still in the hall? With Mr. Howard in the library? Comforting him as Miss Conroy suggests?"

Edith pursed her lips and looked down. "You could say so. He made an advance, and…things got carried away…but I tried to stop it. I tried to s-stop him, but…"

Lewis shifted in his seat. "He was too strong."

"Yes."

"Were you behind the bar or in front of it?"

"Behind."

"*Behind* the bar…the whole time?"

"Yes."

Biting his lip, the chief bobbed his head in thought. Rex knew it was only a matter of time when his father would piece together that inconsistency. But Lewis must've flagged the issue in his mind for a later time, not raising it until he got the story straight. "So then, when you were *behind* the bar, were you standing, or—"

"Yes. He'd pushed me against the counter, and I reached for anything I could find for protection."

"And that's when you grabbed the icepick."

"Yes."

"And that's when you—"

"Yes."

"How many times?"

"I don't know. Several. Enough for him to back away."

"Did he cry out?"

"He gasped and—groaned, I suppose, but he didn't yell."

"Did you?"

"No."

From the way his father gazed around at them all, Rex could guess he was assessing whether someone should've heard all this happening from the next room or not.

Yet he just asked, "So then what?"

"I ran away," Edith said.

"Where?"

"My bedroom."

"So, you also had to cross the drawing room, past everyone else. How'd they—"

"No," she said. "I went through the basement. The stairs behind the bar. I saw no one."

"Except the staff," Lottie corrected. "Right?" Nerves had reentered her voice. Rex wasn't sure if she feared new holes in her adoptive mother's story or the servants losing their alibi. Probably a sad mix of both.

Edith looked past the chief's shoulder and then off to the side, shaking her head yet saying, "Yes. Of course." She closed her eyes and tapped her forehead three times with her middle fingertip. Letting out a single laugh, she shook her head again. "I did. I saw them all working, but rushed past before they saw me. And then, my room." Opening her eyes, she widened them for a second. "No one in my room."

Lewis leveled Edith with a concentrated stare then. Ducking his head, he squinted at her, but without so much as a blink or twitch to break the intensity of his gaze.

"Edith, hon'?" he asked in a more off-the-clock voice. "Are you sure you stabbed him?"

"What?" Edith said, shocked the chief even had to ask. "Yes."

"Actually punctured the skin? Saw him bleed?"

She fought to still her trembling lip. "I don't remember blood. It happened so fast. I ran away as soon as I could. But I know I did it. I could…feel it. I heard it." Like cutting into ripe fruit. If only she could cover her ears to the sound that echoed inside her skull.

"Any sense how deep?"

"No."

"Hit bone?"

Ransom clasped her hand with both of his.

"Yes," she said. "Or, I don't know."

"Meet any resistance when you pulled the pick out?"

"I think so. Yes."

Leaning toward her, Lewis asked, "Mind if I borrow this?" Before she answered, he plucked one of the silver-and-jade pins from her hair.

"Oh," was all she said as she laid a hand on her bun in the pin's absence. She turned around to see where he was taking it. Unfortunately, he made a beeline for the body.

Down on one knee again, Lewis parted Noble's shirt and jacket and delicately pierced the central-most chest wound with the hair pin. He pressed his lips as he eased the sliver of metal in and out of one hole, wiped it against his handkerchief, then repeated on another wound.

Edith vaguely registered how the chief inspected Noble on this side of the bar, *this* side, and not where she'd left him. But she'd last seen him alive, she swore she had, so somehow the man had made his way this far until succumbing to what she'd done. She squeezed her eyes shut.

"Pop?" Rex asked just then, alarming Edith out of her cloudy misery. He appeared as confused by his father's grisly method as everyone else.

"Where's it now?" Lewis said as he wiped the pin clean for the last time. "The icepick."

Ransom cleared his throat and straightened. His already warm palms dampened against Edith's skin.

"I—" he began.

"I think…" she uttered.

Her breath whistled through her teeth as she exhaled, trying to see her exit to the basement again. The silver pick like a flash of white fire, Noble's shocked and silent pain, him stumbling over something as he backed into the wall, her slamming the bar door behind her as she ran, and then the calla lilies in the stairwell, swarming around the walls of her living tomb, platinum streaking into burning gold as she descended into hell.

There she'd stopped, she remembered. Wavered with liquefying muscle until a clang roused her and urged her onward, out of the theatre, past the kitchen, then up the west stairs. Robotically, she'd conveyed herself to her bedroom, to her wardrobe and the skeletons…the skeletons that had chased her into the tub. The skeletons she'd later clawed off her armoire door, letting their bones fall to pieces as she'd watched her husband discover her secret shame. *"No more,"* she'd said.

"I dropped it," she stated now. "I think I dropped the pick in the basement. The theatre?" She turned her face to Ransom, belatedly curious what he'd been about to say before.

"Yes," he said, "you dropped it in the theatre."

"How do you know?" she asked.

"Yeah," Lewis grunted as he got to his feet, leaving the pin wrapped in his handkerchief on the floor. "How *do* you know that?"

"I found it there when Frederick and I searched the basement."

"Colonel?" Rex asked, and Edith's breath held in her chest.

Lewis squinted an eye.

"I didn't know she'd done it," Ransom said, "only that she was so distressed, and then I saw beads from her dress behind the bar. When I *didn't* see the icepick where it'd been before, I feared the worst, and thought maybe she'd taken it with her. I hoped not, but then I saw it. I saw it. And the blood…There *was* blood.

"Your son didn't know," Ransom hastily added for the chief. "I was the first downstairs and found it before he did. My boy," he then said to Rex, "I—well, I panicked. When I heard you coming, I tossed the pick into the other room, hoping you wouldn't see. It was a reflex, a silly one."

"You said you were checking the door," Rex marveled, "making sure it was locked."

"And so I did. Which was the right thing to do anyway."

"If there were an intruder, yes." Hands on hips, Rex nodded toward the floor. "We checked all possible entrances and exits, did everything we could to secure this wing. You gave me a *gun*. When all that time, you knew. You knew that—"

"I tell you, I *didn't!* But the way she looked when I found her…If it was somehow possible, I had to protect her."

"But finding her beads alarmed you enough to throw that caution aside. You had no choice but to lead me right down the way she'd escaped, right in the path of any new clues."

"A knee-jerk reaction, yes, but I just had to see for myself, and—I'm so sorry. I did wrong, but with the right intentions. I swear it, boy."

"Even in her state," Helen murmured, "you left her alone because you knew you could. You knew there was no one else who would harm her. You left her in her room, until we asked you to go back."

"That's the real reason you wouldn't let me phone anyone," Rex said. "Never mind scandal. You were scared."

Sheepish, Ransom dropped his head without another word.

"I see." Lewis's downturned mouth accentuated his jowls. Edith always did think he resembled a bulldog, a loving, loyal creature even if it never looked particularly pleased. And with this renewed interest in her husband, Lewis decidedly did not look pleased. "So, I ask you again, where is it now?"

Relaxing his grip on Edith's hand, Ransom didn't look at the chief directly as he replied, "Still there."

"In the basement?" Helen asked. "But then, on our way to the kitchen, Lottie, we must've walked right past it."

"Into, more like," Lottie said. "I nearly slipped on something in the dark, remember?"

Helen's eyes widened. "That's what clanked when you kicked it. Oh, dear." Her ivory skin looked rather green.

The chief mashed his mouth into his palm like before. He drew in a sharp inhale, then dropped his hand into his trouser pocket. "I don't suppose this icepick has any fingerprints left on it?"

Ransom ran his thumb along Edith's knuckles. "I wasn't thinking. My instinct was to wipe it down with my handkerchief before ridding of it."

"You had enough time to do that?"

"I did."

Lewis looked to Rex, who shrugged in seeming agreement there probably was time.

"Well, I do understand your motivation, Ransom. I do. I also believe how you could do such a thing without thinkin'. You gotta realize, though, not everyone'll see it that way. That seeking out the weapon, wiping it down, and hiding it away sounds pretty well thought out. In doing that, you might've implicated yourself in this crime, too."

"No," Edith moaned faintly, and Ransom wrapped his arm around her shoulders as she sank against the cushion.

The retired chief stared intently at the body. He released his hand from his pocket and rubbed his chin.

"Thing is, though," he said, "I don't think she did it."

"What?" the suspects exclaimed at once. Helen felt Lottie lean on her for support.

"B-But, I did. I did it!" Edith cried as she jumped to her feet. "I know I didn't imagine that!"

The Colonel stood, too, and took his wife back into his arms, trying to still her as she wriggled with incredulity, as if she wanted to be guilty after all.

Perhaps they all wanted her to be, too. Because if she wasn't, then someone else was. Someone still unknown. Maybe someone Edith wanted to protect. Helen looked down at Lottie, whose chest heaved with silent breaths as she just stared straight ahead of her, unblinking.

"I *know* what I did!" Edith insisted.

"Now that's just it, see," Lewis said. "*Do* you?"

"Of course I do! How could you possibly ask me that?"

"Well, now, honey," he said more gently, "if you don't like that, then you'll really have to forgive me for what I'm gonna ask next. And I hope you don't mind that I do so in front of the others."

Wide-eyed, Edith shook her head and gazed at him expectantly.

Walking over to her, he looked deeply into her eyes again as he gestured for her to sit back down while he likewise sat across from her, as before. The Colonel resumed his seat beside her, too.

Leaning over the coffee table, Lewis ventured, "Edith, darlin', how much liquor would you say you consumed today?"

"Oh…dear, I," she stammered, clearly not expecting that line of inquiry. She flittered a hesitant glance at her husband and touched a hand to her beautifully unkempt hair. "Couple cocktails in the afternoon, maybe? Glass of wine at dinner?"

"Well, now," the chief said, "that doesn't sound like much. Not over several hours, anyway."

Helen thought of how out of sorts Edith had looked on the porch that afternoon, though, and Rex had mentioned in the pool how she'd fainted. But they'd blamed the heat and dehydration as much, if not more, than any alcohol Edith might've had by that time.

Even so, she'd appeared a little glassy-eyed and quiet through dinner. Confused, even. And after the whole horrible episode with Noble, the Colonel had only said he'd found her in her bedroom, where she'd claimed to have taken a bath—yet *both* he and the missus had returned to the drawing room looking like they'd gotten wet.

Just what state had Ransom found Edith in? *Was* she reliable as her own witness?

Helen left Lottie's side as she edged closer to the chief, curious how he would follow up. Could inebriation absolve Mrs. Warne to any degree in a court of law?

Reaching across the table, Chief Rainger beckoned for Edith's hand with his open palm. She tentatively accepted it, and he asked, very quietly, "Did you consume anything else tonight?"

Edith's eyes never left the chief's as her face twitched to the side, as if halfway through an unspoken *no*, but rather than complete the gesture, she brought her chin to her chest.

"She doesn't normally drink very much," Ransom blustered, "so what little she has goes to her head quite easily."

Still holding the chief's hand, Edith laid her other palm on her husband's chest, shaking her head again. But when she didn't elaborate, Lewis asked her point-blank if there was another substance he should know about.

Edith's airflow seemed to stop as she emitted no sound and rapidly blinked away tears.

Helen waited for Ransom to comfort his wife, but he only sank his mouth into his hand and stared at the floor.

"Medicine," he muttered into his palm.

"Prescription?" Lewis asked.

"Originally."

Lewis slowly nodded. "How long ago was that?"

Ransom sat up but still looked down at his fingers as they flexed and unflexed. "I don't know, years. Early in our marriage."

"I was given a mild paregoric at first," Edith finally said.

"And what was that for — at *first?*"

Pressing her lips together, she shifted in her seat. "My monthly sickness." She swallowed.

"And then?"

"And then my dosage increased a little, for…" She licked her lips as her chest rose and fell. "When I lost a child." Delicately, she cleared her throat. "*Every* time I lost a child."

Helen's lungs deflated. She flattened her hand on her chest and looked back to see Lottie rest hers on the porch door to steady herself.

All through their year together at university, Lottie would harp on to Helen about Edith never wanting children, never wanting *Lottie*. She'd joke that her reluctant guardian was frigid or using some sort of pessary to avoid pregnancy. And then she would stop because imagining Edith and Ransom in a sexual context was altogether awful. The girls would fall over giggling about that.

Why neither had guessed Edith could be barren escaped Helen. They'd so easily cast her as the villain, they hadn't seen her potential as a victim until tonight. And, oh, what potential she'd lived up to.

Ransom's drawn face and curved back communicated how much he, too, ached over the children he'd never have with his wife, at least not by nature. He'd had Lottie to share with her, though, so it was puzzling that Edith wouldn't have warmed more to the child. Unless the girl had only been a painful reminder of the children Mrs. Warne would never bear herself. Emotional terrain was pitted with all sorts of paths and obstacles, everyone navigating it differently.

Clutching her drying tendrils, the Colonel pressed his lips to Edith's scalp, exhaling shakily through his nose as moisture gathered in his eyes. At the display, Helen tried to swallow down the pressure building in her throat.

"After the last time," Edith continued, "when there'd been such a long stretch of nothing, only for it to take again and then… *be* taken from me again, I…I didn't know how to manage after that. So, I simply kept…"

Listening intently, disbelievingly, Helen found her presence in that library wildly inappropriate. Here, Mrs. Warne had already confessed to infidelity and murder, but what she admitted now was no easier to handle. The journalist stirred to attract Lottie's or Rex's attention, see if either shared her embarrassment and would leave the room with her. But they stood transfixed, their gazes locked on Edith.

Lewis coughed into his hand. "Look, I…I'm sorry to have dredged this up. I truly am. I didn't mean for it."

He hoisted himself up from the sofa and began to pace beside it, alternating between looking at the floorboards beneath his feet and the body beside the bar.

Clearing his throat, he said more authoritatively, "Just answer me this. How much, eh, *medicine* did you consume today?"

Edith sat up and massaged her fingers. "Oh, I don't know. It's been some time since I measured, but...I'd say, a small sip this afternoon? Another before dinner? Perhaps slightly more then. And then more...after."

"After dinner?"

"After Mr. Howard attacked me."

"And when you say you had more *before* dinner, that amounts to what, exactly?"

"I couldn't say. Just — more."

"Enough to impair your judgment around the time Mr. Howard attacked you, ya think?"

"I think it impaired my judgment a great deal in my...interactions with Mr. Howard. That is, *prior* to the point of having to defend myself." Exhaling softly through her mouth, she played with her Mandarin collar. "But when I fought him away — " she looked Lewis in the eye "— I knew exactly what I was doing."

Stuffing his hands in his pockets, Lewis bobbed his head as he kept pacing. "I've asked you a lot of indelicate questions tonight, and for that I'm sorry."

"You're doing your job," Ransom said.

"What *was* my job, anyway." The retired chief shrugged. "And in my formerly professional opinion, I believe you *did* stab Mr. Howard this evening, Edith, but I do *not* believe you inflicted the fatal wound."

Ransom's was the only face to break into a smile of obvious relief.

"I don't have the wherewithal to *completely* rule out the icepick," Lewis went on, "but the wounds are mostly below his left shoulder." He stopped walking and rocked on the soles of his worn brown shoes. "Larger there, too, because they're deepest in that soft tissue, where the shaft could sink to the hilt. But on the chest? No, sir."

He lowered his head with another small bob before he let it hang, his eyes on the floor.

"See, most of 'em there seem to've hit the breastbone or an upper rib. Even where one might've slipped through, it wouldn't be a mortal one." He bit his lip and shook his head. "It just doesn't look like it hit the sweet spot, and not with enough force. That's my hunch, anyway." He gave another modest shrug. "I can't prove it. But I'd guess that after a few jabs were enough to fend him off, the real culprit snuck in and finished what Edith never intended to start."

"But how?" Helen asked.

Lewis hummed. "That blow to the head could very well've done him in. I'm not sure."

"Could it have been an accident?"

"Possibly, Miss Conroy. He could've lost balance, brained himself on that counter. But on which side of it is another matter…"

Before the chief could say more, Lottie exhaled. "That must be it." The sudden relief sounded odd in her voice. "On top of drinking too much, he probably reeled in pain and shock, and stumbled over."

"I did see him stumble," Edith said, for the first time sounding like she believed in her own innocence.

"I'm sure you did, dear," Lewis said. "*Behind* the bar."

Behind. Again, he emphasized that word, and Helen kicked herself for not connecting it before. Beating her to the punch, Rex asked, "So then how'd he end up on *this* side of the bar?"

"Son," Lewis said, "you have read my mind. That's another matter makin' all this pretty peculiar, isn't it? That after sustaining that kind of injury, he'd walk all the way around and into here. Not impossible, I s'pose, or even improbable. But if he did, we've got no trail to prove it. No blood, nothin'."

"Or any reason why he'd then close the doors behind him," Rex said. "They were sealed shut when we found him."

"Edith said he'd closed them before luring her behind the bar," Lottie offered wearily, "so maybe he just climbed over the counter."

"Why?" Rex asked.

Arms hanging limply at her sides, she lifted then dropped her shoulders. "To avoid the broken glass in back?"

"Then why not just sit out here," he said, "where it's more comfortable. He could've lain down, or come to us for help. Why hide in the *bar?*"

"How should I know?" she whined, looking and sounding overtired. "That's where he belongs. He's a lousy drunk. Nothing more." Leaving her post at the porch door, she ambled to the sofas and sank down across from her father.

The chief side-eyed her closely. "Any thoughts on who else could've done this?" he asked her. "Anyone follow you from LA, maybe?"

Lottie grimaced. "Noble does make more enemies than friends."

"Such as?" the chief pressed.

"Oh, I don't know. Studio execs, crew."

"Why?"

"Prima donna stuff. Nothing so bad for anyone to want *this*, though. I wouldn't think so. His bark is usually worse than his bite."

"Was," Helen corrected, wondering just how hard Noble had ever threatened to bite Lottie now that Edith had shared what he was capable of.

"Was." Lottie swallowed, the corners of her mouth drawing farther down. "Anyway, no one took him seriously." She sat up straighter and picked at the fringe on her lap. "Not really. Indulged him, sure, but not in any way that truly mattered. The enemies he made, he kept close."

"Close?" Lewis asked.

"Sure." She waggled her head casually, though averted her eyes from anyone's. "Close to his pocketbook, his influence. Keeping lackeys in line is easy."

"What about another lover?" Helen asked, quickly adding, "Someone he spurned in the past, before you were in the picture?"

"*Past*." Air puffed from Lottie's nose. "Oh, he actually treats women quite well when he doesn't care for them. Nothing his money can't buy, including a peaceful parting of ways."

"So," Lewis began, "you don't think that any women—"

"No. I don't know. Maybe. I don't think that sort would have it in them."

"Their fella might," Rex said, "if made to play the cuckold."

"Or a father," Helen added, "looking to make an honest woman of his little girl." The words were out when she saw Ransom redden. If he was embarrassed or angry, Helen wasn't sure, but she bowed her head when Lottie's quiet glare pierced through her.

"Did you recognize anyone on the train?" Lewis asked Lottie. "Anyone at all?"

"No, but then, I rarely left the compartment. I don't much crave attention from captive audiences when I'm captive, too. Sociable Noble, though, he might've run into someone he knew or made a new acquaintance. If he did, he didn't tell me." Her eyes drifted but appeared to harden again as she said, "He never *is* one to tell me of new acquaintances."

"Was," Helen repeated.

"Was," Lottie echoed, sounding strangled.

"This could've been a crazed fan from the area," Rex said, "if it leaked out you'd be here."

"In any of these cases," Lottie said, raising a hand to shade her fatigued eyes, "I wouldn't even know where to begin to guess. Honestly, I wouldn't." She exhaled loudly, which brought them all back to silence.

Sidling away from the body and the group, Chief Rainger paced the northern end of the room for a spell, past the grand globe and hearth and eventually pausing by the oversized firewood rack. He peered into it like his son had earlier that night, then released a latch. Swinging one of the iron sides open, he took a step inside and knelt, largely obscured from view.

Lottie stayed on the sofa as the others edged toward the fireplace.

"Damp," Lewis said as he pressed his palm to the rack's wooden base. Then he wiped his hands together to clean off any dirt and straw that had stuck to him.

"That could be the ice delivery," Edith said. "We had the kitchen stocked this morning, and since we'd be entertaining all day, I asked that a block be brought directly here as well."

"Huh," Lewis said, looking around at his feet. "Good use for the off-season, I suppose."

Helen knit her brow, assuming by "off-season," he meant the months they didn't require the rack for firewood — but why they'd store ice there instead was peculiar. Why not stock it right in the bar?

Ah, well. Fire and ice, she mused. The chief stood and stepped out of the rack, fastening its latch once more.

Only then did Helen notice a brass panel of buttons on the adjacent wall, probably for summoning servants. She'd noticed something similar in every room. *"When it comes to modern marvels,"* Lottie had said, *"he spares no expense."*

Helen glanced over at her friend, who sat frowning at the space in front of her, not paying any mind to the rest.

"Ransom," Lewis said, "mind if we fetch that icepick? 'Nfact, I'd like to search the basement myself."

"Of course," the Colonel replied. He invited Rex to follow, and the men set off down the hidden stairwell.

Not fifteen minutes later, the chief, Colonel, and Rex rejoined the women in the Liberty Library. The three ladies were all sitting on the sofas, and Rex's cheeks burned as he made eye contact with Lottie. Sitting there, she looked so curious of their findings, so convincing in her naivety. Some actress she was indeed.

"What is it?" she asked, her brow furrowed at his expression. She rose to her feet along with Helen and Edith. "What did you find?"

Glancing to his side, Rex saw Ransom's face had grown sickly pale. They both left it to his dad to reply first.

Chief Rainger jutted out his lower lip as he examined the implement in his hand. He held it with the fresh white dinner napkin that Rex had found for him in the kitchen. Better than the soiled handkerchief Ransom had wiped it with.

"Hm," the chief grunted, holding the pick by the handle and shaking its tip toward Lottie. "Found this, obviously, but funny thing. Also a pair of shoes, stashed under some old firewood."

The line between Lottie's brows deepened.

"Left behind by the help?" Edith suggested, walking to her husband.

"They're women's shoes," the Colonel answered.

"So, one of the maids'?" she asked. "What sort are they?"

"Keds," Lewis said. "White oxfords."

"I don't own a pair of Keds," Edith said defensively.

"Well, I do," Lottie admitted, "but I certainly wouldn't leave them in the basement."

"You *do* own a pair, Miss Landry?" the chief asked.

"Well, yes, I wore them just this afternoon. For tennis. Why?"

"Oh," Edith said weakly.

"Darling?" Ransom asked.

"No, I…it's only that I remember them now."

From the look on Ransom's face, he remembered them clearly enough, too.

As did Rex. Lottie'd been holding them out on the porch that afternoon. He only recalled them from the enthusiastic way she'd thrown them down when he and Helen had arrived.

"And where are they now?" Lewis asked.

"No," Edith said, darting glances between him and Lottie. "Lewis, please. I am obviously the one who—"

"Now, Edith, honey, you've said your piece. Let her answer some questions now." His tone had turned cool. "Miss Landry, where might your footwear be at this moment?"

"Well, naturally, they're upstairs in my—" Lottie squinted. "Or did I never bring them inside?" She turned to Helen. "Did I not bring them in?"

"After our swim, you mean? No, I don't think so. Come to think of it, mine must still be out there, too." Helen rolled her eyes with a self-deprecating *tuh!* of her tongue.

"So, they must be on the porch or the lawn somewhere," Lottie said as she stepped out from between the sofas. "Or maybe one of the maids brought them in, but I wouldn't think she'd toss them in with a stack of wood! I still don't see why it's any concern. Unless they're very dirtied?"

She giggled, nervously it seemed, but no one joined her. Helen seemed to want to, half-heartedly smiling and forming her lips around the beginnings of words, while Rex just clenched his jaw against a sudden pain in his throat.

Lottie looked around at the serious faces. "What?" Her titters petered out, turning into a huff at the others' silence instead. "What does a pair of shoes have to do with—Oh, now you couldn't possibly think—I almost married the man!"

"Well, now, miss, with all due respect," Chief Rainger said, "that in itself makes you a prime suspect."

"Ransom," Edith appealed, wringing her hands as she walked to Lottie's side.

"Now, Lewis," the Colonel interjected, but his old friend raised a hand to him.

"She's the closest to him here. They have history. And from what I can gather about the victim, it'd appear you had motive, Miss Landry."

"But I would never do such a thing," Lottie cried. "And even if I wanted to, I've been with everyone this entire evening."

"Well, now, not *everyone* the *entire* night," the chief said delicately. Rex knew when his father didn't want to get anyone riled, much less disrespect a family friend, yet the man had a knack for catching people off-balance. Exploiting it. There had to be a reason he wasn't coddling Lottie like he had with Edith.

"You all indicated before that you were each in and out of separate rooms through the course of the evening. Is that not so?"

"I only meant I was always with *someone*, here or in the drawing room or—here, and…I don't like what you're implying."

Uh oh. Rex swapped a glance with Helen and knew from her frightened look that Lottie's tone now bordered on *Do you know who I am?* territory. Maybe Lottie didn't always get what she wanted, but between her father and fame, she'd gotten quite a lot—and gotten quite used to that. For all her sweetness and humble origins, fact was, there would always be that side to her that sought the spotlight.

She'd be frying under the interrogation lamp next if she didn't keep her wits about her.

"Lottie," Rex said, "there's no implying. We're all suspects here. That's a fact we've known all night. And we're still all in this together."

Her chest rose and fell with sharp breaths through her nose as she stared at him through watering eyes. "Really? Because it feels like just me versus the Raingers right now."

"Lottie, no," Helen started before her friend snapped her face to her.

"You know it, Helen," she said. "You're too smart not to. What doesn't sound so smart to me, however, is how a pair of shoes in the basement connects *me* to a murder. I wasn't even wearing them tonight!" She began laughing again, a little crazily, even. And maybe Rex had imagined it, but he thought he'd also heard some of her old French accent slipping through.

His father set the icepick down on the nearest table. Hands in pockets, Lewis took a few steps toward Lottie. "You asked if these shoes were much dirtied, and I've gotta say, yes, they are indeed."

"Okay, well, I wore them outdoors on the lawn, as everyone saw, and now they're mingling with a pile of firewood, apparently."

"There do seem to be some scuffs from the wood," Lewis acknowledged. "Also bits of dirt and hay on the soles."

"I was down at the stables, too. But I did not bring those shoes into this house. Not me personally." She pumped one shoulder. "As I said, it's possible one of the servants found them and brought them in to clean. Just tossed them until they could be tended to. The laundry's down there as well."

"Possibly. Though they didn't appear so much 'tossed' as *buried*."

"I —" Her breath caught in her throat. "I don't know what else to say. I don't know how they got there or why it even matters. For all I know, they could belong to one of the maids. You haven't brought them here to show me nor asked me to look for myself. Why not have me try them on like Cinderella?" Her French accent was clearly coming out now, along with that earlier, haughty tone.

"We don't want to tamper with the evidence too much, Lottie," Rex said, "not before the police can have a look."

"Evidence?" she asked sharply.

"S'pose I didn't mention it," Lewis said, "but in addition to dirt are some blood stains on the upper."

"Blood? But I —"

"A light spattering," he went on, "but clearly detectable on white canvas. Doesn't appear to've rubbed off from something else. They look dripped on directly."

"But, but I — I wasn't even wearing them tonight," she repeated. "And if they do belong to a maid, maybe — oh, I don't know, maybe someone accidentally cut herself in the kitchen. Or got dripped on by the raw steak. Or maybe it's not even blood! Could it be wine or sauce? Maybe one of the girls simply set them aside to clean or dispose of later."

"Set them aside beneath a stack of firewood," Lewis remarked, pulling a hand from his pocket to rub his chin again. "In a separate room from the laundry or waste. And tell me, do your maids typically wear sport shoes on duty?"

"Well, I — I don't know, but maybe if her work pair was —"

"Or maybe *you* retrieved *your* shoes from outside at some point before the evening's meal, to change into when the time was right."

"Right for what?"

"Walking more silently on wood. Tile." His eyes glistened as they narrowed. "Better footing in case of struggle or needing to run away. And maybe you hid them there afterward to clean or dispose of yourself. Or for your getaway. Slip out the service doors instead of the main ones. Get away more comfortably." He gestured toward her dress heels.

"What?" Lottie exclaimed on a laugh, glancing at Helen, then Edith. "Me, in this dress and those Keds. Could you possibly imagine?" She giggled again as though waiting for the joke to end. Surely the chief was just having a laugh. But Rex knew better.

"That's precisely what I'm doing, miss. Imagining," Lewis said. "I'm picturing it all in my mind and finding it's not too difficult."

"Oh, now, this is absurd. Rex?" Lottie looked at him imploringly, her trembling smile fighting to stay in place.

Mirroring his father with his hands also in his pockets, Rex shrugged helplessly as he tried to find words. Scanning the library walls as he'd done when he'd first stepped foot within them, he made eye contact with each portrait of the Warne dynasty, felt the weight of their stares.

What do you know? he beseeched them. *What did you see?*

But they wouldn't answer, only waited for his next move for or against one of their legacy. The one who bore a resemblance, Rex just noticed, to a gentleman to the right of Ransom's portrait. So, what she hadn't inherited from her father came from farther down the line. He could see with his own eyes now—she really was one of them.

Edith edged nearer to Lottie and wrapped a hesitant arm around her.

"I agree that it's damn odd," Rex finally said. "But it's there. We saw what we saw, and we have to work with everything we can find at this point—"

"Fat lot of good that does!" Lottie snapped, and Edith flinched out of their embrace. "We also found an actual icepick with blood on it, and not even that's proven anything." She mustered an uneasy yet apologetic glance at Edith before glaring back at Rex. "Yet a pair of shoes is the smoking gun? I suppose you think I stabbed him with the toe of an oxford? *C'est absurde!*" The tears that had amassed in her eyes now fell as she shook. "If I wanted to get away, I would be *away* by now, not standing here on trial."

She looked at everyone around her.

"My God," she sobbed, "*I* was the one to *find* him. Rex, you were right here with me. I led you straight to him! Why would I do that?"

Rex of course wondered the same thing, beyond it being nearly impossible to imagine Lottie doing something so horrendous to begin with.

Getting away with murder didn't typically involve returning to reveal the body right afterwards. And how Noble had been concealed inside the bar, he could've easily remained out of sight at least until the next day — indeed, leaving enough time for the culprit to get away or cover any tracks overnight, make reasonable excuses for Noble's absence in the meantime. In the hideous hypothetical instance that Lottie *did* do this, she could've simply left Rex wondering where the bar door was that night. But instead, she'd opened it wide, just because he'd asked.

Although…

She hadn't opened the door directly in front of Noble. Not at first.

First, she'd opened the left-hand door. Depending on the doors' mechanism, maybe that one *had* to open before the other could. Or maybe Lottie had deliberately risked Rex seeing only the left side of the bar for a quick peek, the right door keeping Noble out of view. Rex had been persistent, after all; he hadn't given her a way out of showing him.

Yet, precisely that. He'd had to persist. Because she'd resisted. Under the pretense that she wanted to talk elsewhere — where they could *"really be alone."* But hadn't they already been alone? Just the two of them in that library, as far as either knew? Or had she only meant to go where the others would be more than a room away, less likely to walk in at an inopportune time?

But then where *else* had she been, when he'd first entered the library and discovered no one there? He recalled how she'd eventually come in through the north hall door. Her excitable state, which led him to tease, *"Caught ya red-handed."*

She'd raised her hands then, looking ready to go quietly.

"Outfoxed by the Red Fox. You got me."

"Where were you before then, Lottie?" he asked now, defeated. Was he really doing this, calling her out in front of everyone?

His father was only doing his job, or at least what they'd asked of him. Ransom, on the other hand, had gone to such lengths to protect Edith and with more damning evidence than this, even stood by her after a full confession. Now, too, when she still wasn't officially ruled out, Ransom took his wife into his arms after Lottie had startled her away. Where was Rex's drive to put love ahead of the law?

But should he have to? Would Lottie honestly ask that of him, if she truly loved him, too?

"Where *was* I?" She sniffed. "Here with *you*. Or have you already forgotten that conversation?" She wiped her nose with the back of her hand but couldn't clear the stunned hurt from her eyes.

"No," he said, wincing. "Oh, of course I haven't forgotten, Lottie." He approached her and cupped her bare shoulders in his hands, gently stroking her clavicle with the pads of his thumbs. "But before *then*," he whispered—not so that the others couldn't hear, but because the grip that his own despair held on his throat made it difficult to say even that much. "When I first walked in, you weren't here."

Her lips parted, then clamped shut, the muscles flexing on both sides of her jaw. The tears had stopped, but her eyes remained glassy. She gazed at him, and all the love she'd seemed ready to give diminished with every second.

Rex couldn't bear it. "Helen?" He looked to her instead with lingering hope. "Had she gone back into the drawing room with you?"

Helen met his eye, frowning. "Why are you first mentioning this now?"

"Because I—just, please, did you see her?"

Gingerly, Helen drew her head side to side, then dropped her eyes to the floor.

Lottie, without another word, glided toward the north hall and vanished from the room. Everyone, even the chief, let her go. The mirrored door clicked softly into its latch behind her, and Rex heard her footsteps echo down the hidden stairs.

No one made a move to stop her. With broken faces, Ransom and Edith just held each other, and Helen pinned Rex down with a saddened glare.

"For that matter," she said with emotion scratching at her voice, "I was alone, too. In the drawing room. At that exact same time. So much for my alibi! All while Colonel Warne was alone in the west wing, Mrs. Warne was alone in her bedroom, Lottie alone wherever she was, and you, too, Rex. You were alone then, too. The only one, as it happens, in the actual room where the murder took place."

Rex's gaze swept side to side across the wood-paneled floor. "I only questioned her because of that access from the hall. The library isn't the only way."

"No, it isn't," Helen said. "So I could've entered the bar just as easily myself from the drawing room, using that same hall. Just like the Colonel could've entered from the west wing using the basement stairs, and Mrs. Warne, too. And *you* were already right here. We *all* could've done what you suspect Lottie did in that same amount of time. Which wasn't much, I might add."

"But if Noble was already down after Mrs. Warne—" Rex said, until he caught Edith's ashamed look.

"True," his father chimed in, though the word's high-to-low inflection didn't carry much confidence. Certainly not as much as his interrogation had seemed to moments before. "It wouldn't take as much time or force."

"But?" Helen asked.

"But, well…look, I'm no polygraph test. I do get a read on people, though." After playing bad cop, Lewis was back to his sheepish, somber mood. "I am aware that Miss Landry is a fine actress. She is also just Lottie. The lovely little girl I watched grow up and play with two ruddy knuckleheads like my boys. If I had to wager, it was Lottie I saw and heard just now. She's suffered a trauma tonight like nothing any of us has seen, and I just don't know that those were the eyes of a guilty woman. I truly and earnestly believe none of you standing here are guilty either."

A statement that should've given joy instead made Helen and the Warnes visibly shrink. Rex, too, curled a little more into himself, feeling like morning would never come. And simultaneously dreading that it would.

"Look now," Lewis said in their silence, "it's late. You've all gotta be beat, the events of this night twisted all up in your heads. And, regretfully, I can't offer you any more expertise. I'm just as outta' my depth, to be frank, and concerned that if I'm here any longer on my own, Chief Thompson'll think I've helped cover up something." Hands back in pockets, he rocked to and fro on the soles of his tatty shoes. "So, I'm gonna bring him and his deputy into this, and they'll take it from here. Maybe even call the sheriff's office, since we're in the county seat.

"You can expect they'll want to question each and every one of your staff, too, in the household and on the grounds, though I don't know that they'll have the resources to get to everyone tonight. Not much left to this night as is. If I had to guess, they'll at least investigate the scene and secure the premises till dawn.

"Now, you all just sit tight while I make the call. And someone please see to Miss Landry. And do give her my apologies."

Nightcap

to wind down before bed

Rex found her in the Gold Theatre.

If only life came with a playbook. He had no idea how to navigate this situation. Even more, he hated that he'd half expected to find Lottie in that utility room, digging her oxfords out from the firewood to rid of the evidence.

Instead, she was standing in the projection booth, absently running a finger along the edge of a reel. She glanced over when he entered the doorway, held his stare for a few heartbeats. Then she said, "Mind turning off the lights?" She pointed back toward the stairwell entrance.

Rex nodded but stalled a moment, wanting to say something, anything. He lowered his eyes, searching for the words, but instead noticed a brandy snifter sitting next to the projector. He hadn't noticed her leave with one.

Following his gaze, she blandly said, "So that's where I left it before. The lights?"

He retreated to the switch panel, and they entered darkness.

But then, with a click, the screen beside him illuminated, a filmstrip counting down as the projector rattled through its reel. In the flickering light, he saw Lottie emerge from the little room in back and take measured steps toward him. He approached her, too, and they met in the middle, where she took his hand and guided him between two rows of chairs.

Seated side by side, they looked at one another until she turned away to face the screen. No music accompanied, but Rex recognized the opening title sequence of *The Renaissance Man*. He laughed in spite of himself.

"How?" he said, leaning into her. "It's barely in theatres."

"A woman has her ways." In the glow of the screen, he saw the corner of her lip curl.

"You arranged this? For me?"

Her lips drew back down. "Uh-huh." Leaning slightly forward, she raked her fingers through the fringe at her knees as she added flippantly, "Otherwise Ransom was going to show one of me in a silly period wig."

No trace of her accent now. He stilled one of her hands with his own, looking at her intently. "There is nothing silly about you."

Fisting her other hand, she sat back and turned her face to him. "So I gathered upstairs. Clearly, when I put my pretty little mind to it, I'm capable of quite serious things."

He watched the play of shadow and light on her face, the film running through its silent frames. This was a talking picture, but it seemed Lottie had wanted them to speak for themselves, with no soundtrack.

Nonetheless, she looked back at the screen without another word. He felt her hand pull out from under his.

"Lottie, please," Rex said. "Don't be angry that I've asked you questions just like everyone else has had to answer."

In profile, the little apple of her throat rose and fell.

"We all agreed, didn't we?" he asked. "That we'd share everything we knew to get the timeline right?"

"Then why didn't you ask me sooner?" she said, still staring forward.

Rex took his turn at silence.

She looked at him then. "Because you didn't want to know. If I'd done it, you didn't want to know. Or watch me lie to you to save my skin."

He glanced down and drew in a deep inhale before meeting her gaze again.

"Well, I wouldn't have," she went on. "I'd have told you the truth if you asked. If you'd only asked." Shaking her head, she began smoothing the fringe on her lap once more. "When I discovered Noble, I —" Her voice caught, and her words to follow quivered as her eyes glistened in the projector light. "One of my first thoughts was that I'd found you alone in the library. You'd been alone in there — with him. And I wondered…and how I hated myself for that."

"Then I guess we're both guilty of not asking."

"Is that *all* we're guilty of?" Looking down to wipe her eyes and nose, Lottie then rolled her head over her shoulder and gazed up at him.

Rex angled himself toward her, taking both of her hands now and bringing them to his chest.

"Lottie, I swear to you — I *swear*, on my mother's grave — I didn't touch a hair on him. You know me. I get tough in the game, but I wouldn't so much as —"

"I know, Rex. Which is why, after that one second, just that one second that I doubted you, I knew I didn't have to ask you anything. Right here —" releasing a hand from his, she flattened her palm to her heart "— I already knew the answer. And hoped you would know it, too."

Rex adjusted in his seat. "So, what does this mean? I'm damned that I didn't ask and now damned that I did? I don't know what I'm supposed to do, Lottie. I don't know what to say, how to act around you anymore, I—I only…" He took another long breath and placed a hand at the side of her face, caressing her temple with his thumb. "I only know how I, that I've…"

Overcome, he dropped his hand and let go of hers, turning to face the front again as he shook his head. A hell of a time this was to even think of making love. "I don't even know," he said. "Just that what I'm feeling, it makes me crazy, and I can't see straight anymore."

What he did focus on was his projected image, the football hero in uniform, dashing across the field with his team and dodging the opponents' blows. Scoring the touchdown before winking at the blonde in the stands. He looked larger than life. What a small man he felt now.

Glancing at Lottie, he saw she now watched the film, too. "You were magnificent," she said softly. "Always magnificent."

"I'm just a man, Lottie."

"As I'm only a woman. Who thought she might show you how she felt by—" She broke off with a derisive laugh. "A simple gesture."

She looked at the movie screen the entire time she spoke, with the same forlorn expression she'd had while staring at the film reel before, when he'd found her down here.

And that's when Rex fully grasped what she'd done for him. Ransom had another feature prepared for this night, but she'd changed it. Saw to it that the projector was loaded with something other than Lottie Landry, Hollywood star. Yanked the spotlight away from herself—and Noble Howard, too—to shine it onto Rex Rainger instead. Fill everyone's eyes and ears with his glory, not hers.

A simple gesture that complicated everything.

The way Rex had found her idly stroking that reel…she'd even loaded it herself, hadn't she? With Noble around, she would've had to do it discreetly. Maybe before dinner, when everyone rested and refreshed. Or *after* dinner, when she'd left Rex's side with her brandy glass and returned without it. After she'd left the drawing room to confront Noble in the library — and found the room empty.

Rex hadn't considered that scenario. But he could picture it now — her puzzled face when she discovered both Edith and Noble absent from the library, the bar doors closed. Then the smile lighting her eyes when her thoughts — dare he hope? — turned to Rex instead. The excitement, maybe, that fueled her swift steps down the hidden stairwell to the Gold Theatre, where she'd set her drink down to swap reels. The giddiness that then caused her to forget the brandy as she ran back upstairs and into Rex, who'd found himself alone in the library, too.

Alone, that is, until he wasn't, when the object of his affection was suddenly there and flustered with some secret. Something she hadn't wanted to tell him, at least not yet. She'd seemed pleased to find him there, though, for the chance to speak with him alone, just as eager as he'd been. And for mutual reasons. Noble had nothing to do with it. It had only — and always — been about her and Rex.

The possibility of it crashed on him, and he turned his body back to Lottie's and clasped her arms. Of course, he couldn't know for sure what had happened, if his imagined scenario *was* the innocent reason why Lottie hadn't been in that library those few minutes in question. He couldn't know without asking, and even then, it would only be her word. Her loving or lying word. And damned if he'd question her again tonight.

She looked at him, startled, perhaps afraid, but before she could protest or question him in turn, he pressed his lips to hers and refused to second-guess his actions or what her response might be. He was tired of playing defense.

The pass wasn't incomplete as she leaned into him, softening against him but not weakening in her kiss or efforts to hold him closer. Her fingers glided around to his back and up and over his shoulders as she slid her body nearer and onto the edge of his chair.

She was practically in his lap, and Rex fought the impulse to lift her and seat her there. His hands roved up her soft arms, along her neck, and into her satin hair, and then he brushed the contours of her cheeks, sweeping her blonde waves out of her face as she clung to him and returned everything that he gave.

Easing a palm back down and along her clavicle, he inadvertently slid her dress strap off her shoulder. Sensing the thin fabric fall, he broke from their kiss.

The two just stared at each other, breathless, Rex looking away only to glide his hand up the back of her arm — so softly, it made her shiver — to raise her strap back into place.

Again, they simply gazed at each other. And though there was so much he wanted to say to her in that moment, all he whispered was, "I'm sorry."

For a moment, she said nothing, just searched his face with her eyes.

Then she whispered back, "Lie with me."

Lottie didn't have to ask Rex twice for him to agree to lie down with her for a while. Without questioning, he took her hand and led her back up the silver stairwell.

Lottie didn't need to beg the others, either, for permission to rest. They felt better that Rex would be with her, too. Hang propriety when protection was priority. His father only cautioned that they wouldn't have very long, so to make the most of it.

Lewis shook with a deep chuckle in his chest then, raising a brow at his son and adding, "You know what I mean. You get some shut-eye, boy. I think it would do the rest of you good to try the same. I already caught a few winks before Freddy called me, so I'll hold the fort here."

Ransom stayed behind with Lewis as Edith rested a hand on Helen's shoulder and invited her to lie on one of the sofas in the drawing room. The chief was adamant that everyone stick to the east wing where he felt it was safe, and instructed Mrs. Warne and Miss Conroy to lock the drawing room door to the foyer.

He'd only made the exception for Rex and Lottie to go upstairs because he sympathized with her and trusted his son. They, too, were ordered to lock the bedroom door, though.

When Lottie expressed her gratitude for his father's leniency, Rex said, "It's just his way. He wouldn't even lock prisoners up."

"He trusted them?"

"Or at least his own strength if they tried to run." He shot her a side-grin as they wound their way up the main staircase and heard Edith latch the drawing room door below. Such a bittersweet déjà vu of the sweet ascent they'd made earlier that day. The infatuated glances, the heady anticipation of having a whole night ahead of them, filled with possibility.

They'd never entertained this one.

Nor had Rex ever expected Lottie to bring him back to her room — though he'd hoped she would, if he were honest with himself. Of course, he was too much of a gentleman to *expect* such an outcome, and, even now, it wasn't exactly how he'd have planned it anyway. *If* he weren't too gentlemanly to plan such a thing, that is.

All he knew now was that after their nightmare of an evening, he'd found himself in his wildest dreams.

But, as in dreams, Rex felt paralyzed once they entered her bedroom and secured the door behind them. He could barely form coherent language, the courtesies he thought in his mind not coming out of his mouth. He just stood there by the door and awkwardly held his arm out toward the bed, as if she wouldn't know where to find it otherwise.

A breeze wafted in from the open window. Evening had taken the dank thickness from the hot air, and though it was still warm, Rex shuddered with a chill, the hairs at his neck prickling. Lottie stroked her bare forearms at the same time.

"Uh," Rex said as he rubbed the back of his neck, "if there's anything you need — to do. Change clothes, freshen up, I'll just…" He pointed his thumb at the door, where he'd stand sentry in the meantime.

"At the risk of sounding untoward, Rex—" she smiled slyly in the moonlight "—I think I have everything I need right here."

His heart leaped at the sentiment, and he smiled back as she stretched and squeaked with a kittenish yawn.

She unbuckled then kicked off her heels and sighed luxuriantly. "Ohh, why didn't I do that sooner?" She stepped over to the bed and looked back at him, expectant.

He wiped his palms on his hips as he walked to the bed's opposite side. Silently, simultaneously, they sat on the mattress and eased one leg up after the other, mirroring each other as they inched toward the center. Rex stretched an arm under her neck as she curled into him.

"Sleep," she said.

But Rex couldn't. As his body relaxed beside Lottie's, his mind refused to stand still as it continued to rove downstairs, walking the perimeter of the library and checking every window and door lock once more. Round and round he went, his imagined self concluding each lap at the north fireplace, his phantom legs butting up against that large rack every time.

Lottie stirred against him. As she used his bicep for a pillow, he raised his forearm and let his fingers fall into her hair, gently combing the soft waves. She purred a little hum when he pressed a light kiss to the top of her head, but then her breathing deepened as she seemed to drift off.

Rex drifted, too, but back downstairs. To the basement. In his mind, he walked the entire theatre again and then along that narrow hall leading out to the pool. Room by room, until he stopped beside the firewood. Lottie's shoes. Rex squeezed his closed eyes to see more of the utility room in the dark. The dusty equipment, the flecks of straw and dirt, the unusual contraption with pulleys running the height of the wall.

The height of the wall.

Pulleys, conveying something to somewhere. There was no going down, so there was only up.

The height of the wall. Up to the basement ceiling, which became the library's floor.

The library's floor.

Firewood.

Fire rack.

"Even the firewood has its own elevator," Lottie had said. Hours that felt like days ago, in the drawing room, right after dinner. *"Like the dumbwaiter in the pantry. When it comes to modern marvels, he spares no expense."*

Rex stopped stroking Lottie's hair as his body turned rigid. The hairs on his forearms stood on end as his breathing nearly stopped, too.

Easing his arm out from under her, he whispered words of comfort to her snoozing form and glided his other hand along her side. Bringing it to her face, he held her cheek and kissed her softly on the lips.

"Mm," she moaned drowsily as he quietly told her to keep sleeping and promised to return.

She remained sound in bed while he delicately let himself out the door and turned the key in its lock.

Rex tiptoed to the other end of the hall, where he found a door to the west-wing stairs. Removing his wingtips, he took the wooden steps all the way down, which creaked slightly beneath his weight.

Stepping out near the kitchen, he laced his shoes back on to cross the dark basement, retracing the thoughts that had already wandered back there. The door to the utility room stood open.

Chief Rainger met his eye when Rex reached the open doorway.

"The elevator," Rex said.

"The elevator." His dad nodded down toward the iron railings that fenced him in.

The chief was standing directly in the center of the firewood rack and a glow from above. Rex looked up through the rectangular hole in the ceiling to see Colonel Warne's stricken face hovering from upstairs in the library.

"I'm such a fool," Ransom said. "It never occurred to me that—"

"Me neither," Rex said, looking from one man to the other. "I noticed it before but didn't know what I was seeing. I didn't—"

"None of us did," his father said, glumly, "and I was even lookin' right at it, talkin' about ice and firewood. Too fixated on the function to see the possibilities. Appears we got ourselves a culprit cleverer than us. Was just testing to see how it might work."

Widening his stance, the chief fisted his hands on his hips.

"And now we gotta think who would've had access."

Lottie came to at the touch on her shoulder. She opened her eyes to see a silhouette in front of the moonlit window.

She smiled. "If I'm still sleeping, then you'd better kiss me. Make it a good dream."

Standing beside the bed, Rex didn't move, other than to bend and give her shoulder a gentle squeeze. She could feel his palm grow hot against her skin.

Arching her back, she hummed out a long, contented sigh with the stretch. His hand left her side.

"Come, now. You know not to be shy with me." She propped her head up on her hand. "Is it time already? We have to go?"

She could just make out his nod, and she sighed again, this time disappointed—and terrified of what was to come. How she wished it had all been just a nightmare, starting with Noble lying here, in this very bed, mere hours ago. If it could've all just been her imagination, except for lying here now with Rex at her side. He was wrong when he'd said life wasn't like the movies; they *could* write the happy ending they wanted if they willed it enough.

But first…

"All right," she whined. "Then wake me with a kiss, my prince, before you whisk me away."

He hesitated again but gradually did bend down farther and lean in. Feeling his lips against hers and his hand on her cheek, Lottie was ready to melt into the kiss when instantly something didn't feel right.

Not the cushion of his lips nor the scent of his skin.

Not the stubble on his face nor the callouses on his palm. They scraped her, and with a gasp, she sat up and scooted away, pulling the sheets to her chest as a flimsy shield.

Silver-blue light still cloaked his dark form, but Lottie's heightened alert helped adjust her eyes to his stature.

Not so tall, but built like a baby grand, just as Rex had said.

"Please don't be afraid, Miss Lottie. It's only me."

The air eked out of her lungs in small tremors. Looking around her empty bed, she couldn't understand where Rex had gone. She prayed not far.

"Please," the shadow said. "You know you can trust me."

"Ernie," she whispered.

"Yes, miss. And I'm afraid we don't have much time."

"But, what are you doing here?"

He extended his hand to her. "Making good on my promise."

"Promise?"

"To run away."

"Run away!"

"No, no, shhh…" He sat at the edge of the mattress and pressed his finger against her lips. "They'll hear us."

Breath held in her chest, she froze against his touch.

"It's not like I planned, so we have to go this way." He removed his finger from her mouth to point it at the window. "I've got the ladder lowered."

Lottie glanced past him at her vanity table and thought of the rope-and-wood fire ladder that Ransom had installed behind it years ago, as precaution. It had stayed rolled up there so long, she'd forgotten about it.

"You got any comfortable shoes to wear? I grabbed the ones I found outside, but I can't get to 'em now. Stashed anythin' else you need, though, down at the stable."

"Stable," she said slowly.

"That's right. I hope you don't mind I took the liberty of choosin' your things. Just figured you wouldn't have time. We really do have to go now."

"The stable," she repeated, trying to think of Ernie making any promises while they'd talked there that afternoon. If she'd asked for any in the first place. She remembered fantasizing about running away on the horses, but surely he knew that wasn't serious? That she'd just been talking, voicing her thoughts as they came. She'd felt so silly about it afterward and made him pinky-swear not to tell anyone. Which only made her feel sillier, how she'd actually held her little finger out to him and made him —

Oh, no.

"You did promise," she said. "You pinky-swore to help me, didn't you? To run away."

"That's right, Miss Lottie. And I'm a man livin' up to my name, just as you said."

Ernest Hart of the Earnest Heart, she'd declared him as kids. Born to act, she'd bedecked herself in one of Edith's exotic robes and jewelry and pretended to be queen, knighting Ernie her esquire with a fireplace poker. She had always meant it, too — that his heart was good and true.

And apparently so had he. Only, he'd gravely misunderstood what she had actually asked of him. What she'd never asked out loud, she realized now, leaving him only what she *had* said to work with. How foolish. She should've remembered how literal her old friend always was. Distilling everything down to its simplest meaning.

"Ernie," she said with more compassion. "I didn't mean—"

She stopped when Noble's cold, dead face filled the darkened space where she still couldn't quite make out Ernie's features. Noble, lying there as the ice melted on him. His bright light snuffed out.

She shivered with the breeze blowing in from the window.

"I didn't mean," she repeated, "that is to say, I…" Try as she might, she couldn't offer him the clarity she should have before. She didn't dare. Not now that she knew this man could be dangerous. Capable of carrying out what Edith hadn't done after all. But could Lottie be sure of that? Sure that Ernie didn't simply want to run away? That this timing wasn't just awful coincidence, as he clearly wasn't capable of…

"Forgive me," she started again, desiring to be safe either way. "I don't even know where to begin to thank you. I should've known you'd come through for me."

Ernie exhaled with excited relief, and every breath after came out like a pant. Reaching for her face again, he leaned in for another hard kiss.

"You never have to doubt me, miss—I mean, Lottie. I really can call you that now, can't I. Now that we're—"

"Yes," Lottie said before he could articulate whatever he thought they were to each other, "you can of course call me that." She patted his hand where it still held her cheek and gently lifted it away before edging to the other side of the bed. "I'd better dress." She stood as if to walk to her wardrobe and gauged if she could beat him to the door.

"Lottie, my sweet, we don't have time. Told you, I got everything in the stable. Dusky's all saddled up, too. You're probably better off barefoot on the ladder anyway, and I'll be carryin' you from there."

She inhaled a shaky breath. Lying in Ernie's arms, those brutally strong arms, as he snatched her away. Those hands on her body, what could be a killer's hands…

"Um, but, oh, but I, ah…" She glanced at the door, hoping he couldn't see her eyes in the dark. In the stillness, she listened for Rex's—anyone's—steps and felt desperately alone when she didn't.

Oh, Rex. Why'd you leave me?

"Yes, Ernie," she said breathlessly, "I...think I can do that. I'll follow you out." If she could get him outside the window first, then she could reach the door in time.

"No, sweetheart," Ernie said to her dismay. "Ladies first."

"But if I fall, I'll need you to catch me."

Standing silent a moment, he seemed to only stare at her, and she feared he was sizing up her motives. Then he rounded the bed and walked straight up to her.

"Lottie." He took her face in his calloused hand again—funny, how fast he'd grown comfortable doing that—and curled his other arm around her waist. She dreaded another kiss until he stepped aside and turned to guide her toward the window, with his palm at her back. "You have to trust me."

She felt his hand push her forward with more urgency to the side of her vanity table, which he at once lifted from both ends to shift over a few feet. How he could lift it so easily frightened her even more, and she lamented that he didn't drag it, so the noise could alert someone downstairs. But then, of course, that's probably why he didn't.

She now saw the rope ladder hanging over her sill from where it was bolted to the floor. With her back to the wall, she tried to root herself against it, make it impossible to move her until she could sprint across to that door.

But even if she reached it, if it was locked, she'd never get it open in time. Not unless she hurt him first.

Glancing at the vanity, her silver hairbrush glinted back at her. But Ernie stood between them, and even if she could will the brush into her hands this second, would striking at him be wise? What if that wasn't enough to slow him and only incited his anger? Once more, she had to remember the potential danger he posed, had to tragically continue the charade.

By the time she could even collect these thoughts, he was right by her side and guiding her to the sill.

She hiked up her dress and raised one trembling leg over the window frame. Her toes found a wooden rung. Adjusting to the ball of her foot for leverage, she lifted her other leg and eased herself down until she hung completely outside of the house. The massive roof and columns of the Madison porch stood next to her like an imposing yet silent witness, powerless to save her. Lottie's entire body tensed against the fear that shook her, and despite every ounce of her better judgment, she raised her face to smile up at Ernie, praying he wouldn't see through the act and push her from the ladder.

Lottie never had cared for heights. She was loath to look down, but it gave comfort to see faint light from the drawing room below. Someone would have to see her from there, right?

But as she descended, and Ernie followed from above, she saw the ground-floor shades were drawn down.

Of course. Edith had closed them while they'd waited for Rex's father to arrive. Certainly that's why Ernie could lower the ladder to begin with. And maybe she and the others had been in another room or too distracted to notice the sound of it dropping.

With a dizzy sigh, Lottie dropped her forehead against the back of her hand, squeezing her eyes shut and fighting the tears. She was nearly to the ground now. She could pound on the window. She could run once her feet touched the earth. But Ernie was nearly to the ground, too. Close enough just to hop down and grab her. Silence her. Even if they caught him, would they find her dead or alive?

She tried to shake the thoughts from her mind and just let her feet sink into the grass. What a decadent sensation that had given her before, the soft and warm blades tickling at her skin. What met her now was cold and damp. In the distance, the allée of elm trees loomed large and black, walling in her upcoming death march to the stable.

Maybe if Ernie did force her all the way down there, made her mount her dear Dusky first, she and the horse could flee without him, ride to safety. Back to the house in time to alert Chief Rainger and, God willing, reinforcement.

Ernie was at her side before she realized, and he took her hand. Gulping, Lottie started to walk if it meant avoiding him carrying her.

But he didn't move when their arms ran out of slack, tugging her back to him instead.

"What is it?" she whispered, hoping he'd had a change of heart.

He pointed overhead. "This is where I heard you," he breathed back. "I heard *him*, yelling. Saw you struggling. I don't know what all that was about, Lottie, but I heard enough."

Looking up to where the ladder hung out the window, she understood that he meant Noble. When they'd come in from the pool, Rex had mentioned running into Ernie on the east terraces. The worker must've still been on the grounds when the actor had hissed his ugly threats up there, where he'd pinned Lottie to her vanity table and shoved her head over the mirror, into view. She could still feel the wooden frame boring between her shoulders, her golden locks probably catching the sunlight as she'd fought to catch her breath.

Absently, she drew her fingertips to her lips, reliving the scene from the outside looking in.

Ernie took her hand from her mouth and cupped it against his broad chest. "I just need you to understand why the plan changed. Why we didn't just run away. I, I heard how that man talked to you, and I couldn't allow it. No, miss. Especially when I heard him and Mrs. Warne—"

"Stop," Lottie croaked.

"It's just that, I could get *you* away, but I couldn't leave her behind with him. *No* one was safe with him around."

"Please stop, Ernie," she begged, unable to hold back the tears. "You don't need to explain anything to me."

He shifted closer to her. "Now, now. I didn't mean to make you cry, sweetheart." He caressed her hair. "Please don't."

"Only…tears of joy, Ernie. I'm—" She gasped the night air into her hardened lungs as she shuddered. "I'm so—" she swallowed "—grateful."

"Oh, Lottie." He wrapped his thick arms around her, crushing her to him as he wrung her side to side. "My love, my heart."

Then, before she knew it, she was off her feet and in his arms, distancing from the house at a gallop.

She'd just delivered the performance of her life, but all control shattered now as she screamed with everything she had — *for* everything she had and had lost.

Lottie screamed for her father, screamed for Rex, for Noble, for the broken sanctity of Belleau. Screamed for her life, for Edith, for chances to do better, to *be* better than all the heartache she'd brought down on everyone. For loving the wrong people, letting the wrong people love her. Craving the attention she never properly gave back. If she could survive this, she vowed to do it better. Rex wasn't the only one with a mother's grave to swear on.

She cried out for it all, though Ernie's rough hand now muffled her screams. He kept running, feverishly asking her why, why she'd want to do that, why go and ruin his plans, *their* plans. "Lottie, I love you, don't do this." He wept as she wept. "I don't understand why you'd wanna do this!"

But he still ran, ever faster, and Lottie's hurting heart rattled inside with every jerky bound he made. Sobbing, she wrapped her arm around his neck and cried into his chest, the smells of sweat and horse hide consuming her senses. "Oh, Ernie, Ernie... why did *you* do this?"

He didn't answer. Just kept running while his warm tears dripped on her face.

She wiped them away, but noticed a dark stain on her fingers. When she looked up, Lottie saw blood streaming from his nose.

So he still got them. The nosebleeds. Always at the worst times, when he was most stressed. The other kids' laughter at "Bleeding Hart" would then only add insult to the original injury. Lottie's own heart couldn't help but still go out to him when she thought of the torment he'd endlessly endured in their past. Nothing that excused what he'd done in the present, though.

When they reached the stable, Dusky was rearing outside, tied to a post. The stallion sensed her distress, Lottie knew, and had riled all the other horses. She could only hope the commotion would buy more time and raise more attention for her rescue.

She, too, finally struggled against Ernie, who dropped her to her feet but still held a firm grip on her wrist. He grabbed her other one when she swung at him and dragged her inside the stable, where he pinioned her within one muscled arm while he groped for a rope. He nearly knocked a lantern off its nail as he did so, causing shadows to shift in the low golden light.

The rope's rough fibers scraped at her arms as he bound her up and tied her to a stall. Betty's, Lottie realized, and she turned her head as far as she could to seek comfort from the mare's big warm eyes.

The space was empty. Lottie craned her neck farther to peer over the door.

Her eyes had barely adjusted to the pale mound on the ground when Ernie said, "Wasn't her time yet." He stepped up to Lottie and, pressing against her, looked over at the dead horse as well. "But it was close enough. And I'd promised to take care of it myself."

Lottie deflated with a feeble groan, dropping her head.

Tucking a finger beneath her chin, he raised her face back up. "I wouldn't've been able to after tonight, sweetheart. You know that. And I promised you it'd be me."

Though tears still flowed, she calmed, trying to catch her hyperventilated breath.

"Aw, Lottie," he murmured into her hair as he pressed little kisses up and down her hairline. "It's okay. I forgive you. We're gonna be happy, you and me. Soon as I calm that horse and we're on our way."

Her face screwed with a new crying jag coming on. But she knew he couldn't see as he kept stroking and speaking into her hair.

"The others'll be okay. They'll miss ya for sure, just like I always have, but they'll get along. You'll see. Rex, too. I know you were gettin' sweet on him, but I forgive you for that, too.

And I wouldn't hurt Freddy. He's a good man, and who could blame him for wantin' you. But you shouldn'ta brought him to your bed like that. It's not decent, Lottie. It dirties a girl like you. But I'll forgive ya for that, too, if you promise it was only protection. I know I gave you all a scare tonight, so I couldn't fault ya there. I certainly could not."

Eyes closed and mouth open, Lottie's head and shoulders shook on each exhaled breath.

"Shh," he cooed, "be still. You're safe. Ernie's here, ready to forgive you."

Dusky continued kicking up a fuss outside but gradually settled down. Lottie opened her eyes and rolled them in the horse's direction.

There, she saw Chief Rainger, Rex, and Ransom — creeping in through the stable door, fingers to lips for her to keep quiet. Glancing to the other side, she saw two officials emerge from the shadows where another door led.

She slowed her breathing and rested her head against Ernie's. Then she kissed his cheek before whispering in his ear.

"I love you, Ernest Hart of the Earnest Heart. Please, please do forgive me."

And then she watched him pull back and smile, seconds before he was apprehended from both sides.

21

Earlier that evening,
approaching half past eight o'clock

He wanted to harm Noble, that was certain. Though he didn't know if he actually would. He probably wouldn't if he didn't have to. But if he did, he'd knock Noble out so Lottie could get away.

For now, Ernest Hart was only delivering ice to the library.

He'd done so that morning, by way of the firewood elevator for convenience. Much easier than that narrow, winding stairwell. He always feared scraping that pretty silver wallpaper. Not that he couldn't take the stairs himself after sending the ice on its way and meeting it in the library, but if the lift could hold his weight as well, why not?

The Warnes often did ask him to deliver a block directly to the library after stocking the kitchen. And as they'd be entertaining all weekend, he was to replenish the bar the next morning. Only, Ernie knew he wouldn't be around by sunrise.

So, with the ice block pinched in large tongs and hoisted atop his broad shoulder, he once again conveyed himself upstairs from the basement on the elevator. Should he be seen, he'd just make his excuses that, in this heat, and after a long day of drinks, he figured they might need more for the evening. He'd just play dumb as everyone always expected anyway, since he didn't have to play at it very much. That much Ernie did know, for all that he didn't.

Luckily, no one was there. Or at least he didn't think so until he heard the murmur within the wall.

"No, Noble," he heard a woman say. He slowly set the ice block down on the elevator floor.

It turned his stomach if his Lottie was stuck canoodling in there with that rat. If he could strike Noble down now, maybe he and Lottie could already get away.

Detaching the metal tongs from the ice, Ernie gripped them, just in case, as he crept closer to the bar. He stepped right up to the wooden wall and pressed his ear to the panel, listening and realizing it wasn't Lottie but Mrs. Warne inside. And from the protests to follow, he understood she did not desire Mr. Howard's company any longer.

His heart sped up. Ernie knew the bar opened from inside the library somehow, but he usually made his deliveries through the back, to store ice beneath the counter. He wasn't sure where exactly to unlatch the front entry. But he tried, and once he found it, he threw one panel open.

But it was already too late.

Mrs. Warne must have escaped out the back, thankfully. And Noble stood there clutching his chest, leaning against the wall and heaving with agonized breath. In his startled pain, he didn't appear to notice Ernie in the open doorway, just swiveled to lean his back against the counter instead, where it seemed he could partially sit on a shelf below. He now had his back to Ernie, and he hunched as he continued rasping.

Gingerly, Noble bent down, and Ernie wondered if he'd fall to the floor, if Mrs. Warne had injured him that badly. But then Noble sat back up, and a tuft of white peeked over his shoulder.

A cloth he may have retrieved from the floor and now pressed to his shoulder.

His presence unknown, Ernie debated what he should do. Noble was already slowed down, weakened, so Ernie could just quietly close the paneled door as he'd found it and retrace his steps to the elevator. Go back to the basement, where he'd left Lottie's Keds. He could try to find her, get away with her now — but how was he supposed to do that? She was probably with the others and would be until bedtime, when it would be easier for him to rescue her after hiding in her room. He needed to wait.

Stick to the plan.

The tips of Ernie's fingers twitched from where they looped through the tongs handle, and he began to quietly step back.

Until he heard nasty obscenities hit the air. Grumbled, by Noble, against the women who'd scorned him.

"I'll show 'em. I'll show 'em," he bitterly spat.

Another tremor ran through Ernie's fingers as he watched the man's curved form rock in place. Now and then Noble hissed with seeming sharp pain, and he turned his head slightly to spit.

Grunting, the actor next fished around with his free hand for a bottle of liquor, which he opened with his teeth before spitting out the cork and taking a swig right from the neck. After another chug, he brought the white cloth to the bottle's opening and saturated it with the clear fluid. Then he looked down as he seemed to fiddle with the top of his shirt. He hissed again in searing torment when he pressed the cloth back to his shoulder.

Ernie took another slow step back, ready to leave the man to his business. He could only hope Lottie wouldn't take pity on the rat, that the Colonel would find out what had happened and throw him out without another word.

The floor creaked beneath his boot.

"Eh?" Noble groaned as he turned his head to the right. "Who're you?" he said over his shoulder when his eyes met Ernie's.

"Just a hired hand," Ernie replied as he took another step back.

"Well, whaddya think you're doin' in here?"

"Only making a delivery, sir. Got a block back there." He pointed his tongs at the ice he'd left behind.

Noble whistled. "Strong one, aren't ya? Got a good back for labor, I bet. Like a mule."

The tips of Ernie's fingers twitched yet again, and he squeezed them around the handle in his hand. The sturdy metal that could hurt but not kill.

"If ya don't mind," he said, "I'll just do my job and head out, sir."

Noble cocked his chin up. "You do that." Then he looked away to resume tending to his wounds.

Instead of walking back to the fire rack, though, Ernie eyed the chipped and melting ice block already sitting on the bar. "Anything I can help with, sir?" he asked after Noble let out another moan.

The man's head shook with sardonic laughter. "Mind your potatoes, will ya?" he said without looking back around. "Go on, now. Do what they pay ya for and beat it."

But Ernie didn't budge. Just stared at the back of Noble's head, gauging where it'd be softest. He took a step forward, not caring if he wasn't quiet.

"Aw, c'mon now," Noble said, his head dropping toward his chest. "I said scram already."

Ernie took another gradual step forward.

And then he advanced closer, faster. He clamped his tongs around the chipped block and tried to gain a good grip.

He got it.

With a firm hoist, he yanked the block from the countertop and swung it like Babe Ruth up to bat.

Brought it down just as Noble turned his head and said, "Aw, hey, look, pal. I'm so —"

The apology died with him.

The present hour

They had the full story by dawn.

Ernie swore he hadn't planned to kill Noble. But in the moment...

The moment.

He knew. He'd known that man did not deserve to live. That no one would've slept a safe night in that house so long as he did. It was time to put him down.

Ernie'd hit him with enough impact to split off part of the melted ice block. The broken chunks flew back and coasted on the library's wooden floor, where he'd left them to melt. The bulk of the block he'd simply set back in place on the counter before closing the paneled door and hopping behind the bar to grab the body and drag it down the stairs in back.

Except, as he'd fussed with Noble's limp form, tried to get the right leverage to lift him, he heard Lottie's voice out in the library. *"Noble? Edith?"*

He'd ducked his body down behind the counter with his victim as he heard her swiftly open then close one of the bar's front doors. A cursory look, to his relief, just long enough to confirm no one stood in there—but that relief was short-lived as he next heard her unlatch the door from the hall. He shoved his hand against the bar's back door if it could keep her from opening it, but he only heard her tap her way down the stairs. So much for that route, then. He'd have to take Noble down on the elevator. But he didn't want to risk dragging him out into the hall.

It'd been all Ernie could do to lift Noble and get both him and himself over the countertop. He'd left Noble slumped against the wall there until he could catch his breath, but then he'd panicked. If Lottie had come in looking for the others, it might only be a matter of time before someone else did. This was not how the plan was supposed to go. He didn't know how he'd get Lottie out of the house now with a body to reckon with, but he'd have to think about it later as he first fled to safety.

Gripping his tongs, Ernie slipped out of the bar and closed the door behind him, concealing Noble from view before running back to the firewood elevator. He covered his finger with a clean corner of Noble's bloodied handkerchief to press the down button on the brass wall panel, then pressed the cloth to his nostril as the lift descended. Some time for a nosebleed. His pumping heart only made the blood gush harder, and he unfortunately got it all over Lottie's white shoes after he'd scrambled out of the rack to send it back upstairs. He tried wiping the canvas to no avail and just shoved the shoes beneath some firewood until he could sort out how to get Lottie back in them and running away beside him. The block of ice, meanwhile, he dropped in the pool.

Ernie described how he'd then run back inside the house via the servant access door to the west wing, where he'd stashed his tongs away and hidden in one location or another until he could pull together another plan. He'd had no idea how his flight had almost framed Edith for murder.

He wept over that now. Over his betrayal of the family he wanted so badly to be a part of. Over what he wanted with Lottie and would never have. Over the reality of what he'd done. Lottie'd been his entire focus. Take her away, and all he had left was the blood on his hands. He'd had nothing to lose and yet lost it all.

Inconsolable, he eventually wore out his welcome and everyone's patience. At least as far as what they could accomplish at the house. Chief Thompson and his deputy escorted him out, with retired Chief Rainger close behind.

The last thing Ernie Hart saw before they drove him off to county jail wasn't the Colonel and his wife, holding each other tenderly as they looked on from their front steps.

Nor the handsome football star holding hands with the love of Ernie's life.

And definitely not the yawning young reporter who'd quipped at the end of his confession: "Fire and ice," as if typing the headline already.

No, in the end, he saw only Miss Lottie Landry, with the golden glow of sunrise reaching to kiss her golden cheek.

Keeping her in the spotlight.

EPILOGUE

the hair of the dog

Tap, tap, tap...

The young reporter's fingertips plunk out the words on her typewriter, finishing the story of the century.

Fire and Ice, she's titled it.

A crime novel, loosely based on the events of Noble Howard's murder. *Very* loosely, out of tremendous love and respect for the living. After promising all the liberties she'd take with the facts, she received the blessings of all involved.

All those so very tragically involved in that incident. But rise from it, they have.

Helen, for one, has been taking her first crack at fiction, in stark contrast to the journalistic pieces she's been assigned the past year — ever since her debut interview with the Red Fox earned Miss Conroy her transfer to the *Chronicle*'s sports department. She's done many interviews with him since then, covering the Chicago Cardinals' 1929 season. Finishing fourth in the league, they crushed the Bears in the standings. So much for "wasting" himself on a "losing team." Good thing Rex didn't take Noble's advice last summer to move across town.

It's good to see the Red Fox do so well. See his loyalty pay off. Helen's sure it eventually will with Lottie, too. Once the Warnes return from their year-long sojourn abroad. Europe, where they've ventured with their daughter to make peace with the past and build a new future together—as a family.

Lottie's needed this. To escape the American press and visit her French roots, see her home village again and pray at her mother's grave. To have the time and space to heal and grow, learn to trust and stand on her own feet, not someone else's coattails. Become not who she wants to be but who she is.

Hollywood star it isn't. Helen thinks it's marvelous how Lottie has returned to the stage, her holiday giving her a whirl at West End theatre in London. A modest theatre, where she had to audition and Ransom has no pull.

In her letters, Lottie writes of how lovely and intimate the acting experience is with an audience, the staging wonderfully austere and the stories so much more poignant than anything the studio churns out. How it's so liberating to pursue her passion without celebrity in tow—though how she does still enjoy the warmth of those spotlights. Maybe this will turn into something longer term. Maybe she'll stay overseas. Maybe she doesn't have to figure it all out right now. Romance, for the time being, has taken backstage.

Thank goodness she could break her contract with the studio. The circumstances with Noble helped, of course, inevitably tarnishing Lottie's name with that bad business. One of Ransom Warne's connections helped facilitate the negotiations, too, in tandem with William Randolph Hearst's efforts to put his dear Marion in Lottie's place. Finally *something* got ol' R.W. and W.R. to cooperate with each other.

Meanwhile, Rex is done with Tinseltown, too. *The Renaissance Man* shall remain his one and only picture, though he's still having to turn down offers. "Athletes make awkward actors," he will humbly quote from Noble time to time.

He and Helen have become extraordinary pals since that hot summer day of '29. If amateur sleuthing taught them one thing, it's how well they jive. Outside of their interviews, they spend a lot of time together around the city when Rex is in town, playing tennis and cycling, and enjoying long walks along the lakeshore. Yet whatever whispers might swirl around the social circles, Helen and Rex have the stuff of great friendships, and that's that. And that's wonderful. Helen's so happy to have him in her life in this way and to know that he still has a chance to make her friend so happy, too.

He clearly already has the Colonel's approval, and to this day, Helen's sure that's why Ransom had invited Rex for that August weekend while Lottie was in town. Bring in the fox to chase away the snake.

If Lottie comes home and she and Rex finally do court in earnest, then Helen will be the first to cover the story of their nuptials. It'll be fun, writing a society column again for old time's sake. And she's held on to that headline she once imagined: "Red Fox Raids French Hen's Coop." Oh, but Lottie would kill her. That's what makes it all the more enticing to use.

Yet it remains to be seen if Lottie *will* come back. And what she wants to come back to. In the meantime, Rex might visit but can't very well abandon his team to join her over there. He feels it's not his place, anyway, that the Warnes need their time as a family, and Mrs. Warne in particular deserves her rehabilitation in privacy. She's doing quite well, according to Lottie's letters. Healthier, happier. As is the Colonel after confronting his ghosts on French soil, the real Belleau. The Colonel and his wife have forged their own fond memories in Paris as well, honoring Clothilde's work there but placing Edith's own stamp on the city and Ransom's heart.

Chief Rainger, too, has made his strides, coming out of retirement to enforce law once more. He savored his break from it all but couldn't deny that investigating at Belleau got him itching for action again. He's known as Deputy Rainger these days, working for the county sheriff's office. His other son Henry has also successfully installed himself as an associate at Evanston's

Scientific Crime Detection Laboratory. Crime never sleeps, and neither do the Raingers.

It's a wonder and a blessing that any of them are getting on as well as they are given the events of the last year. Starting, naturally, with Noble's death in August and all the mourning and awful publicity to follow. Not exactly the attention the actor had hoped would come of his fateful trip to Illinois. It really is a shame, when Helen thinks about it — and she does think about it a lot, not only because of her book. It's just sad that Noble Howard couldn't have enjoyed the anonymity of Howard Noble and carved out a more decent life for himself.

But, oh, who is Helen kidding. Howard Noble the salesman was probably just as big a snake, selling his own oil. Some people simply can't be saved from themselves.

Then came Black Thursday in October, when the stock market crashed and sent everyone for a spin. The Warnes, Conroys, and Raingers all took their hits but, all in all, fared okay. It got Helen drinking her liquor a bit stronger, though, that's for sure.

She's sitting with a manhattan at her desk right now. Celebrating the conclusion of her first novel manuscript and toasting the anniversary of its unfortunate inspiration. Noble made for an unlikely muse, and Helen hopes her fictionalization of his sad tale shows tremendous respect for the dead, too.

Because, after all — snake or not — he didn't deserve this.

Sighing, Helen sits back in her chair and kicks her bare feet up beside her typewriter, swinging her toes as she looks out the window.

It's a balmy day outside, milder than a year ago but just as lovely, and Rex will be picking her up to breeze in that breezer of his — all the way back to Wheaton.

To Belleau.

The Colonel has entrusted them with looking after the estate, with the aid of Chauncey and the staff that didn't accompany the Warnes overseas. They've been getting on without Ernie well enough, his mortified and apologetic father picking up the slack if it means in any way repaying the Warnes for all that his son wrought upon their lives. Ransom can't find it in his heart to dismiss the elder Hart, it not being his fault that the apple fell so very far from the tree.

When Rex has the chance, he delivers the ice himself.

But tonight is not for any duty beyond the one owed to what happened one year ago today. Call them morbid, but both Helen and Rex hope to find their own sense of peace by revisiting the scene of the crime. By making happier memories within it, filling the space with a better energy for the Warnes to return to.

And this way, they can also load up one of Lottie's silliest movies in the Gold Theatre and have a harmless laugh at their dear girl's expense without ruffling her feathers. *She* always performed brilliantly; it wasn't her fault she wasn't given much to work with.

Helen's looking forward to a good swim, too. The Warnes' travels have delayed their plans to fill in the pool, and Helen might even bring a bathing suit this time.

Chuckling to herself at the thought, she holds her martini aloft.

"Cheers," she says out into the ether, where Noble may or not dwell. Where he may or may not have found peace.

"To coattails and cocktails. Covering what ails, though never curing."

The End

Author's Note

In writing historical fiction, I draw from historical facts but inevitably take many liberties (that's where the "fiction" comes into play). And for this book, it's no different.

As my first entirely historical novel, *Coattails and Cocktails* comes largely from imagination, yet I would be remiss not to tip my hat to Colonel Robert R. McCormick and his first and second wives, who very, very loosely inspired the characters of Ransom and Edith Warne. Rex and Lewis Rainger likewise very, very loosely stem from Wheaton's own Red Grange and his father Lyle. I did want to pay homage to these historical figures by acknowledging their Wheaton, IL, roots and reflecting their traits to a degree. But my intent was never to fully nor accurately portray anyone in real life. My characters' personalities, backstories, and dramas are all their own!

But to the extent that art imitates life…

Robert McCormick ran the *Chicago Tribune* like Ransom runs the *Chronicle*. Both men were involved with the Illinois National Guard. McCormick also named his Cantigny estate for his experience in WWI, in which he served as a citizen-soldier who fought in the Battle of Cantigny in France, whereas Ransom was a war correspondent at the Battle of Belleau Wood. That aspect of Ransom's backstory takes after Floyd Gibbons, a *Chicago Tribune* correspondent sent to cover the First World War. Gibbons lost an eye to German gunfire when he tried to save an

American soldier in the Battle of Belleau Wood, for which he earned the high honor of France's *Croix de Guerre* with Palm. Ransom's contributions to cryptology likewise reflect Colonel George Fabyan of Geneva, IL, not McCormick.

I will note as well that, for a time, McCormick was guardian to two daughters of a Chinese politician so that the girls could receive an education in the States. This gave me the idea for Lottie as Ransom's ward, but none of the scandal speculated in this work of FICTION has any basis in McCormick's reality. My mind went there purely for a plot twist.

Edith Warne draws in part from both Amy and Maryland McCormick, her penchant for Asian art and antiques coming from Maryland and her artistic talent from Amy (as well as the "skeletons" in her closet, which I actually saw during my tour of the McCormick house!).

And then there's football-hero Rex, who mirrors Red Grange in that he once worked for a local ice company (Red worked for L.C. Thompson, not my fictional R.C. Johnson), played a football player in a film, and played actual football for Wheaton High School and the Fighting Illini.

But to all the Bears fans out there, my sincerest apologies for taking your beloved Galloping Ghost and placing his fictionalized counterpart on the Chicago Cardinals team. I did so for one reason and one reason only: my dad, who's been a loyal Cardinals fan from Chicago to St. Louis to Phoenix. For what that man has been through these past few years, this is the very *least* I could do for him. And, hey, my dad, brother (also a Cardinals fan), godfather, husband, and I all attended the University of Illinois, so we have that historical pride in (and claim on) Red, too. *I – L – L!*

*cups hand behind ear to hear all fellow U of I alumni reply, *I – N – I!*

Team rivalries aside, Red's "Galloping Ghost" nickname transferred to Helen as the "Gliding Ghost" of tennis. Grange was also the son of a lumberjack-turned-police chief, but after his mother's death, his family eventually moved to Illinois from

Pennsylvania, not Wisconsin (the latter being my little connection to the Ashby lumberyards of *Seven for a Secret*, my debut novel that also takes place in 1920s Chicago, in part).

Where Lewis Rainger is concerned, the city of Wheaton is also the county seat of DuPage County, so it would have had a sheriff's office as well as its own police department. For the purposes of this story (and based on my understanding of the traditional roles of police chief vs. sheriff), I have assumed that the local chief would have jurisdiction over this crime's investigation, only calling in the sheriff's support as necessary. Any inaccuracy in that is my bad. And the head of Wheaton's police department in 1929 may have held the title of "Marshal," but I've opted for "Chief" purely for more punch.

So, again, where the characters go, they're just that: characters. Fictional. Any similarities to actual people don't go much beyond what I've just mentioned.

For as much as I strayed from facts, there's much that remains the same, notably the Cantigny estate that became my "Belleau." Located in Wheaton, IL, Cantigny Park was Robert McCormick's gift to the public. To this day, you can walk through his house and gardens, as well as the First Division museum now standing on the property. The adjacent forest preserve is actually called Belleau Woods, though I never realized that until after I'd already named my setting. Fate!

I inevitably took some liberties with Cantigny's landscape and architecture, such as the east and west wings that weren't added to the mansion until the 1930s, and I don't know if Mc-Cormick ever had a tennis court — he did have a pool at one time, though, that was eventually filled in. Some descriptions of floor layouts, décor, and furnishings were improvised for the story's purposes, and I admittedly don't know the exact inner-workings of the firewood elevator, but there *is* one that you can see with your own eyes!

In fact, I tried to stay mostly true to key settings like the Liberty Library (based on Cantigny's Freedom Hall, complete with hidden bar), the dining and drawing rooms, Madison and

Jefferson porches, and the Gold Theatre. These spaces were already so perfect for my little mystery, why mess with much? And I want to offer readers a chance to follow the fictional footsteps of these characters in case you ever get a chance to tour Cantigny. If not for this story, then you must go for its actual history and beauty.

Which, again, I fudged with. And though I did my best to capture the 1920s and crime elements authentically, any and all factual inaccuracies are my own!

Thank you, Dear Reader. You're the bee's knees!

~ Rumer

Acknowledgments

Time to take to the podium again and gush my countless thanks to those who've helped me get to this point. Earlier this year, I had the honor of delivering the keynote speech at the 2017 Upstate Eight Literary Festival in Illinois. Me, talking about writing as if I remotely know what I'm doing. I still have so much to learn, and always will. But one thing I could tell those aspiring authors with certainty: "For as solitary as the act of writing is, we can't do it alone."

Ain't that the truth.

And so, I begin by thanking my editor extraordinaire, Bev Nickelson, for her infinite patience with my incessant emails, encouragement of my weird brain, and expert guidance that strengthened this story. I thank Sarah Allan, editor extraordinaire #2, who also edited *Seven for a Secret* and knows how to buff and polish my words like no other. Coreen Montagna likewise returns on interior design after her deco delight for *Seven*. Visually telling the story is Gina Dickerson of RoseWolf Design, whose stunning cover art manages to make the Roaring Twenties *purrrr*. And the cherry on top is the monkey at the bottom — the new logo for Fallen Monkey Press that I'm still going ape over, designed by Marlena and Aaron Clark. These folks are truly the *crème de la crème*, and I'm over the moon to have scored such a dream team.

Infinite gratitude to Shani Struthers as well, one of my all-time favorite authors who is also a friend and mentor. Additional thanks and warm hugs to Shannon Von Essen and Sue Schiller, for believing that I had something valuable to say to a new generation of writers. I must of course thank authors Aubrey Wynne and Melissa Storm, too, as the reason this novel exists in the first place!

Massive thanks to Cantigny Park and the memories of Robert R. McCormick, Amy McCormick, Maryland McCormick, Red Grange, Lyle Grange, Floyd Gibbons, and George Fabyan for lending some local spirit to my setting and characters. I toast some gin to Lon Ashby, too, who fed the gossip at Ransom's dinner table as a crossover with my novel *Seven for a Secret*.

It should also never go without saying that I give heartfelt thanks to my husband Ryan and our family, for continually supporting me in every way possible.

And to the Fallen Monkey, for getting me back up in that tree.

About the Author

Rumer Haven is probably the most social recluse you could ever meet. When she's not babbling her fool head off among friends and family, she's pacified with a good story that she's reading, writing, or revising — or binge-watching something on Netflix. Hailing from Chicago, she presently lives in London with her husband and probably a ghost or two. Rumer has always had a penchant for the past and paranormal, which inspires her writing to explore dimensions of time, love, and the soul. Her novel *What the Clocks Know* won 1st Place in General Fiction for the 2017 *Red City Review* Book Awards.

Visit Rumer at:
www.rumerhaven.com
@RumerHaven

Also by Rumer Haven

If you enjoyed *Coattails and Cocktails* and want to read more history-n-mystery by Rumer Haven, be sure to check out her novels *Seven for a Secret* and *What the Clocks Know* — two subtly supernatural stories in which present-day mysteries unlock past secrets.

Who was Alonzo Ashby? And did he jump or was he pushed? Return to 1920s Chicago and see the Jazz Age tragedy that continues to haunt a young woman in the New Millennium. *Seven for a Secret* is where historical fiction meets contemporary rom-com — from the Roaring Twenties when the "New Woman" was born, to the modern Noughties when she really came of age.

Then travel across the pond (and farther back in time) as an American expat's "soul search" seems to actually find a ghost. Woven between 21st-century and Victorian London, *What the Clocks Know* is a haunting story of love and identity that won 1st-place in General Fiction for the 2017 *Red City Review* Book Awards.

Both titles are available from Amazon in paperback and e-book format.

Seven for a Secret

It's the year 2000, and twenty-four-year-old Kate moves into a new apartment to find a new state of independence in a new millennium. Almost immediately, she starts crushing on a hot guy who lives in her building. Deciding to take a break from her boyfriend Dexter, Kate believes the only thing now separating her from the fresh object of her sexual fantasies is the thin wall between their neighboring apartments.

A former 1920s hotel, Camden Court has housed many lonely lives over the decades—and is where a number of them have come to die. They're not all resting in peace, however, including ninety-year-old Olive, who dropped dead in Kate's apartment and continues to make her presence known.

For Olive has a secret she's *dying* to tell. One linking her to the sex, scandal, and sacrifice of a young dreamer named Lon. As the past haunts the present, Kate's romantic notion that the thrill-of-the-chase beats the reality-after-the-catch unexpectedly entwines her modern-day love life with Lon's Jazz Age tragedy.

What the Clocks Know

Twenty-six-year-old Margot sets out on a journey of self-discovery—she dumps her New York boyfriend, quits her Chicago job, and crashes at her friend's flat in London.

Rather than find herself, though, she only feels more lost. An unsettling energy affects her from the moment she enters the old Victorian residence, and she spirals into depression. Frightened and questioning her perceptions, she gradually suspects her dark emotions belong to Charlotte instead.

Who is Charlotte? The name on a local gravestone could relate to Margot's dreams and the grey woman weeping at the window.

Finding a ghost isn't what she had in mind when she went "soul searching," but somehow Margot's future may depend on Charlotte's past.

67678092R00162

Made in the USA
Lexington, KY
18 September 2017